THE ASSOCIATION

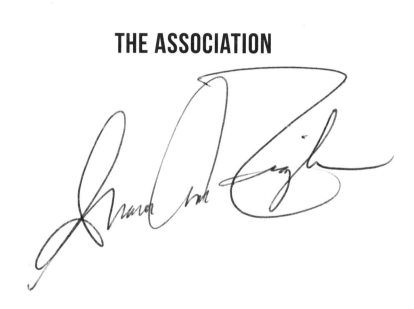

THE ASSOCIATION

SHARON ANN ZIEGLER

Palmetto Publishing Group
Charleston, SC

The Association
Copyright © 2018 by Sharon Ann Ziegler
All rights reserved

First Edition

Printed in the United States

ISBN-13: 978-1-64111-129-4
ISBN-10: 1-64111-129-1

Library of Congress Control Number: 2018952891

Hey Paul,
Love You

Silence the angry with love. Silence the ill-natured with kindness. Silence the miser with generosity. Silence the liar with truth.

—Gautama Buddha

CONTENTS

PROLOGUE

In my years of practicing law, I was confronted with three basic types of attorneys: nerd attorneys, cause attorneys, and hack attorneys. The nerd attorneys were generally true geniuses. They often involved themselves in corporate law cases or in cases having anything to do with math. Most of the federal appellate court judges I came in contact with were nerd attorneys. Cause attorneys, on the other hand, were devoted to their particular cause, be it political or social, and they fought tooth and nail to that end, often to the brink of bankrupting themselves or their firms. Hack attorneys were all the rest.

The hacks I knew had various characteristics, like sweet and charming, flashy and loud, mean and condescending, reserved and meek, or insensitive and boorish. They represented anyone or any company. They represented criminals and some were prosecutors. They represented both defendants and plaintiffs. The generic hacks read very little, if at all. They always took shortcuts, but that did not mean they lacked intelligence. The hacks were shrewd and cunning. Some lied, cheated, stole, defamed, and perhaps even maimed or killed to defeat their enemies. All hacks had one thing in common; they were in it to win it. It was all about the money and the power and how much they could greedily seize.

Usually, I could easily tell if a person was a nerd, cause, or hack attorney. Sometimes, however, it was not so easy because an attorney could possess a combination of characteristics. Take me, for example—definitely a legal nerd, always wanting to analyze the law correctly, never wanting to get it wrong; but since I grieved when a wrongdoer won, and since I took each case to heart, I also had the characteristics of the proverbial cause attorney.

The worst type of attorney was the true genius hack. They were extraordinarily rare. I was only exposed to one, maybe two, during the course of my legal career. It was daunting to be confronted with such an attorney because where wits, common sense, and integrity were my available weapons, deceit, chicanery, and malevolence were the weapons of the genius hack.

CHAPTER 1
THE DISMISSAL

I arrived half an hour early despite having an unshakable reputation as a steadfast latecomer. It was a windy, cool day in mid-March when I entered the gothic-style building and proceeded through the metal detectors manned by armed guards. Quite unsure of where I needed to be, I was obliged to ask one of them for directions and notwithstanding my best efforts at politeness, the stern-looking gatekeeper from whom I sought guidance did not verbally respond to my plea for help. Instead, he dismissively pointed in an easterly direction, refusing to look at me. I thanked the guard for his assistance, such as it was, then I hesitantly followed the dimly lit corridor east, as gesticulated. Trudging along, I intuitively sensed that my spiraling descent into a mysterious rabbit hole had been decidedly set in motion.

Room 113—I'd found the proper location. Relieved, I tiptoed into the musty auditorium and sat down on a wooden bench in the second row, thrilled to have scored an exceedingly unobstructed view. Unfortunately, I was not lucky enough to retain my great seat because moments later, a tall man with an enormous head rudely sat in front of me, which forced me to slide over a little to get a better perspective.

The man's rudeness was not upsetting. Like it or not, he was entitled to sit where he wanted. It was merely the bigness of his head that was bothersome. Big heads always sat in front of me; that was my reality. Mentally brooding over my sad misfortune, I quietly tried not to fidget by folding my hands prettily in my lap, while whispering people ceremoniously filed into the austere chamber filling it nearly to capacity.

As time crawled forward slower than it should have, I scrutinized a huge painting that hung crookedly on the wall directly opposite the main entrance to the auditorium. The skewed painting suffered from visible areas of delamination, and was an awfully yellowed portrayal of the building in which I sat. Its crookedness was more than distracting. I desperately wanted to straighten it, but since that consuming inclination was not possible, I scanned my surroundings and noticed that the room, like the painting, was also shabby and untidy. Crazed plaster peeled near the ceiling line above the crooked painting, exposing powdery dust; cracks spidered from the wall corners around several soot-covered windows that were hard to see through; and the wooden benches were scratched and worn smooth from years of wear and tear. Taking into account the run-down condition of the building and the tatty condition of the painting, I fancied that the local community had taken prodigious pride in the landmark at one time, but over the years, wanton neglect and concentrated distrust of the business conducted within its confines rendered the decrepit building just as ugly as the painting that featured the same.

I looked at my watch as the hushed voices of the congregated crowd intensified; the proceeding should have started almost twenty-five minutes ago. The temperature in the room increased appreciably, and since I did not wear any stockings, my bare legs dampened and kept sticking to the wooden bench. I shifted in my seat several times during the oppressive wait, which grew longer and longer, just as the crooked painting looked more and more crooked. I began to feel overcome by a foreboding impression that the proceeding would never commence, when, suddenly, a tremendous bang, accompanied by a chilling breeze that blew upon my back, thundered through the room. A baritone-voiced officer ordered all of the attendees to rise after a new arrival busted through the heavy set of mahogany double doors and moved through the audience like an iron-fisted dictator. His white, kinky mane flapped ferociously as he blustered past my row.

The spectators watched in silence as a subservient man helped the newcomer climb a podium and slip a dark, silky robe over his short-sleeved polo shirt that matched his tawny, mustard slacks. Once bedecked in his formal regalia, the husky man seated himself on a throne behind a raised desk situated beneath the crooked, yellowed painting while two other men and one woman scurried about him preparing his papers and effects, all in an effort to do anything necessary to bring him comfort. No smile, no hello. The throned one only displayed an attitude that he did not want to be there and that he would finish very quickly.

Then there was the Invocation. Everyone was ordered to remain standing while an unexpressive pastor gave a toneless speech instructing the audience members to embrace Jesus Christ as their Savior and pray for justice. The circumstances surrounding the demanded prayer were positively disconcerting and I feared if I did not succumb, the seemingly disagreeable tyrant would penalize me. I prayed frequently, both alone in my mind and openly in church, but I had never been forced to pray at the behest of an omnipotent dictator. Nonetheless, although I was not there to pray, I was there to win, and whatever it took, I was determined to succeed. Therefore, I closed my eyes, swallowed an air bubble that developed in my throat, bowed my head, and pretended to be lost in deep, devotional prayer until the pastor concluded his sermon and asked the audience members to take their seats.

An edgy stillness overtook the room after everyone sat down, but it was coarsely cut short when the tyrant shuffled his papers and grumbled nastily to his underlings prior to the official commencement of the session. That was when I scoured the room searching for my adversary. I looked to the right and I looked to the left, but to my dismay, no one in attendance closely resembled the photographic self-portrait he had posted as part of his online profile. Driven by sheer will, I refused to give up. I looked again to the right and again to the left, then I did a double take when someone conspicuously averted my glance. I knew in an instant that the glance avoider had to be my man because I was well aware of the disdain he held for me that boiled to the surface during our previous email communications.

My adversary's internet headshot depicted a man approximately thirty years old with a defined chin, plump cheeks, and smooth, caramel-tinted hair, which was not in keeping with the truth. In person, he was a bushy-haired, ashen brunet with a pallid complexion. Small-framed and diminutive, he looked much older than thirty, perhaps even as old as forty-five. His droopy face with wide-set eyes, backward sloping forehead, protruding nose, and disappearing jaw left one feeling confused by the incongruency of his countenance; his attributes more closely personified a cold-blooded piranha rather than a warm-blooded human.

I eyed my adversary for a protracted period jarred by the stark difference between his online photo and his actual appearance but my awkward staring was not returned even though the object of my obsession seemed manifestly conscious of my gawking. In lieu of inspecting me, he firmly looked toward the tyrant with his head held high, projecting calm assuredness, while his thick-knuckled fingers fiddled with a black and gold embossed pen. Mercifully, my cringeworthy fixation was finally disrupted when the officer who called all to rise introduced the throned tyrant.

"Please come to order, ladies and gentlemen. The Superior Court of the Third Judicial District, Lakewood City, Carson County, Georgia is now in session, the Honorable Judge Doyle McMurray presiding."

Everyone heeded the command and came to attention. The judge breathed a listless sigh into his microphone and stroked his expertly shaped Elvis sideburns, then he slumped his head between his hands and started the session by calling the calendar. He announced each case by name and asked the attorneys how long they were going to take to present their arguments.

Once my case was called, my adversary jumped up and exclaimed, "May it please the court, Your Honor, I will be quick with oral argument on my motion requesting the court dismiss the complaint filed against my clients. I will only need about ten minutes of the court's time."

The judge was delighted and he laughingly snorted, "That's fine. Succinctness is a virtue, especially today. The weather forecast calls for calm winds and sunshine later, so I scheduled an early afternoon tee time . . . I'm already dressed to play."

The dank room filled with sycophantic snickers in response to the feeble attempt at comedy. Seconds ticked by as I waited with apprehension for the crowd to come to order.

When the last snicker trailed off, the tyrant turned to me and pointed a gnarled arthritic finger at my face. "How much of the court's time will you take?" he asked in a tone that metaphorically indicated any time taken was a theft of precious moments of his life that could never be replaced.

"Your Honor, I will need at least thirty minutes for my side of the argument due to the complex legal issues involved."

"Are you telling me this motion will take forty minutes total—ten minutes for the defendants and thirty minutes for the plaintiffs?!"

"Yes, the legal issues are significant and need to be discussed in detail," I said trying to keep a stiff upper lip and remain resolute.

The tyrant surveyed me with noticeable disgust, then he vigorously shook his head no, and proceeded to call the rest of the calendar in order to determine how much time he would have to spend in that courtroom awaiting his afternoon tee off.

Judge McMurray was unequivocally very unkind to me. He treated the other attorneys in the room, all older white males, with much greater respect than he treated me. The reasons for the inferior treatment could be many. Maybe Judge McMurray did not like me because it was the first time I had appeared before him, and he despised tenderfoot outsiders, or perhaps it was my dress; maybe he did not like my dress.

I liked my dress. I had spent a lot of time choosing the dress I wore that day. Originally, I purchased a different dress to wear but I ended up returning it for a store credit because I did not want to risk regret by testing a new dress in a new environment. Instead, I chose a tried and true dress I had had for years, and loved wearing. It was not only comfortable, but also comforting because it was festooned with abundant ruffles that thankfully covered all of my bodily imperfections. I even had my hair cut a few days before the hearing to reduce the chance of having a bad hair day. Having a bad hair day can distract a girl from doing any job.

Overall, it was patently peculiar how I was the only one in the courtroom who seemed to care about their appearance, aside from a standout lawyer with a clean-shaven face and a full head of neatly trimmed silver hair who worked the room like a politician soliciting money and votes. The standout lawyer was so dynamically alluring and coolheaded, I nicknamed him "Perry Mason" because he reminded me of the fictional attorney character of the same name who almost never lost a trial. Lucky for me, Judge McMurray called Perry's case first, so I was gifted with the opportunity to see if the debonair attorney was deserving of the iconic nickname I bestowed upon him without foreknowledge of his actual abilities.

Perry did not disappoint. He took center stage with considerable fanfare, turning to the audience with a wave before starting just to make sure all of the onlookers were paying close attention. He dominated the room with his proportionate colossal form and his refined gentlemanly panache. His head was big, his nose was bulbous, his hands were huge, his arms were immense, his shoulders were broad, and his accentuated southern drawl was polished. During his opening statement, he recounted the facts of his case in a rhythmic cadence inundated with powerful inflections that left his listeners wanting more. Perry explained that he represented an old pig farmer who sought to have an adjacent landowner's fence torn down because the fence encroached two inches onto the pig farmer's property. The adjacent landowner countersued for nuisance due to the putrid fumes emitted from the vile swine. The feud between the neighbors had been years in the making and culminated in a tense standoff that day in court.

Perry called the defendant as his first and only witness, designated him hostile, and proceeded to question him in a bellowing manner with accusatory undertones. Opposing counsel objected that Perry was badgering the defendant when Perry leaned on the witness stand and riveted his hypnotic, movie-star eyes on his cowering prey with intimidating force. Judge McMurray, awestruck by Perry's performance, did not take the bait—he overruled the objection. Perry was allowed to have his way with the defendant and he successfully coerced the whining encroacher to admit that his fence was built two inches over the property line and that the pig farm smells were not intolerably vexatious.

Grandstanding a bit after the successful cross-examination, Perry spread his peacock feathers, strutted back to his seat at counsel table and rested his case. Thereafter, opposing counsel questioned his witnesses but not with the flare capable of defeating the proficient display demonstrated by his predecessor. At the close of the proceeding, Judge McMurray smiled adoringly at Perry and granted judgement in favor of his client. The victorious Perry rose from his chair, thanked the judge, and exited the courtroom, impeccably dressed in a gray gabardine suit he complemented with a sleek, expensive watch, a twinkling pinky ring, and a dainty gold chain bracelet that was strikingly too small for his explosively large frame.

I watched Perry with laudable admiration during his showboat departure. He flaunted distinguished decorum when he winked at me with charm in his eyes just before he flashed a smile that exposed his decayed, tar-stained teeth. As he swaggered past, I inhaled a markedly memorable, burnt camphor aroma that pungently wafted around his imposing figure. I did not learn Perry's name that day because no one uttered it; everyone exclusively called him "Sir," which led me to guess he commanded a lot of respect in Lakewood City.

The tyrant called the next case, and a raggedy, bearded man behind me stood and tried to balance himself on splintered crutches. In the process, he dropped a stack of unopened postmarked letters and haphazardly littered the room. I came to the rescue straightaway, but when I rose, I slammed my knee into the bench before I picked up the scattered mail from the unswept floor and arranged it in a neat pile. As I stepped toward the man, I inadvertently glimpsed the return address imprinted on the envelope on top of the stack—the sender was the Georgia State Bureau of Child Support Enforcement. I jerked my head upwards, and when I entered the personal space of the hapless man to deliver his mail, I inhaled the grotesque scent of ammoniated urine. The man did not thank me; he just snatched his mail from my hands and hobbled toward his anxiously waiting attorney.

Once the outwardly feeble man steadied himself from teetering on his crutches, his attorney explained that his client was not a deadbeat dad. To the contrary, he was an invalid without any means to pay child support. That was when I knew the attorney had told his client not to bathe, to dress in filthy clothes, and to act disabled. It was all for show, drama, to make the case visually stimulating. And that smell, that was a really nice touch; the client exuded the stench of destitution. At the gavel, the despot refused to award back child support payments to the crying mother who cradled the invalid's infant daughter in her arms. The deadbeat dad won, a big success for the deadbeat's attorney, Cedric Holmes.

Cedric Holmes was a skinny, tallish man, about fifty-five years old, with greasy sable hair that garnished a compact head connected to an outstretched, attenuated neck. Although categorically displeasing, Cedric's giraffe-evoking characteristics were duly mitigated by his oval face and square jaw, but like his neck, his elongated nose, which slightly hooked over his withered lips, gave him a ghastly appearance that made one take a second look. Cedric was not a leader; he was somewhat submissive, mild and soft-spoken, possibly a pushover, clearly a follower. He was not flashy, not like Perry. Cedric was surely amiable and helpful. Boy, was he helpful. Cedric walked out of the courtroom dragging his invalid client, while simultaneously holding the invalid's unopened mail and one of his crutches. I wondered if the stench of destitution rubbed off on Cedric as he left the building.

Judge McMurray finally called my case—batter-up. I wasn't nervous anymore, but my knee started to swell. I did not need sympathy, not like the urine-smelling deadbeat dad who had just walked away with a win. I needed to project strength and determination, so I confidently approached the bar without limping, gracefully entered, and elegantly sat at plaintiff's counsel table. The dictator did not acknowledge me. Rather, he turned to my adversary who had taken a seat at defendant's counsel table and quizzically demanded, "What the hell is going on?"

I was shocked! The holier-than-thou ruler had not read the briefs?! I submitted a reply brief, a statement of undisputed fact, numerous exhibits, and a motion for summary judgment. I had spent at least $300 binding and tabbing the documents and mailing them overnight delivery to the defendants and the court. I had even sent a courtesy copy directly to Judge McMurray's office, but he had not read a word—*nada*. How could I explain the intricacies of the law with regard to my lawsuit in merely thirty to forty minutes when the judge had not read the briefs?

It didn't matter. I learned in the short run, that preparedness was not a quality the judge cherished, and that being the case, he permitted my adversary to speak first and uninterrupted for more than fifteen minutes. My adversary answered the judge's what-the-hell-is-going-on query by presenting a one-sided version of what my case was about. He mischaracterized the facts, distorted the issues, cited the wrong law, and told the judge it was a frivolous case brought by two disaffected individuals. I tried to interrupt when my adversary prevaricated, but Judge McMurray snarled a sadistic rebuke. "Silence! I'm not talking to you. Sit down or I will jail you for contempt!" Clutching counsel table with a trembling hand, I did what I was ordered to do. I sat down to the realization that the hearing had devolved into a pathetic circus act, wherein the purveyor of justice prejudicially doled out impartial bias.

After my adversary's tiresome opening soliloquy, Judge McMurray permitted me to speak. I tried not to squander my time, so I jumped to my strongest argument first, but that technique did not work. As soon as my argument crystalized, the judge stopped me, turned to my adversary, and asked him more questions about my case. Minutes later, I was allowed to begin again, only to be instantly shut down by another halt-speaking command. The fix was surely in. I barely got a chance to present the necessary elements that would support my claims. When I tried to speak for the last time, the truculent dictator brashly cut me off and proclaimed he was ready to issue a final decision.

Silence fell upon the courtroom. I heard a bird shriek in the distance. Judge McMurray drew in an unrestrained breath and slowly turned to my adversary, pointed his gnarled, arthritic finger high in the air, and spiritedly said, "You win!" Afterward, he turned to me, pointed the same gnarly finger offensively at my face, and loudly yelled, "You lose!"

That was it! My case was summarily dismissed without any reason given. To top things off, as a last kick in the face, the tyrant ordered my clients to pay the defendants' attorney fees and costs. I informed the court I would appeal, and in response, Judge McMurray savagely growled, "Go ahead. Maybe the appeals court can tell me what to do!"

As I left the courtroom, trying not to appear disappointed, I looked to my right and made a mental note of each individual my adversary represented. They were all present, five defendants and two additional representatives. The five defendants consisted of four aged men and one woman who had just pushed past her prime. The two additional representatives were young men who should have known better.

The four old men were creaky and completely nondescript. They all looked similar, so similar in fact, I knew it would be difficult to distinguish between them at a later date. Each round-faced crony had chalky hair tinged with sickly, jaundiced streaks and unexceptional facial features overlaid on blotchy, sun-damaged skin. They all stood in a hunched over way, which exemplified their stooped physiques, and they all flaunted distended bellies that hung over their belts, making them look bloated by hardened impotency. The attire the cronies modeled was similarly nondescript. They all wore tan pants, different colored golf shirts and dark-hued sport coats, the designated male uniform for their exclusive fraternity, I speculated.

The well-seasoned female defendant was escorted by one of the young men representatives and the couple was contrastingly distinct compared to the old men. The older woman called the young male who accompanied her "Dylan." Clearly, Dylan was the woman's son. They looked so much alike: same raven-black hair, same wide eyes with black curled eyelashes, same straight nose with aristocratic attributes, same voluptuous, rose-colored lips, and same smallish stature with medium-build frames. The two even possessed the same mannerisms, particularly in the way they walked with a slinky bounce to their step.

The singular characteristic that drastically distinguished the raven-haired duo from each other was their coiffures. The woman proudly wore her tresses loose and brushed back, highlighting her sharp widow's peak. Dylan wore his hair short, a tad longer than a crew cut, with bangs he spiked upwards with gel. Although a grown man, about thirty years old, Dylan seemed childish and unaware. He did exactly what his mother told to him to do without any disagreement, and all the while he displayed a mysterious yet pitiful persona.

The other representative with the group seemed a bit younger than Dylan. His facial features were not completely discernible because his straw-colored hair fell into his eyes, masking the windows to his soul. He was lanky, bow-legged, and shabbily dressed in a wrinkled flannel shirt and torn jeans. His work-worn hands were swollen and calloused; his chipped fingernails were embedded with brown grime. He seemed thoroughly grubby, just as if he had been working in a field right before coming to court. The young man had a quiet demeanor. He did not speak to anyone during the course of the morning's events.

My adversary, and those he represented, stared at me with mocking condescension as I left the courtroom. Humiliation set in as I retreated down the dreary hallway and raced to the parking lot. Charcoal clouds circled overhead and the whooshing wind had picked up speed during the time I had spent indoors. The wind was so brutal when I rushed to my car, my skirt blew up, exposing my underwear. I impulsively tugged it downward so it would not blow up again, all to no avail. Despite my valiant struggle, my unmentionables revealed themselves once more. I felt my face flush with fast pumping blood, and I wished I could melt into oblivion. Anyone watching saw the high-waisted briefs I was forced to wear because I hadn't thought to wash my more attractive undergarments before the hearing. As I got into my car, I wondered whether Judge McMurray would get to play golf later that day; maybe he had been misinformed about the afternoon's weather outlook.

It took longer than expected to drive home because I had to stop several times to wipe away periodic waterfalls of tears that obstructed my vision. During my final stop, I looked into the rearview mirror, and it reflected a person I wished I did not know. My reddened eyes were puffy from rubbing; my blemished face was streaked from weeping; my makeup had already washed away; my salty tears burned. Somehow, in spite of my despondency, I eventually arrived home. My husband, James, did not ask what happened. He just hugged me . . . he knew.

I always shed a few tears after I lost anything: a case, a bet, my dignity, or even a simple argument. But the worst tears, tears of confounding failure, came after working diligently for a cause or concern, only to later see it crushed by an undeserving opponent. Such circumstances left me feeling heartbroken and ironically, lonely. There was an aching sense deep in my core that it was me against the world and no one cared.

It took a couple of days of wound licking to realize the case I had lost was not about me or the unfair way I was flattened in the courtroom. There was much more going on—of that I was sure. I had two options: continue to feel sorry for myself and lay down my arms, or deliver a powerful counterblow and attempt to vanquish the wrongdoers.

CHAPTER 2
THE BEGINNING

When I was in law school, I went to a psychic tarot-card reader with three of my law-student girlfriends on a whim one afternoon after classes dispersed. The reader we had chosen operated out of a modest house located near the greasy spoon where we spent hours pouring our hearts out to each other while drinking bitter, sludgy coffee and eating sugary, stale desserts.

At first, I was eager to embark on the spooky adventure, but when the psychic collected upfront non-refundable fees from us before offering any pearls of wisdom, my enthusiasm waned and my pessimism waxed. As a result, I did not anticipate hearing any supernatural details about my future that would prove informative, but I stayed in the game and waited my turn for a reading. The psychic called my name last and summoned me into a back room with a doorway shrouded by filmy red fabric. After I ducked into the chamber of foresight and sat at an old Formica table, I watched the fortuneteller shuffle an oversized deck of illustrated cards. She dealt the first card from the pack and flipped it over. It was the card of Justice.

The reader peered into my eyes and before she turned over any other cards, she asked, "Are you from the South?"

Thinking she should know where I was from, I jokingly replied, "Oh yes, South Jersey."

Unamused, the clairvoyant stiffly clarified her question. "I want to know if you are from a southern US state?"

"No," I replied in a more serious vein.

Recalling the psychic's response to my revelation years later, I will always believe in a person's ability to prophesy the future because she convincingly prophesied mine when she said, "You are a southern girl at heart, and I feel as though you are from the South."

James and I had relocated to the South after working for a number of years in the big city where we both attended college and professional school. Exhausted by the drudgery of the rat race, we needed a change of venue, so we moved to small-town America and briefly settled in North Carolina. Soon after relocating, James received a lucrative proposition to work in a rural town in north Georgia. He was interested in the position, but he wanted me to see the town before he made any final decisions. So one scorching hot summer weekend, we loaded up the car and headed to Champaign, Georgia, a hamlet located in Davis County, approximately one hour northeast of Atlanta in the southern Appalachian foothills. Once there, we discovered Champaign was truly adorable, and inhabited by friendly residents, so we embarked on a house-hunting venture.

James brought me to a divine blue colonial situated in a secluded neighborhood, perched atop a steep, sloping ridge with a For Sale sign propped against the garage door beside the front entrance. The lawn and flowerbeds were perfectly manicured, and three mighty oak trees provided soothing shade, protecting the homestead from the harsh summer sun. As I got out of the car, I was enchanted by the delightful aroma of August jasmine mixed with the scent of fresh-cut green grass that permeated the air. The garnet-red front door beckoned us to enter, so James punched a code number into the lock box, retrieved the key, and unlocked the bolt. He motioned me to open the door, so I turned the textured-glass knob and unveiled a foyer with rustic hardwood floors and a stairway that vaulted heavenly to the second floor. Stepping through the threshold, my presence was met with an invitation of immediate occupancy; the former owners had already emptied the house of its contents.

I began my tour in the living room, left of the foyer, then I moved into the chestnut paneled den, where I spontaneously visualized myself happily living in the glorious home with James. I skipped into the kitchen next to the den and gazed out the bay window above the sink and to my astonishment, our yet-to-be-born children were cheerfully playing hide and seek in the densely wooded backyard. I deliberately proceeded through each room, and upon viewing every nook and cranny, my excitement percolated and bubbled over. I could not contain it, my veins vibrated with an overwhelming tingling sensation that stoked my euphoria.

I returned to the foyer for a second time, and as I looked up the stairway, I watched our lovely future daughter gracefully descend, all dressed up, ready to attend her senior prom. My heart pulsed with exhilaration as I toured the upstairs bedrooms. The home was more than perfect; there was even an impressive home office with built-in barrister bookcases adjoining the downstairs den that would enable me to continue my freelance legal brief writing business.

At the completion of my intoxicating exploration, I rushed to find James waiting in the living room. I jumped into his welcoming arms and whispered softly in his ear, "I love it!"

James twirled me around and whispered back, "It's ours!"

James had already purchased the house and, unbeknownst to me, he had already accepted the job offer in Georgia after he took a solo trip to interview for his new position. James gave the house to me and our future family as a present. I was stunned and incredulous.

How on earth had he been able to pull off such a surprise? Amazing! Most people might find it unacceptable for their partner to make such monumental decisions without consultation, but James chose right—I was ecstatic.

James and I settled into our new home and our new life quite easily. We spent time decorating, laughing, and having a lot of fun. Our new neighbor, Evelyn, was an aging, sweet-natured Hispanic lady with a slight accent, who lived alone with three pint-sized dogs. She was supremely pretty, altogether petite, and a masterful cook, which was evidenced by her rotund midsection. Evelyn was an absolute dream to have as a neighbor, quiet but ever attentive and helpful. She watched over us with the enveloping love of a mother hen. Frequently, Evelyn would stop by and deliver a casserole, always with the same excuse: "I made too much, and I know you two are busy, so I thought you would like some dinner."

Once sunny spring afternoon while Evelyn and I discussed gardening techniques in her front yard, James returned from work earlier than usual.

"Oh, there's James. He's early," I said to Evelyn.

"I wonder why," Evelyn added as we walked towards his vehicle.

James slowly rolled down his window.

"Hi, James, why are you home so early?" I asked.

"Aren't you glad to see me?" he replied, brandishing a sneaky, full-toothed smile.

"Oh yes," I said, just as I noticed a shoebox resting on the passenger seat.

"I have a surprise for you," he announced.

"What's in the box?" I gushed.

"I love surprises," Evelyn imparted.

James opened his door, gingerly grasped the surprise-containing box, and coyly slid out of his seat, careful not to shake the box he held.

Evelyn and I cozied up to James and his mystery box, and prodded him to open it. James slowly lifted the lid in an effort to savor the occasion, then he let us peek at the surprise. The box contained an adorable white kitten with golden mosaic eyes, odd black and gray spots, and a tail that looked like it belonged to a raccoon.

"I found her underneath my car in my office parking lot. She looked so tiny and scared; I had to bring her home. Can we keep her? Pleeeease?" James teased as he deposited the tiny kitten into my arms.

"She is so sweet," I cooed as I held the soft, purring animal close to my heart.

"She should thank her lucky stars you found her. She is so cute," Evelyn cheerfully remarked.

James and I simultaneously cried, "Star!"

Star was the perfect name for the newest member of our family.

I had practiced law for some time before I stepped into—or I should say, stepped *back in time into*—the antiquated courtroom in Lakewood City, Georgia. I was at the top of my game for a while writing freelance legal briefs, working mainly in federal courts. Most of the cases I handled dealt with constitutional discrimination issues and equal protection, but for the most part, there wasn't any type of federal case claim to which I could not speak. Numerous attorneys from all over the country sought me out for consultation and asked me to write briefs for their federal court cases. I collected the lion's share of my contacts when I lived in the city up north and I was careful to nurture those relationships so my attorney contacts would continue to refer work my way even after relocating.

I carried on my brief writing business for a number of years, working out of my well-equipped Champaign home office while James steadily built a thriving medical practice. I kept myself busy writing when James was away; I often worked well into the night and on the weekends. Legal research and brief writing was tedious, but when I won a case, I felt a sense of earnest satisfaction because I represented those without a voice. I was thankful to be helping others. I was gratified to be working on cases with meaning. I was also appreciative that James was helping the sick recover, even though his excessive hours meant less time for him to spend with me. The sacrifices we made were wholly worthwhile.

Notwithstanding all outward appearances, one day, I abruptly stopped practicing law. I completed work on my active cases, I refused to take new cases, and I let lapse all of the contacts I had had with the attorneys with whom I worked and consulted. I could not do it anymore. I was done. I was tired of the lack of civility and integrity in the practice of law. I could not listen to anymore lying, cheating attorneys who would do anything to win. I could not listen to anymore lying, cheating clients who would say anything to win.

Right before my exodus from the legal profession, I phoned a client—who had been fired and replaced by a man half his age—to ask him what he wanted in terms of a resolution to his age discrimination case. The client paused briefly in order to carefully select his words, then he maniacally stated he wanted to see the man who discharged him clutch his chest, fall to the ground, writhe in pain, and die an agonizing death as a result of a massive heart attack. That was the last straw that broke the proverbial camel's back. I knew it had happened; my impression of the practice of law had turned into a hackneyed cliché. I had become a commonplace cynic, who thought all lawyers were cheats and all clients were either greedy or just plain crazy.

I needed to get out, take a break, and make a change or something. However, things were a little more complicated than just having severe disillusionment with my chosen profession. I was also experiencing serious personal problems. The old adage that things are not always what they seem certainly rang true for me when I learned that my perception of my own stability was founded on false beliefs in security, love, and happiness. Nothing was right in my life. My serious personal problems brought on the fight-or-flight response, and I chose flight. Not only did I quit my practice, but I also took off—I guess you could say I ran away, I just checked out.

On the morning of my departure, after I packed a bag with all the necessities I would need for an indefinite stay, I carried Star to Evelyn's house and knocked on her door.

"Hola, how are you today, mija?"

"I'm okay. Can you look after Star for a while?" I mumbled.

"Yes, I would love to. What's wrong? You look so sad. Are you going somewhere?"

"Yes, but I don't want to talk about it."

Evelyn pressed, "When will you be back?"

"I don't know," I said as a tear slipped down my face.

Knowing Star was safe, I returned home, grabbed my suitcase, and proceeded to my car, but right after I locked the front door, I reopened it and went into the kitchen. I retrieved one of Evelyn's homemade lasagna casseroles from the freezer and left it on the counter to defrost so James would have something to eat when he got home. Then I skipped town for good, believing I would never return to Georgia.

I ended up at my law-school girlfriend's house. Her name was Sandy, and she stayed up late waiting for me. I had driven for more than ten hours to her massive, chateau-inspired mansion, which was located in an upscale town twenty miles due north of Philadelphia, Pennsylvania. Upon my arrival, she showed me to a handsome guest room with a four-poster bed draped with a down blanket encased in a velvety plum-colored duvet. Sandy gave me clean towels and said we could talk in the morning. James had no idea where I was and I did not answer my phone.

As I unpacked my bags, I realized the only things I had lugged to Pennsylvania were gaudy, sparkly party dresses and cheap, ugly jewelry;

I had not packed underwear or pajamas. How could I wake up and put on a party dress? I lay down in my clothes, attempting to rest after the exhausting drive, but rest was elusive and sleep was impossible. I could not stop shaking. The shaking was a manifestation of my overwhelming anxiety that began an hour into my drive to Sandy's house, and could not be controlled. My body was overcome by intermittent throbbing spasms that forcefully surged through my muscles indiscriminately and would not cease. Perhaps I needed to be in a hospital rather than the safe comfort of my friend's house. After several intense moments of twitchy repose, I rose from the bed and left the guestroom.

I silently went downstairs and picked a book off the shelf in Sandy's study, hoping that reading would quell my acute distress. I chose a book of Irish limericks. Kind of cute and cheery. I had never read a book of limericks. Notwithstanding the upbeat nature of the limericks, the rhymes did not provide the necessary cheer. My shaking continued and grew stronger as the hours passed. I felt like I was hooked to an archaic electrotherapy machine that administered punishing shocks every time I moved my body. I needed to stop shaking. I thought a breath of fresh air might do me some good, so I decided it would be a nice gesture showing gratitude if I went to the mini-mart and bought breakfast for Sandy and her husband, Connor. People up north typically went to the nearest mini-mart and bought breakfast rather than make the meal at home because everyone was so busy.

I headed out at five thirty; it was a rainy, bone-freezing Tuesday morning. The mini-mart parking lot was packed so I had to wait for someone to leave before I could park. Eventually, I found a spot and got out of my car. When I entered the mini-mart, my nostrils were immediately slammed with the pervasive smell of spiced coffee and fried eggs that hung in the air. I licked my lips. The thick aroma was so overtly intense, I could actually taste the acidity of the dark-roasted coffee and the lard-laden greasiness of the eggs on my tongue.

The people in search of breakfast were standing in three separate lines. Each line served a different purpose: one for pouring the tasty coffee, one for selecting the yummy breakfast sandwiches, and one for making the payment. You were supposed to move rapidly through each line. Do not spill the coffee that would cause a break in the flow; the coffee girl would have to come out and clean up the mess. Do not take too long to select your breakfast sandwich; no one liked waiting. Pay quickly and do not stop to chat with the cashier; she might get distracted.

Remarkably, the practiced people moved through each line in perfect unison, like dancers on a stage performing a bewitching ballet. Their movements were swift yet graceful, hurried yet composed. I was mesmerized by the dazzling spectacle and for a short time, my mind was satisfyingly disconnected from my emotional pain. But then, a thought shook me loose. It dawned on me that the mini-mart customers were not people. Au contraire, they were nothing more than caffeine and fried-food-addicted automatons. Yes, robots programmed to rhythmically follow a sequence of simple movements in order to satiate their early-morning cravings.

As I waited in the third line lost in thought, a gruff man in a green uniform with his name embroidered above his front left shirt pocket lightly nudged me indicating it was my turn to pay. A cute checkout girl, whose fingernails were painted black and embellished with white cat faces, took my money and returned my change without looking at me. Moving toward the exit, I noticed that my spastic shaking had miraculously stopped during the time I had spent in the mini-mart because I was preoccupied with the fascinating event of buying breakfast.

Sandy and Connor were grateful for the delivery of the early morning food and James showed up at Sandy's house about twenty-four hours later. I was not surprised he was easily able to find me; he was friends with Sandy and Connor, too. I was surprised he had canceled his patients and took time off work to bring me home. James rarely canceled patients and he never canceled them at the last minute.

Back in Georgia, I believed my search for answers relating to my personal difficulties might be found at one of the mammoth stores that purveyed millions of books. I did not live near such a store; the closest one was located almost an hour away, just outside Atlanta. Nevertheless, undiscouraged by spatial distance, determined to solve my dilemma and cure my angst, I had diligently set out on the pilgrimage early one morning after James left for work. Regrettably, however, the day I embarked on my journey to mindful resolution, I considered aborting the mission because inclement weather moved in, and nearly separated me from finding needed answers. About ten minutes into the drive, viscous fog fell from the sky and distorted my perception of the cars and objects on the road. I significantly slowed my speed and plugged along until perseverance won the morning. Although I arrived later than anticipated, I reached my destination unscathed, ready to find my truth. I located the self-help section after I entered the book emporium, then I searched the shelves, pulled a number of publications, and carried them off to a quiet area where I could conduct my research in relative privacy.

"Well, look who it is! What are you doing all the way out here?" was the first thing I heard after I sat in an armchair located in a cloistered corner near the rear of the store.

Startled, I dropped two of my books on the floor . . . then I looked up. I could not believe my eyes. I gaped at the face of the nosey, gossipy, loudmouth of my neighborhood who was disliked by many. My stomach began to churn and my mouth became dry, I could not speak for an instant, so I looked away to pick up the books that had fallen. I tried hiding the titles to my books. I could not let her see the titles. Then she would know, and so would everyone else.

"Hi, do you mind? I'm busy, I can't talk right now."

She looked at me with surprised eyes and a frowning expression. "What are you busy doing?"

"Nothing that would interest you."

The nosey gossip glared at me, waiting for me to say something else, but when I did not, she flung herself around and turned towards the exit. Then, without a goodbye, she angrily marched out of sight, wearing an orange beret that matched the orange patches on her faded bell-bottom jeans, a hideous outfit she had probably bought at a thrift shop because I doubted such clothes could be purchased anywhere else. It seemed like an eternity, but the busybody disappeared and I started my research.

I did not expect to find what I did in fact find. I did not expect to react to the findings in the way I did in fact react. Each book I perused informed me it was time to get a divorce. A relationship cannot survive an affair. I tried choking back the tears; I did not want anyone to see me cry, but my tears streamed anyway. Numerous, published, all-knowing mental health professionals soberly notified me I should begin preparing for a new, different, and perhaps challenging unmarried life. Each treatise declared there were no other options.

I had paused and stopped reading when I became overcome by the immutable directives put forth by the experts. I took a cleansing breath, cleared my mind, and closed my eyes. I tried to conjure up the innumerable instances of blissful joy James and I had experienced during our marriage, but I felt a rock slam upon my heart and crush it. Oozing pain spurted forth. My miserable torment made me think for a transient flash that nothing could stop my emotional agony. As the ache in my heart palpitated in an irregular rhythm, I realized I loved James and I did not want to divorce him. I had been with him since I was in college. Sobs broke free, so I repeatedly sucked in and huffed out hyperventilating breaths, trying to abate my profound sadness. When the heart-wrenching pain eased slightly, I opened my watery eyes and reached for the last book in my pile.

The book had a blue cover and bold black letters trumpeting the title, *He Belongs With Me*. Wiping tears from my flush cheeks, I opened the self-help guide and began to read. It was a concise manual published by a reputable male psychiatrist and oddly, his divorce-attorney wife, which advised women how to save a marriage after an affair. A divorce attorney advocating for staying in a marriage marred by adultery seemed absurd, but I paged through it anyway and to my relief, my mood had changed from one of despair to one of hope. The book turned out to be an inspiring blow-by-blow tutorial informing a wife how to get rid of the other woman, forgive her husband, and move on to a life with more love and respect than one could ever imagine. Bingo! I found the answer to all of my problems. I hastened to the counter, purchased the book, and continued reading it in my car.

I heeded every instruction contained in the book. I never deviated. I did everything the authors told me to do. Some days were better than others. It took many months for me to decide not to leave. I knew I was going to stay with James forever when one day, out of the blue, he fell to his knees, grabbed my legs, and wept, "I'm sorry!"

That was it—those two healing words sealed the deal and made me reflect positively on my relationship. As I looked at my husband with hope for the future I thought, *I'm sorry means so much, it acknowledges your pain, validates your feelings, and asks to begin again.*

CHAPTER 3
THE CASE

After my hiatus—my sabbatical, or my nervous breakdown, whatever one called such an episode back then—I realized it was time to jump back into the legal game. The first order of business involved getting new clients. I could not rely on my longtime legal contacts anymore because most of them held grudges against me for earlier abandoning them during my "extended vacation." Therefore, it had become necessary to cultivate new clients on my own. Thankfully, James recommended me to one of his patients named Gloria, and as soon as she called for a consultation, I hopped in my car and drove over to her house.

Gloria lived nearby in a terribly dilapidated mobile home situated in the rear lot behind her brother's house. When I arrived, I parked in the driveway and made my way to the backyard, which was an utter mess; I had to walk around piles of garbage and discarded household items to reach her front door. It took some time after I knocked on the dirty door for my potential client to answer because she was extremely obese and had trouble ambulating. After she answered, she invited me inside, offered me a seat at her wobbly, water-ring-stained dining set, and told me what happened.

The week before she contacted me, Gloria had traveled with her sister to JollyWorld, a popular amusement park resort located in Atlanta. She attempted to rent a medical mobility scooter at the kiosk located within the park so she could use it to visit each attraction. Unfortunately, as soon as she selected a scooter and tried to mount it, it took off, causing her to fall and scrape her knee. She could not remain at JollyWorld because she was in too much pain. The accident forced Gloria and her sister to end their vacation before it even started.

I decided to take on Gloria as a client because she was sweet and I felt sorry for her. I knew I could win a case like Gloria's and maybe, depending on the amount of the settlement, she could use the proceeds to clean up her yard and perhaps buy a new dining table. I photographed Gloria's mostly healed knee, and she thanked me with a hug before I left her home.

The following weekend, I went to JollyWorld with James to investigate the infamous scooter-rental kiosk in order to determine why Gloria's scooter had failed. The kiosk was located past the entrance gate on the right, so after we purchased our tickets, we approached the rental attendant, a muscled guy who was friendly and helpful. I told him my aunt was interested in renting a scooter on her next visit to the park and he showed us some for hire. Right away, I noticed there weren't any safety cut-off switches on any of the rentable scooters, and none of the scooters had a park gear that would prevent the vehicles from moving while being mounted. Hence, since the evidence we discovered was inculpatory, James videotaped the scooters highlighting the lack of safety features, while I distracted the accommodating attendant with numerous questions about the age and mechanical capabilities of the scooters.

Subsequent to the successful completion of our clandestine mission, James and I spent the rest of the day riding high-speed roller coasters, eating delicious, albeit high-calorie, theme-park fare, and playing kitschy, nearly impossible-to-win carnival games. James loved carnival games. He was completely undeterred by the unlikelihood he could win a prize, and against my sage counsel, he gambled heavily on one game he chose to play. He spent dollar after dollar throwing baseballs into baskets and produced no winning results. He tried longer than I thought he should, but he was his own man, and could not be convinced to stop until he ran out of money, an outcome that occurred not long after his compulsive competitiveness kicked in.

Dejected and cash poor, James trailed behind me on our way toward the exit out of the carnival attraction.

"Hey, wait up! Do you have any dollars I can use?" he pleaded after stopping near a game called Shoot out the Star.

"Really? All these games are fixed. No one wins them. You are wasting your time and money," I replied in a dissuading tone.

"Pleeeease . . . I'll prove you wrong."

"Oh . . . okay," I said, handing James a twenty-dollar bill.

After James snatched the bill, I followed him to a game counter where a tween-aged boy was using an automatic BB rifle, attempting to shoot out a black star pictured in the center of a paper target. The boy shot the rifle with fast-clipped jolts, not stopping till it died an empty death, and although he tried with dedicated persistence, the youngster failed to claim victory.

"This game is really tough," the boy groaned, hanging his head in defeat.

"You did a great job. You just need more practice," James said, patting the boy on the shoulder.

"Let's see if you can win," the boy sassed with an impish grin.

"Sure, let me try. I'm a great shot."

"When did you ever shoot a gun?" I asked, disbelieving James ever shot a gun.

"I used to hunt with my father every summer when I was a kid before he left me and my mother," James recalled.

"Oh," I said, wishing I'd never asked the question.

"By the way, this is called a rifle and not a gun because it has a long, grooved barrel for better precision," James explained as he picked up the rifle and positioned it to fire.

"Oh, I didn't know," I said.

James did not respond. He shifted his attention to the gun and the game, and after he scoped the perfect shot, he proceeded to methodically shoot out the entire star with the composed accuracy of a professional sniper. Astonishingly, he accomplished the endeavor by taking systematic breaks between the dislodgement of every pellet, careful not to hurry the process. At the end of James' performance, the game attendant grabbed the target, and both he and the boy examined it closely. The boy's mouth dropped open and both he and the game attendant murmured in unison, "Wow!"

Joyfully triumphant, James claimed the coveted reward for proficient marksmanship: a fluffy white bear sporting a red bowtie.

"See, I told you I could win, and you didn't believe me. I think I should keep this cute bear for myself."

"I'm sorry. I'll never doubt you again," I said as James nestled the well-deserved award into my arms.

The day after our amusement park adventure, I contacted JollyWorld's risk manager and gave him my damning evidence. JollyWorld agreed to pay Gloria $5,000 to settle the matter. It was a quick, easy, and lucrative conclusion to the case. I was in high spirits when I drove over to Gloria's home to give her the news. Gloria's brother was picking up trash around her trailer and putting it into a black plastic trash bag when I pulled into the driveway. He stopped what he was doing and met me at my car. Gloria was in the hospital.

I felt hot when I walked into the hospital. The sharp scent of disinfectant permeated the wide corridors as I looked for Gloria's room. I had never cared for hospitals, so the visit was more disagreeable than

I would have liked. I found Gloria's room after a wrong turn, then I lightly tapped on her half-opened door.

A woman sitting by Gloria's bedside softly said, "Hello, I'm Gloria's daughter, Pam. Come on in."

Gloria was in extremely poor health. At age sixty-two, she was approaching end-stage renal failure and she could no longer speak. She was using a pad and pencil to communicate, but despite her condition, she seemed upbeat.

I apprised Gloria about the settlement offer. "JollyWorld has offered to settle your case for $5,000. Isn't that terrific?!"

Gloria scribbled on her pad of paper and held it up: "OK JOLLYWORLD PLATINUM PASS."

"Do you want the $5,000?" I asked.

She nodded yes.

"And you want me to get you a JollyWorld platinum pass, too?" I replied, rolling my eyes in disbelief because I had never been presented with such a wacky request.

She perked up and again nodded yes.

I turned to Pam, and she said, "My mother felt robbed of her JollyWorld vacation when the scooter injured her and she would love to see the Christmas lights at JollyWorld this year."

Gloria closed her eyes, so Pam showed me to the door and whispered, "I think the only reason my mother is still alive is because she's determined to go to JollyWorld in a few weeks."

It was a cloudy day in late October when I left Gloria's sick bed.

The next day, I cut a better deal for Gloria. Not only did I get the $5,000, but JollyWorld also agreed to give Gloria a $100 platinum pass. A free annual pass to JollyWorld, Gloria could visit as much as she wanted. I returned to the hospital to impart the news of my conquest and I found Gloria alone in her room. I asked a nurse who was passing by if a notary was available and the nurse said she would send one up.

Shortly thereafter, the notary arrived. Gloria understood what was going on, but she lacked the strength to write. She did, however, muster up just enough momentum to sign the settlement agreement.

Gloria was gone when I returned to the hospital to deliver the settlement money and the JollyWorld platinum pass. She had been transferred to a long-term care facility because she had fallen into an unresponsive coma. I issued the proceeds and the platinum pass to Gloria's brother since he had power of attorney. It was two days before Thanksgiving and icy weather had moved into the area. Three weeks later, Pam phoned to tell me Gloria died alone, hooked to a ventilator. She expressed anguished guilt that she was not with her mother at the time of her death. I did not go to the funeral. I did not know Gloria very well. Instead, I prayed there were Christmas lights in heaven for Gloria to enjoy.

The week between Christmas and New Year's Day of the same year, 2013, James and I visited a common interest development community called Covington Commons for the first time. The community touted itself as a luxury lakeside cooperative established in 1995, located one hour northeast in Lakewood City, Georgia right below the South Carolina border, overlooking breathtaking Carson Lake in the northern part of the Chattahoochee-Oconee National Forest.

Covington Commons consisted of five thousand developed and undeveloped property lots situated in three distinct neighborhoods, Mockingbird Heights, Peacock Plains, and Eagle's Nest. In addition to the luxury homes and homes sites, the entire community was benefitted by a bevy of enticing amenities. The cooperative boasted a yacht club with a sumptuous lakeside restaurant, marinas, boat docks, a complete equestrian park with an event arena, fifty miles of riding trails and boarding stalls, two Greg Norman eighteen-hole golf courses, one nine-hole golf course, two golf-club restaurants, tennis and racquet ball courts, swimming pools, gymnasiums, workout equipment, exercise classes, tetherball courts, etc. You name it, Covington Commons had it all. Anyone could build a house in the community and be on vacation for the rest of their life. There was even a funeral parlor and a cemetery conveniently located within the enclave. Essentially, you could check in and you never had to leave.

The purpose of my trip to Covington Commons was to meet prospective new clients, Jonathan and June Wainright. James tagged along since he had the day off and nothing to do, but I permitted his accompaniment only after he agreed to two non-negotiable conditions: that he not meddle in my dissemination of legal advice, and that he act only as my subordinate. I did not need anyone leaning over my shoulder second-guessing me, which happened to be one of James' least endearing qualities. I desperately wanted to sign the Wainrights as clients in order to fortify my caseload that had become non-existent after I had settled Gloria's claim.

The Wainrights lived in Mockingbird Heights, a neighborhood with many undeveloped lots and less than fifty completed houses. No other houses appeared to be under construction the day we visited, and the roads were woefully cracked, bumpy, and pothole damaged. As I inspected the neighborhood onward to the Wainrights, an uneasy sensation imbued my sensibilities because Mockingbird Heights projected an undeniable feeling of stark abandonment and unthriving neglect. The common areas were overgrown with weeds, the streets were dirtied with debris, and one of the stop signs was toppled to the ground. I was bewildered by the condition of Mockingbird Heights because it could have been so much more. James jolted my thoughts out of a pensive state when he pulled in front of the Wainrights' homestead and announced, "We're here!"

I alighted from the car and walked to the front door, traversing an inlaid-stone walkway, followed by my subordinate. After I rang the doorbell that emitted a joyous little tune, an attractive, elderly couple courteously bid us entrance into their immaculate home. Jonathan was tall, slender, and physically fit. He had salt-and-pepper hair, scarcely any wrinkles, and a smile that put people at ease. June, or "Ms. June," as she preferred to be called, was statuesque, elegant, and also physically fit. She had smooth white hair cut into a shoulder-length bob, a sweet, pinched nose that crinkled upwards when she laughed, and a soulful, lilting voice. Stepping through the doorway, June grasped my hand with a hospitable hold while Jonathan gave James a hearty handshake that lasted a trifle too long.

After the amiable introductions, Ms. June delicately placed her hand on my back and led us to an authentically recreated eighteenth-century English tearoom, wallpapered in a Wedgwood-style blue and white hibiscus pattern.

"Do sit down, please," she said as she offered us chairs around a resplendent table covered with an embroidered white linen tablecloth and set with fine china and silver flatware.

"Thank you for making the drive to our home. We appreciate you coming today," Jonathan remarked when he entered the room after us.

"No problem. We are glad to be here," James said.

"How long have you all lived here? Your home is beautiful," I asked as I beheld Chinese porcelain platters atop the table filled with sweet-smelling treats and steaming biscuits.

"It will be fourteen years next month," Jonathan replied.

"Yes, that's right," Ms. June said, pouring tea from a sterling pot, polished to a gleaming, mirrored shine. "We are originally from Champaign but we moved here after Jonathan retired so we could be near the lake."

"Carson Lake is gorgeous and it is so close to your house," I said.

"We do love the lake," Jonathan averred.

"Everything looks delicious," James declared.

"Please help yourself. There is plenty for everyone," Ms. June said.

I chose a lemon bar, and after I devoured it without finesse, I said, "The lemon bars are delicious. These are the best I've ever tasted."

"My grandmother gave me the recipe on our wedding day. It has been handed down for many generations in my family."

"Everyone loves June's lemon bars," Jonathan added as he stroked Ms. June's forearm.

"Would you like more tea?" Ms. June asked after I gulped my first cup.

"Thank you, I would love more tea." I did not tell Ms. June the tea was not hot enough because she was so sweet. "Your son was nice to recommend my legal services to you. He is a friendly man and a fantastic store manager. He makes grocery shopping a lot easier."

My glowing review of their son's services was met with gushing pride by both of the Wainrights. "Thank you, we are very proud of both of our sons," Ms. June stated as Jonathan smiled in agreement.

After a few more polite exchanges, James became restless with the chitchat. "I think it's time you tell us about your case."

"Oh, yes," said Ms. June.

"Where do you want us to begin?" asked Jonathan.

"How about at the beginning," I suggested.

Mockingbird Heights was the first neighborhood built in Covington Commons, which included a gym and a marina with boat docks. Right after the lots were partitioned and the amenities were built, the developer subdivided the much larger Peacock Plains neighborhood, and annexed to it a new gym with tennis courts, a bigger marina, more boat docks and a nice nine-hole golf course with a putting green. There were thousands of homes built in Peacock Plains post-millennium because people relished the additional recreational comforts. The Eagle's Nest lakefront mansion neighborhood was built after the developer handed over the management of Covington Commons to the Covington Commons Homeowners Association, a.k.a. the Association. The Association spent millions on the lavish amenities in the newest

Covington Commons neighborhood, and most of the amenities about which the Association bragged were located within Eagle's Nest.

The Wainrights sought my counsel because they were concerned that the Association was not properly maintaining the entire Covington Commons community, even though all of the residents paid exorbitant $500 monthly assessment fees for amenity use and infrastructure maintenance. They believed the failure to care for their neighborhood negatively impacted property values and disastrously affected sales, and that was why their neighborhood had not been fully developed. The Wainrights had purchased their home for $320,000, and a recent appraisal indicated its value had dropped to $180,000. The appraiser based the low valuation on the lack of community growth and the failure to properly maintain the neighborhood amenities and basic infrastructure.

The Wainrights agreed with the appraisal report. Ms. June stopped using the nearby gymnasium because she felt sick when she entered the women's locker room due to the strong smell of mold and mildew. She said the bathrooms were filthy and in a state of disrepair. Jonathan complained that the nearby boat docks were similarly in a state of decay, with missing boards on the galley ways that could easily injure residents who sought access to their boats. The couple further lamented that the Association failed to maintain the Peacock Plains amenities, which had also fallen into disrepair. The infrastructure in Peacock Plains continued to deteriorate, just like the infrastructure in Mockingbird Heights. They opined that the Association expended its revenue only on the well-kept Eagle's Nest neighborhood, the affluent subdivision where all the Association board and committee members lived.

The main reason the Wainrights solicited legal assistance was because they feared their sons would not be able to sell their home after their deaths, and they did not want to leave them with a valueless piece of underwater property.

At the close of the eye-opening critique, I advised my hosts that they had a claim for breach of fiduciary duty against the Association and its individual board members for not suitably maintaining the amenities, roads, and other community necessities in Mockingbird Heights. Accordingly, the Wainrights promptly signed the legal contract I had brought with me, hoping for ameliorative relief from the worrisome legal obstacles that stood between them and their serenity.

The couple escorted us to the foyer after I bound myself to their cause. Right before we left, Ms. June said, "Please wait, I have something for you before you go."

"Oh, sure," I said.

Ms. June disappeared but swiftly returned. "These are for you," she said, presenting me with a hand-written copy of the lemon bar recipe and a jar of canned jalapenos. "I always keep copies of the lemon bar recipe on hand because many of my friends ask how I made them. Also, I thought you might enjoy the jalapenos I canned last summer. I still have quite a few jars left over."

"Thank you so much. I'll try to do my best to make your lemon bars as delicious as you make them. Thank you for the jalapenos, too."

I was touched by Ms. June's kindness; she hugged me with grateful sincerity.

After leaving the Wainrights, James and I went to the gymnasium closest to their house. We spoke to the receptionist at the front desk and she said the gym would remain open until eight o'clock for the property owners. We told her we were interested in purchasing property in Covington Commons and as a result, she let us freely walk around the facility.

No one was there. No one was working out. It was a weekday. Most gyms were always filled with people working out, socializing, or otherwise having fun. Aside from the receptionist, we did not see any other workers. The dusty exercise rooms were equipped with aged nautilus machines, rust-speckled free weights, thinned yoga mats, and deflated exercise balls. The indoor pool was drained of its water and the outdoor pool was blanketed with a threadbare mesh cover and closed for the season. The two indoor tennis courts had tattered nets and faded boundary lines. The bathrooms were disgusting, just like Ms. June had said. The entire facility was foul and unkempt.

On our way out, the receptionist eerily disclosed, "Not many people use this gym anymore. Most people drive a few miles down the road and use the newer gym near the yacht club, if they can afford it."

"Afford what?" I asked.

"Afford the admission fees," the receptionist said.

"What admission fees? I don't understand. I thought every household paid monthly assessment fees that allow the residents to use all of the amenities," I said.

"No, not exactly. Initially that was the case, but after Eagle's Nest was built, the board members required all residents to pay additional admission fees to enter the Eagle's Nest amenities in order to defray the building costs for those new amenities."

James asked, "Are the admission fees expensive?"

"Yes, very expensive."

James and I visited local realtors to see the list prices for the Covington Commons homes and lots for sale before we headed home.

One of the realtors revealed, "There are thousands of undeveloped lots for sale in Covington Commons."

"Why are there so many undeveloped lots?" I asked.

James added, "Are the lots hard to sell?"

"Historically, the lots in Covington Commons sold like hotcakes when the community was first developed in 1995. People flocked in droves to buy the lots for investment purposes, or to build their dream retirement homes on Carson Lake. The boom lasted for a while but then the market collapsed in 2008 and many people fell into arrears on the payment of their monthly assessment fees. The Association foreclosed on thousands of lots and took title to those properties. Now, Covington Commons lots in Mockingbird Heights and Peacock Plains are almost impossible to sell. No one wants to pay monthly assessments fees in those failing neighborhoods. The Association has been left holding the bag on thousands of valueless lots for years," the realtor said.

James speculated, "I guess the home values have significantly decreased as well?"

"Home values in Mockingbird Heights and Peacock Plains have radically dropped in value over the years. The communities are stagnating. The roads, utilities, and amenities in those neighborhoods are dilapidated and continue to deteriorate."

"What about Eagle's Nest?" I asked.

"Eagle's Nest is an exclusive well-maintained luxury neighborhood in Covington Commons. Eagle's Nest is not failing. The home values in Eagle's Nest have consistently increased upwards of twenty percent since the neighborhood was developed in 2005 because of the development and maintenance of numerous amenities," the realtor explained.

We went to three different realtors that day and they all said the same thing. The lots and homes were not sellable in Mockingbird Heights or Peacock Plains because no one wanted to pay the expensive assessment fees to live in dying communities the Association refused to maintain.

CHAPTER 4
THE ASSOCIATION

The day after my trip to Covington Commons, I began research-ing common-interest development communities in general and Covington Commons in particular.

Approximately sixty million Americans lived in more than three hundred thousand common-interest developments in the United States, which were governed by non-profit homeowners associations operated by a cadre of board members. The communities were based upon utopian lifestyle choices where property owners shared the costs of both necessities and amenities in either traditional neighbor-hood or apartment settings. The cost sharing enabled the residents to enjoy numerous luxuries that might have been prohibitive under other circumstances. Basically, the communities were managed in the same manner as city governments, wherein homeowners were charged fees for services such as water, sewer, road maintenance, and recreational amenities. Common-interest developments had been growing in popularity since the middle part of the twentieth century, and the number of such communities was predicted to increase expo-nentially in the future.

Specifically, Covington Commons was governed pursuant to the same framework set forth by earlier community cooperatives, but since Georgia laws had relaxed competition and allowed homeowners associations the ability to compete in the private sector, Covington Commons Homeowners Association amassed millions more dollars than the typical association because it engaged in a plethora of unconstrained capitalistic ventures. The Association's lofty $25 million annual budget was partially funded by the monthly assessment and amenity admission fees paid by the residents and lot owners. Another portion of the budget was funded by fees charged to nonresidents who used the yacht club, golf courses, marinas, and restaurants. The remainder of the budget was funded by earnings from a host of other undertakings, like land leases, equestrian events, golf tournaments, vacation rentals, catered parties, weddings, and gas sales to public boaters.

Covington Commons' Bylaws and Declaration of Restrictive Covenants dictated how and by whom the community was governed. Most notably, the promulgations mandated that the community was to be governed by five volunteer board members and six committees staffed by nonpaid residents appointed by the board. The Association committees included a building permit committee, a marketing committee, a long-range planning committee, a recreational amenity committee, a finance committee, and an infrastructure improvement committee. Each board member headed up at least one committee, with the president heading up two committees. The board president was charged with overseeing the finance committee and the infrastructure improvement committee. The finance committee controlled the Association's treasury and the infrastructure improvement committee controlled the construction, maintenance, and improvement of all of the recreational amenities, community utilities, and neighborhood roads.

Detailed voting regulations were also laid out in the Association's governing documents, and instructed that each Association board member be elected by the residents to serve for a two-year term on a rotating basis, with two, then three, board members up for reelection every other year. There were no term limits in place, so a board member could theoretically serve indefinitely up to his or her death, provided he or she could continue to be elected. The sole prerequisite to becoming a board member was being a resident of Covington Commons. No formal training or education qualifications were required. The election rules granted each lot entitlement to one vote, and prior to each election, the board issued code numbers to the property owners so they could vote on the internet. In view of the fact that the board knew all of the individual voting codes, the board could easily discern whether a lot had been voted and how each vote was cast. Therefore, knowing all the code numbers, the board indisputably had the ability to vote an unvoted lot or to change a ballot, which meant the board could conceivably rig an election in favor of the candidates it wanted in office.

Board elections aside, one of the most important aspects of any symbiotic commitment between the governing and those governed is communication and how it is effectuated. In the case of the Association board, it utilized a variety of social media outlets to allegedly keep its residents in the know about board activity, including Facebook, Twitter, and an email-alert system.

I logged on the Association's Facebook page and perused the posts for the prior year. All of the information distributed to the residents was gushingly positive mumbo jumbo stating what a wonderful job the board members were doing. There were no meaningful issues presented, such as how much it would cost to renovate the fitness gymnasium, or what the budget for the yacht club would be for the succeeding year. Only ridiculous things were discussed: The oleander just started blooming at the pavilion near the marina and around the yacht club; if you need a brand-new shirt for your next golf outing, head to one of the pro shops for a stylish find. Nothing I discovered after hours of probing explicitly illuminated specific board behavior— until I came across a website called Locus, a geobased forum that permitted users to log in and blog about issues facing their community. I read many comments posted by the Covington Commons residents on the forum and what I found was completely shocking.

The Covington Commons residents complained incessantly about the Association and its ruling body. The residents accused the Association board of stealing and mismanaging community funds, and they contended that the board exclusively paid for improvements and maintenance in Eagle's Nest to the detriment of the infrastructure in Mockingbird Heights and Peacock Plains. The board members were not the only targets; there were also allegations that the Association committee members and employees were stealing everything from gas, food, merchandise, and even toilet paper from the clubhouses and restaurants. None of the allegations were new; the residents had been making similar indictments for multiple years.

Now normally I would not have put too much stock in criticisms made by disgruntled residents about a board with which they disagreed, but the situation in Covington Commons was different. First, there were hundreds of residents making the claims. Second, the residents were naming the alleged offenders directly, calling them thieves guilty of fraud and other crimes. Third, the residents did not hide their identity on the Locus page. To the contrary, they stated exactly who they were, which would have made it easy to sue the residents for defamation if the statements were untrue. However, after I cross-referenced the names of the board and committee members on a reputable lawsuit data-collection site, I could not find a single case where a board or committee member had personally sued anyone.

Why didn't the board or committee members sue to stop the residents from making "false" recriminations? It was not as if they were unaware of the barrage of criminal accusations; they often logged on to Locus to defend themselves against the claims. Maybe the allegations of criminal activity were not false. Maybe the allegations were true and that was why the board and committee members did not file defamation lawsuits against the residents who charged them with corruption.

The most impactful complaint I read on Locus was posted by a woman named Eula: *Please, someone help us. We are old people who were lured to retire here in Covington Commons. We believed we could live in peace and happiness during our retirement. They are stealing our money and charging unfair fees. Our property values have declined. Now we cannot afford to pay our bills. We're all struggling, that's unless you are part of the board's inner circle. There must be an attorney out there who can help us. Please.*

I stared dumbfounded at Eula's post for a lengthy period. Perspiration began to gather at the nape of my neck. My heart started to beat faster and louder. A burning sensation flared in my sternum. My palms moistened, so I wiped them on my pants. The epiphany struck me with unyielding force: *Could I be the one who could correct the situation?*

I wrote a compelling complaint against the Association and its board members who were identified on the Association's website. Primarily, I asserted that the Association, by and through the actions of its bureaucratic leaders, had breached its community fiduciary duty of care because it had failed to maintain the infrastructure in Mockingbird Heights and Peacock Plains, thereby depriving the property owners of the fair market values of their homes. Secondarily, I insisted the Association breached its fiduciary duty to act fairly because it had only preserved Eagle's Nest and it had failed to distribute the financial assets equitably between all neighborhoods. The singular objective was to force the Association to fix up Mockingbird Heights and Peacock Plains.

On February 13, 2014, I filed the complaint in Carson County superior court, located in the county seat, Lakewood City. I selected February 13, 2014, as the filing date for two reasons: One, when I added all the numbers in the date as per generic numerology methodology, the sum totaled thirteen, a karmic number that portended "upheaval followed by groundbreaking change resulting in future security." Two, the number thirteen had always been a very lucky number for me. I was born on the thirteenth day in May, and Elvis married James and me on a Friday the thirteenth in a cute Vegas chapel just before midnight and just after drinking one too many. There was no question; February 13, 2014, was the perfect day to file an important lawsuit. All the stars were aligned for success. I could not possibly lose based upon my reasonable reliance on infallible theories of superstition.

Fast-forward one month; I was at the point where I needed to tell the Wainrights that I had lost their case. In a nutshell, I had filed a complaint against the Association, neither money nor control was sought, only the even-handed distribution of Covington Commons assets for the benefit of the community at large. The singular goal was to force the Association and its board members to act in a responsible way. The Wainrights did not owe anybody anything. In a cruel turn, howbeit, besides losing the actual lawsuit, my sweet clients owed the evil entity we sued $7,222 for attorney fees and costs the Association allegedly incurred in defending the case. The outcome was ridiculous.

As I was driving to impart the bad news to the Wainrights, I remembered another legal defeat that occurred weeks after graduating from law school. Armed with a JD degree, I had decided to represent myself, hoping to obtain a dismissal of one of my many speeding tickets. The ticket I tried to quash was a citation for speeding sixty miles per hour in a forty-five-mile-per-hour posted zone, which cost a whopping seventy-five dollars. I needed to beat the wrap because I was a poor law school graduate without employment.

I showed up early for my first trial. When the municipal court judge called my case, I asked the ticketing officer to take the stand and instructed the clerk to administer the oath.

"Who do you think you are? A lawyer?" the judge mocked.

"Yes, Your Honor, I am a lawyer," I replied with pride.

The judge motioned me to proceed, and for a short time, I peppered the officer with rapid-fire, blistering questions. I felt strong and confident. I thought I could not lose. Being a lawyer, I would never have to pay another speeding ticket. That belief, however, was not a reality, and my self-possession was a farce. Despite my legal prowess, my confidence evaporated when the judge ordered me to pay the seventy-five-dollar fine and an additional seventy-five dollars in court costs. Ironically, that ten minute, unremarkable trial taught me two of life's most important lessons: overconfidence was never a good thing, and lady justice had a tendency to be a sphinxlike hellcat.

I did not mince words when the Wainrights invited me into their home. I told them forthwith that I lost them $7,222. They did not seem mad, and they did not show any disappointment in the outcome or in my abilities. The Wainrights kindly offered to pay the penalty, and they wanted to compensate me for the work I had already done but I refused to take any money. I advised the couple that we could appeal which meant the payment of the $7,222 would be stayed and not payable until the conclusion of the appellate process. The Wainrights were fully on board and gave me permission to appeal if that was the best course of action.

I slowly motored past Eagle's Nest on my way home from the Wainrights and inexplicably turned into the neighborhood. I stopped near the entrance sign and looked up. My eyes feasted upon a palatial hilltop mansion towering above all the magnificent homes on the lake. The house had to belong to a Covington Commons VIP; maybe it belonged to the Covington Commons board president.

A number of discouraging days passed, and although I had the Wainrights' approval, I had not affirmatively decided to appeal because I was still in the everyone-is-so-mean-to-me mourning stage. Moreover, since my self-esteem was shot asunder with no immediate hope of revival, I feared losing an appeal and possibly exposing the Wainrights to additional monetary penalties. It was clear I needed an ego boost because I was unable to pull up my bootstraps and forget my courtroom degradation on my own. So, I did what I had always done under comparable circumstances, I called my friend Sandy. She was definitely the one to call when the chips were down. She helped save my marriage by giving me a top-notch place to crash during my breakdown, and she always knew what to say to provide warming comfort.

I told Sandy about the case, the ultimate dismissal, and my complete defeat. I ranted about the board member defendants, I ranted about the lawyer who defended them, and I ranted about the judge who had granted them an unjustifiable win. I immoderately vented and Sandy quietly listened to every word. At the close of my tirade, Sandy said something for which I will always be thankful: "Oh my God, the Association has no idea who it's dealing with. The board members will regret the day they ever heard of you. Remember that quote: Failure is a godsend; it ignites the flame of self-improvement in those with a desire to succeed. That applies to you now. You are the best lawyer for the case. I have never known you to give up. You will win."

CHAPTER 5
THE ALLIES

One showery afternoon, soon after Sandy gifted me with encouraging words, I resolved to appeal Judge McMurray's ruling, so I Googled each board member to discover any information that might help with the time-consuming and potentially expensive undertaking. Interestingly, I came across a story published in the local Lakewood City newspaper almost three years earlier. Two Covington Commons residents, Alfred Mertz and Bill Collins, had hired an attorney and brought a lawsuit against the Association and its board members. The suit requested the production of receipts and records substantiating certain expenditures made by the Association. The Association and its board members filed a motion to dismiss, and the presiding judge, the infamous Judge Doyle McMurray, dismissed the case at the first hearing. As I read the article, I wondered if Judge McMurray had waived his gnarled finger high in the air and growled, "You lose!" when he ruled against the two residents in favor of the Association.

I found a phone number for one of the residents who had initiated the lawsuit and called him.

The phone rang three times before a man answered, "Hello, Alfred here."

My voice quavered when I identified myself. "Hello, I sued the Covington Commons Homeowners Association and its board members on behalf of the Wainrights."

Mr. Mertz's cordial words lessened my disquiet. "Oh yes, I heard about that. Please call me Alfred."

"I read about your case against the Association on the internet and I was wondering if I could ask you a few questions?"

"Sure, I hope I can help."

"I think we might be able to force the Association to renovate Mockingbird Heights and Peacock Plains. That's if the appeals court reverses the decision rendered by Judge McMurray."

Alfred listened patiently, then, in a voice laced with depressed cynicism, he said, "I don't think anything will ever change here at Covington Commons. Believe me, we tried to hold the Association and its board members accountable."

"But what about the monthly assessment fees? The residents of Mockingbird Heights and Peacock Plains pay the fees but they don't get anything in return. Their neighborhoods are declining."

"Yes, I understand. No one likes paying the monthly assessment fees because the fees are only used for the upkeep of Eagle's Nest."

"Since those don't provide residents in Mockingbird Heights or Peacock Plains with any benefits, the residents should not have to pay them."

"I agree with you, and did you know that in addition to the monthly assessment fees, each resident must pay admission fees in order to get into each Eagle's Nest amenity? Membership in the Eagle's Nest golf clubs costs in the tens of thousands of dollars each year."

"I heard about the admission fees."

"The board doesn't maintain the amenities in Peacock Plains and Mockingbird Heights so we can't use those amenities, and the extra admission fees in Eagle's Nest are so expensive most people can't use those amenities either. The residents of Eagle's Nest have the best amenities all to themselves."

Outraged by the extortionate admission fees, I spontaneously came up with an additional plan of attack. "Let's contact as many property owners as possible and have them sign a petition requesting that the owners be permitted to eliminate the payment of the excessive admission fees by voting on the issue."

"No one will sign a petition. People who live in Covington Commons are old. Most are in their seventies and eighties. Many residents are on fixed incomes, and many lost a lot of money when their stock-invested retirement accounts shrunk in 2008. The only people not affected by the market crash were the Association board and committee members—they all live in Eagle's Nest."

"We have to try something,"

"No one has the money to fight the board, and no one wants to be ostracized like I was for years. After Judge McMurray dismissed the lawsuit me and my friend Bill brought against the Association, the board started a full onslaught campaign to chastise us. They told the residents at the open board meetings that we were troublemakers and losers. No one wants to be hated by the board and the committee members like we are."

"Maybe some people will help and try to bring about change. I read a lot of resident complaints on the Locus website."

"Sure, a lot of people complain about the board on the Locus site, but it's impossible to go after the board. It is just the way it is. Nobody can do anything. We already tried and failed. I don't want to fight anymore. I just want to live as peacefully as possible. I can't move because my home in Peacock Plains is not marketable anymore. I owe more for it than it's worth."

"I understand," I responded softly.

"How about if I give you Bill's phone number? He is smart and has much more information than I do. Maybe he can help you."

"Thank you, I appreciate your help."

"Wait, let me give him *your* number. I don't want to give out his number if he doesn't want to talk to you."

"Thank you for speaking with me. Please give my number to Bill," I said dolefully as the call ended.

It was five, six, then seven days, and Bill did not call. On the eighth day, I checked my messages and there it was, an audio recording of Bill Collins' resonant voice. I returned his call at once. Bill first asked if I worked for the Association, to which I replied no. His apprehension was more than understandable. After I assured Bill of my sincerity and clarified my role, I garnered his trust, and then the floodgates gushed open.

Bill was an absolute treasure trove of information. He knew all the players, and he saved every document from the lawsuit he filed against the Association. In addition, he saved every written statement and every audio/video recording ever issued by any Association representatives since he moved to the community ten years previously. Bill told me that all of the documents and recordings were stored in boxes in his basement. When I heard that, paranoid thoughts jumped into my head. What if his house burned down, or his basement flooded, or something worse? I was ready to jump in my car and drive an hour to retrieve the whole lot.

Bill advised me there was no hurry, and he proposed I meet with Alfred and himself the next week for lunch at the halfway point between our homes because he didn't want me to drive the entire distance. He suggested having lunch at the Vidalia Café, a comfort-food restaurant located in Canton in a remodeled Victorian house that was painted with a whitewashed exterior and a green-stained roof to evoke Georgia's treasured onion. Bill explained that the Vidalia Café was always busy, but if we went at the right time of day, we could sit uninterrupted for hours. He recommended dining after the dispersal of the lunch crowd at one thirty.

I arrived at the appointed location thirty minutes early, and they were already there, sitting outside on the spacious porch, rocking in oversized white chairs. I knew it was them, just like they knew it was me, even though we hadn't exchanged descriptions of each other. Alfred was a sweet, chubby man, who wore faded jeans, a purple T-shirt, an olive-green bomber jacket, and a Detroit Tigers baseball cap. Bill, conversely, was a much taller, slim man, who walked with a noticeable limp. Bill sported dark slacks, a blue polo shirt, and a gray fleece jacket. Bill and Alfred both jumped out of their rockers, and each shook my hand with the endearing two-handed method after I approached. Both men had friendly faces, expansive smiles, and bright white teeth. The men escorted me into the restaurant and a hostess led us to a table near the kitchen and gave us menus when we sat down.

Before reviewing the menus, Bill handed me a thumb drive and said, "You will need this." He also took a thick binder stuffed with papers out of a backpack he carried and slid it towards me. "These copies are for you."

"Thanks, this is great." I felt like a secret agent on a highly classified mission.

Seconds later, a waiter with splatters on his apron intrusively came to our table and demanded, "What will you have?"

I responded with an unsettled look that the waiter returned with a glare. Clearly, he did not want to come back later to take our order, so I scrambled for my menu and pointed to a photograph of a Caesar salad. Bill and Alfred each asked for the same salad and cups of coffee.

The waiter frowned at me with impatience. "Do you want a drink?"

"Water, please," I said, feeling unfairly bullied.

As the waiter plodded off to place our orders, Alfred observed, "That boy does not seem very happy with us."

"Do you think he'll spit in our food?" Bill joked.

"Oh no, now I don't think I can eat anything for lunch!" I cried.

"Bill's a tease. He won't spit in our food," Alfred said without conviction.

We talked about our personal lives while we waited for our lunch. The more we talked, the easier it was to admire both men.

Alfred had been a school bus driver in a humble town near Saginaw, Michigan for more than forty years. He was the father of twin girls he raised alone because his first wife died when his daughters were in grade school. Alfred's face reddened with blushing pride as he spoke of his beloved children. One daughter was an accountant who lived in Seattle, Washington with her husband and three children; the other was an award-winning chef who lived in Sherman Oaks, California with her wife and their dog Sally. Alfred relocated with his second wife, Susan, to Covington Commons in 2004, four months after Bill relocated with his wife, Eva.

Bill, the tease, had valiantly served his country as a private in the army after he graduated from high school. He was a field radio operator who was sent to the Vietnamese frontlines in the late 1960s. He seriously injured his left leg when he was gunned down by Viet Cong forces during a sneak attack near his unit's base camp. In spite of his injury, during the continued siege, Bill called for help and protected the other members of his unit from a barrage of shelling. He was awarded a purple heart and a silver star for his distinguished service. Bill had gone back to school on the GI bill and earned a degree in math and economics after he was honorably discharged from the military. He taught at a junior college for more than thirty years in a tiny town near Albany, New York. In addition to his lovely wife, Eva, Bill had two children and three grandchildren who he adored.

The waiter brought our food fifteen minutes after we ordered, and that signaled an end to the exchange of pleasantries. Over the next two hours, Bill told me about the Association, the board members, the committee members, the employees, and even the Association attorney. He knew everything about Lakewood City, and he knew everything about every mover and shaker who lived there. To say that Bill had his finger on the pulse of the Lakewood City community was a gross understatement. I felt dizzy toward the end of our meeting because it was difficult to fully absorb the vast amount of information Bill had unloaded on me in one sitting. Consequently, over the course of many months to follow, I called or emailed Bill regularly with questions.

When the time came to leave the Vidalia Café, Bill insisted he pay for my lunch, and he did so using his senior citizen discount card. Bill and Alfred were kind, sincere men, two benevolent heroes. I was no longer demoralized. I was certain the advent of something good was on the horizon.

CHAPTER 6
THE ADVERSARIES

My attorney opponent in the Covington Commons Homeowners Association case was Herschel Marks, a true Georgia boy who had grown up in the southwest region of the state, hailing from the Macon area, where he attended both college and law school. He migrated to northeastern Georgia right after graduation when he was hired by Hunter, Munson, and Handle, a small law firm located on Center Street in the west end of Lakewood City, two blocks behind the courthouse. The firm's name changed to Hunter, Munson, Handle, and Marks when he was promoted to partner five years after his hire, but the promotion did not engender feelings of loyalty on Herschel's part. He left his namesake law firm six months after his promotion because he was lured away by the Association to be in-house counsel with guarantees of higher wages, better benefits, luxurious offices, and a substantial expense account.

One thing that was evident to the entire Lakewood City community was that Herschel craved the finer things in life. He displayed his love of material comforts when he purchased and painstakingly renovated a late-nineteenth-century neo-Palladian revival mansion approximately one year after he became the legal fixer for the Association. Herschel's stately brick manor, situated in the east end of Lakewood City in the revitalized historic district, abutted a busy side street and showcased a classical pediment held up by four robust columns affixed to a blue painted-wood porch. The ample backyard was enclosed by a high brick fence that surrounded a stand-alone guesthouse Herschel rented for additional income.

On the surface, Herschel was the epitome of the upstanding Lakewood City resident, but local chatter claimed he possessed an un-gentlemanly quality; he harbored the unique ability to deceive, which made him a terrific lawyer and a not-so-terrific person. Herschel often lied about things he need not have. One unworthy deception he sus-tained for years was hiding his homosexuality from his community, the members of his law firm, and the Association because he likely did not want to risk any backlash should anyone not approve of his sexual preferences. Notwithstanding his attempted concealment, community members were aware of but did not care that Herschel was a homo-sexual, and that David Clifton, the good-looking, young renter of his guesthouse and a guard at the local county jail, was his lover.

The Association board and committee members for whom Herschel worked were all close friends, and all had been serving in their unpaid positions for at least seven to nine years. The influential friends fre-quently golfed and exercised together, and they traveled to property owners' association conferences all over the country, allegedly at the Association's expense. The elites were so tight knit, they were even part of an exclusive monthly dinner club, a trend wherein one couple prepared a gourmet meal for the other couples on a rotating basis. The Association's upper echelon was a nice cozy group. They were enjoying retirement the way everyone should—but how not many could.

The Association board member who wielded the most power was Gerald Lavine, a purebred Detroiter who had formerly worked in middle management for a car-manufacturing company. It was rumored Lavine never made a lot of money, chiefly due to his lack of ingenuity, but he was most certainly loyal—maybe not to his wife as reputed—but he did work for the same company for more than three decades. After retiring with a paltry pension, he moved into an unpretentious Peacock Plains home with his wife in order to take advantage of Georgia's clean air, low taxes, and southern lakefront lifestyle. Relocating to Covington Commons, and thereafter volunteering for numerous unpaid governing positions, proved productive for Lavine. He built an impressive resume charitably serving the Association for three years as finance committee member, then two years as treasurer, then he secured the respectable spot of vice president. He had completed his admirable rise in the ranks when he scored the enviable post of Association president, a position he would never relinquish of his own volition.

Following his commendable ascent to absolute power, Lavine built an expensive waterfront compound with a pool, fountains, docks, and boat slips. His dwelling sat high atop a hill and overlooked all of the other Eagle's Nest lakefront homes. Lavine was finally living large and crazy; he had become important for the first time in his life and he loved flaunting his significance by driving his customized waterski boat extremely fast up and down the lake on warm summer days.

Lavine's best friend was Cedric Holmes, the attorney who had successfully represented the deadbeat dad the day my case against the Association was dismissed. Cedric lived in boundless splendor with his wife in the posh home situated beside, but just beneath, Lavine's exalted residence. He was a sole proprietor attorney, and although he advertised that he handled all civil matters, his main area of practice involved representing deadbeat dads. He counseled the deadbeats that working for a living was not always the best way to obtain money. Instead, he helped them get social security disability insurance payments. Later, in order to help them retain their disability benefits, he appeared in court on their behalf and got them off the child-support-payment hook, of course with the chivalrous help of Judge McMurray. Life was sweet for Cedric. He was richly compensated by the deadbeats, purportedly from the illegal proceeds they received from street selling their pain medication to the highest bidders. Cedric was not a board or committee member, but he did assist the Association whenever his services were solicited.

Raven-haired Cindy Matthews was the second-most influential board member. She was a divorced middle-aged woman who had re-settled to Covington Commons from New York City with her only child in tow, her adult son Dylan, after accepting an early retirement package from the Wall Street firm for which she had worked as a stock analyst. Cindy lived alone in her Eagle's Nest mansion, and it was no secret she had countless affairs with much younger men, most of whom were Association employees who were routinely fired from the Association after their sexual services were no longer desired. Cindy was known to be tough and vengeful if she did not get her way; it was not pleasing to cross paths with the abrasive vixen and be on the receiving end of her vicious wrath.

Cindy's thirty-four-year-old son, Dylan, was educated at the best elementary and secondary private institutions in New York City, even though he was not a particularly ambitious or grade-driven boy. His admissions into the soi-disant highly regarded schools were obtained purely due to the contacts Cindy had made over the years that guaranteed for her and her offspring coveted seats at the table of New York's preeminent citizenry. Dylan received a college degree from one of the nation's top-ranked universities, and an MBA from a similar institution, despite his love of cutting classes and his addiction to performing well below his God-given abilities. After receiving his MBA, Cindy secured for her son the position of operations manager at the

Association. Dylan was an irrefutable mama's boy. He had even lived with his mother until he assumed the operations manager position, which was when he, at long last, cut the apron strings and moved into a rented apartment in downtown Lakewood City.

Possibly the most important employee at the Association was Haywood Martin. Martin's importance was not based on any endearing quality or innate talent. He was important simply because he did exactly what he was told to do by the Association board members. The twenty-eight year old with flowing blonde hair had been working for the Association for approximately six years when I first saw him in Judge McMurray's courtroom.

Martin grew up in Lakewood City but had moved to West Virginia after dropping out of high school to work in the coalmines. He had returned to Lakewood City after he was laid off due to a downturn in the coal industry and started a small landscaping business. Fortune smiled on Martin's industriousness and many of the board and committee members who lived in Eagle's Nest hired him to landscape their properties. Lavine, in particular, was exceptionally impressed with Martin, so much so, that he rewarded him with the full-time position of director of maintenance for the entire Covington Commons community. Martin was not a resident of Covington Commons; he lived by himself less than ten miles away on a tract of land upon which he parked a mobile home.

CHAPTER 7
THE VANS

A mere two days after meeting Bill, I called him with numerous questions, and after he supplied me with edifying responses, he divulged the specific reason why he and Alfred had filed the lawsuit against the Association in the spring of 2011.

It was common knowledge that the Association purchased one dozen utility vans every three years to be used solely for Association business. In 2010, when the Association vehicles turned three, the board, as usual, purchased a dozen new vans, and claimed that the old vans were traded in for discounted volume pricing. Bill and two other residents had witnessed the delivery of twelve shiny new 2010 vans to the employee parking lot adjacent to the yacht club, the same location where the vans were kept when not in use. Approximately one month after the delivery, Bill noticed there were only four utility vehicles regularly parked in the lot—eight were missing.

Bill's concerns intensified when he discovered that a used car dealership had sprung up and opened for business near Covington Commons just after the vehicles went missing. He learned that the dealership was selling twelve older-model utility vans, similar to those the board claimed to have traded in, and eight brand-new ones. Bill asked about the missing vehicles at the following board meeting, and Lavine insisted that only four new vehicles were purchased in 2010. He stated that eight of the vehicles were returned to the manufacturer after delivery in an effort to reduce expenditures for the benefit of the community. In addition, Lavine asserted that the board decided to re-sell the older vehicles rather than trade them in because more money would be realized on a resale as opposed to a trade. Bill asked to see the original sales receipt for the purchase of the twelve new vans, and he asked to compare the vehicle identification numbers of those vans in the used car lot against the numbers on the receipts. The board chided Bill for making unfounded defamatory allegations, and he was asked to leave the board meeting before the completion of the board's business.

Months later, the Association's 2010 annual accounting statement was released, and it established that the board spent more than $500,000 on new utility vehicles. Bill called a respectable dealership and learned that each new cargo van would have a retail sales cost of approximately $42,000. This validated his original belief that twelve vans had been purchased, and that eight were not returned to the manufacturer. Moreover, a sale of multiple vehicles would have generated a significant discount, reducing the cost of each vehicle to approximately $38,000, which meant the total sales cost should have been closer to $450,000. Bill speculated that someone was skimming money by recording a higher purchase price for the vehicles than what was paid and pocketing the difference. Any person with the authority to make bank deposits and withdrawals on behalf of the Association could easily manipulate the books and embezzle the cash. And the question remained, where were the missing vehicles?

Again, Bill brought this information to the board's attention at another meeting only to be summarily dismissed and more harshly admonished. Undeterred, he once again asked to see the actual sales receipts, but the board refused. Bill became increasingly wary. He suspected insidiousness was seeping into all aspects of the Association's business dealings.

As I listened to Bill's story, my attorney instincts told me that even though there was a lack of smoking-gun evidence to support a claim of wrongdoing, Bill should have been permitted to look at the receipts and bank deposits relevant to the transactions involving the vehicles. I would have thought the board would have been eager to produce the receipts and lift the veil of suspicion, but that was not the case.

Ultimately, Bill had contacted Cedric Holmes for advice specifically because Cedric was friends with Lavine. Bill believed Cedric could persuade Lavine to allow the community members to inspect the Association's books and records without the need for court intervention. Bill said Cedric seemed more than helpful at their introduction. Cedric met him in the waiting area, escorted him to his office, opened the door, and offered him a seat and a freshly brewed cup of coffee. After accepting the coffee, Bill explained the case of the missing utility vehicles and asked if anything could be done to rectify the situation.

Cedric checked the notes lying in front of him, then he looked up and declared, "My secretary wrote down your name and noted that this consultation had to do with utility vans. I thought this was a personal injury matter involving commercial vehicles. Sorry for the misunderstanding." Thereafter, Cedric cautioned, "Mr. Collins, I think the board was right when they said you made a mistake. I'm sure the board purchased four vehicles, not twelve, and I'm sure the board properly sold the older models. I don't think it would be worth your while to pursue the matter any further."

Bill left Cedric's office dispirited after having been shamefully cast aside, but his mood changed to concern when he passed the secretary's desk and overheard Cedric bark an order: "Get me Gerald Lavine on the phone right now!"

Bill was not one to drop anything without a fight, so he and Alfred had pushed on and hired Roger Blessures, the former district attorney for Carson County. Mr. Blessures had served as the district attorney for approximately sixteen years, and each election year he ran unopposed as the Republican candidate. No one ran against him after his first election because he was deemed an effective district attorney and a man of integrity. His public service career ended in controversy, however, right after he got into a disagreeable tangle with Cindy Matthews.

In March 2010, Cindy Matthews' son, Dylan, was arrested for drinking and driving in Lakewood City late one night before he became the Association's operations manager. The gossip indicated Cindy Matthews called District Attorney Blessures the day after the arrest and asked him to drop all charges against her son. Blessures refused, then Cindy Matthews threatened him. She warned if the charges were not dropped, the Covington Commons board would not donate to his upcoming fall campaign, and without the board's financial support, he would not be elected district attorney for another term. Blessures refused once more, declining to submit to coercive intimidation and blackmail.

Subsequently, Cindy Matthews retained the legal services of Robert Cobb Jr., a politically connected Lakewood City attorney, who convinced Blessures to continue Dylan's case based on promises that Dylan would attend rehab and put himself on the path to sobriety. Notwithstanding the assurances made by Dylan's attorney, many Covington Commons residents speculated that the true motivation for the continuance was not to rescue Dylan from his demons, but to delay the case until after the fall 2010 election for district attorney.

At the behest of Cindy Matthews, the Covington Commons board did indeed endorse a Democrat to run against Blessures, and Blessures did indeed lose the election. By design, Mr. Cobb obtained a plea agreement on behalf of Dylan from the newly elected district attorney, Andrew Wilson and Dylan pled guilty to the lesser included offense of reckless driving. Soon after the plea deal was finalized, Dylan moved away temporarily and obtained his MBA. He returned when his mommy got him the operations manager position for the entire Association.

As an interesting aside, Bill revealed that the last murder case Mr. Blessures tried during his tenure as district attorney was, *State of Georgia v. Theodore Milton*. The sensationally gruesome murder occurred on February 20, 2008, and the victim was an elderly Covington Commons architect and homebuilder named Ed Weatherly, who was allegedly murdered in his Eagle's Nest home by his friend and business associate, Theodore Milton.

Cedric Holmes represented the accused even though he was not a potent trial attorney, and that fact set off considerable surprise in the community at the onset of the case. Moreover, as time advanced toward the commencement of the trial, baffling shock waves reverberated among the Association residents when information surfaced that Cedric had never participated in any criminal case—ever— which explicitly indicated he was not qualified to represent a defendant accused of first-degree murder. Weirdly, on the morning before he was to take the stand in his own defense, Theodore Milton was found dead in his cell at the Carson County jail as a result of a massive heart attack he suffered the previous evening. The trial was terminated in the summer of 2008 and the investigation into Weatherly's murder was permanently closed.

Bill knew the Miltons well. Theodore's wife, Vicki, and Bill's wife, Eva, became close friends after joining the local quilting guild, where they honed their skills and mingled with other women who endeavored to preserve the delicate art. Bill had his reservations concerning Milton's guilt, but he did not elaborate on his conjectures.

After the termination of the Milton prosecution and the ensuing death of his public service career, Mr. Blessures had moved to neighboring Green County, and quietly opened a general legal practice in the town of Webster. Mr. Blessures had agreed to represent Bill and Alfred pro bono because he also believed the Association board was up to no good. Therefore, in pursuit of justice for the Covington Commons community, he filed a complaint in the Carson County superior court in May 2011. It was concise, straightforward, and simple, a scant number of pages outlining the facts relating to the utility vans. Mr. Blessures demanded that the Association produce the receipts and provide them to the community members as required by Georgia law. In response, Herschel Marks moved to have the complaint dismissed one month later. On the day of the hearing, Bill and Alfred were surprised to see every board member in attendance, along with Dylan Matthews and Haywood Martin. They all supported the dismissal of the case.

Bill was confused. He had his doubts about the honesty of Gerald Lavine and Cindy Matthews, but he assumed at least one of the remaining board members would want to know who was stealing from the community. Surely, the non-complicit board members would stop the thieves and punish the culprits if they knew about it. Right? Wrong! On that bright May day, while seated in Judge McMurray's courtroom attempting to do that which was right, Bill realized that all of the board members were colluding in the theft and resale of the vehicles to an unscrupulous used car dealer. Judge McMurray summarily dismissed the case against the Association.

Bill and Alfred did not appeal the dismissal because it did not appear that the Association elites cared about the financial dilemmas facing Covington Commons. Nonetheless, even though the ruling body did not act to probe the potential fraud that worried Bill, he continued to examine the tax returns and financial disclosure forms the board posted on the Association's website over the succeeding months. He noticed numerous accounting red flags and he kept records of each discrepancy. Bill made a variety of requests asking for receipts for purchases made and services rendered, but the board refused to provide any documents or information.

CHAPTER 8
PERRY MASON

My notice of appeal was required to be filed in Carson County superior court within thirty days after the date of the final order dismissing my case. The court rules directed the superior court clerk to serve my notice of appeal on the Georgia Court of Appeals in Atlanta with the entire record of the lower court proceedings. I filed my notice of appeal a week early, in person, late one day, just before the clerk's office closed for the evening.

Predictably, when I entered the clerk's office I was met with the same obese woman who originally accepted my initial complaint for filing. I smiled at the woman and I recollected that she was nice the first time we met. Affability, however, was not her strong suit during our second encounter. I could not fathom what caused her turnabout. Perhaps she was ready to leave for the day and she did not like end-of-the-day filings, or maybe my approval ratings in Lakewood City were less than stellar because I was viewed as an interloper who crashed a party to which I was not invited.

In any event, regardless of my wholly irrelevant societal standing, the clerk seethed a little and expelled perturbed anger when I handed her my notice of appeal. She sifted through my carefully arranged papers, then she glowered at me with stubborn resentment. When she spoke, her voice cackled like a crow. "I cannot include all of the papers in the court's file when I prepare the record for delivery to the appeals court. It will take too much time to copy hundreds of pages and attach them to the record. I'm understaffed as it is. Here, take your appeal papers back."

I gathered the papers she had tossed on the counter and said, "You are required to file *all* of the documents I originally filed with the court, including my reply brief, my statement of undisputed fact, all of my exhibits, and my motion for summary judgment." As I continued, my voice grew louder and louder. "You and your office will be subjected to various financial sanctions if you do not prepare and file the entire record."

The clerk fired back, "Well, we will see about that!"

Right then, before I could defend my position to the insolent woman, the frosted-glass entry door shook lightly and slowly jingled open. An overwhelming campfire odor drifted into the clerk's office. I turned to look behind me and, to my astonishment, Mr. Perry Mason sauntered in, holding an extinguished cigar in his right hand and a briefcase overstuffed with papers in his left hand. I did not look into his eyes or consider his face. My eyes were immediately drawn to the dainty gold chain bracelet he wore on his left wrist. It was the exact same bracelet he had worn the first time I saw him.

I redirected my attention to the clerk and lowered my voice. "My case is serious and needs to be dealt with appropriately. You must prepare and file the entire record with the appellate court—it is the law."

The clerk kept shaking her head no, when Perry interposed, "Helen you know she is right, so why don't you go on and confirm that the entire record will be prepared and filed."

Helen hesitated for a moment, then she deferentially bowed her head and responded, "Certainly, sir."

Thereafter, she turned to me, grabbed my documents, time-stamped them, handed one copy of each document back to me, and scoffed, "The entire record will be filed as designated and requested. I'll need the designation in writing."

Thank you was all I said.

I walked out of the clerk's office and skidded a bit, then I dropped my time-stamped copies on the floor of the courthouse lobby. I scrambled to pick up my documents and as I did so, I once again smelled the residual odor of cigar smoke. I looked up, and there was Perry, bending down to help me retrieve my papers. After we had collected my documents, Perry remarked, "I heard about your case. You are fighting the good fight. The Association is tough to go against. I admire that in an attorney."

"Thank you, sir," I said as he pulled a business card from his jacket pocket and handed it to me.

"Call me. I have a feeling you will need someone in your corner as your case moves forward. It isn't easy for an outsider to take on such an important matter in Lakewood City."

Perry held the door when we exited the courthouse. He bid me farewell, then he jumped into a double-parked late-model sporty coupe and roared off. I looked at his card. The flashy, grandiose attorney was Robert Cobb Jr. His firm was Cobb and Associates, and it was located on Piccadilly Street in Lakewood City. As I walked to my car, I could not stop thinking about the dainty gold chain bracelet he wore.

It took a considerable amount of time to drive home due to the ongoing construction on the highway between Lakewood City and Champaign. The early evening sunlight combined with the twinkling reflectors in the construction zone caused me to squint, which made me think I needed to get a new eyeglass prescription; I did not feel as though I could see clearly.

I was tired and thirsty when I entered my house, so I poured a glass of wine and sat down at my desk to search Mr. Cobb's website.

James was attending a hospital staff meeting so I had some time to myself.

Mr. Cobb's website indicated that he had been practicing law for thirty-six years and that he was sixty-three years old. He maintained a general legal practice with an emphasis in personal injury and DUI law, but it was clear his firm handled any type of case. I remembered Bill had told me Mr. Cobb represented Cindy Matthews' son, Dylan, in a DUI case. Mr. Cobb's firm listed one other attorney as a member, a woman by the name of Susan Fitzgerald.

I did not glean any telling information about Mr. Cobb until I clicked on a Lakewood City newspaper article written in 2012, titled "Tragedy." Directly under the title was a photograph of an adorable girl sitting on the lap of a beautiful woman. The child had sparkling blue eyes and shoulder-length, apple-red hair that fell in ringlets framing her heart-shaped face. The woman had similarly colored hair and a similar heart-shaped face. The angelic girl's smile, frozen in photographic time, projected a tender glow of happiness that radiated unassumingly into my soul.

The accompanying article relayed that a woman and her daughter were driving a midnight blue, compact hybrid south on local Lakewood City Route 132 on the evening of December 22, 2012, returning from a holiday shopping trip to Atlanta. An unknown assailant traveling in the opposite direction crossed the median and plowed into their vehicle head on. The woman survived the crash, but her eight-year-old daughter did not. The woman was identified as Susan Fitzgerald, Mr. Cobb's daughter, and the little girl was identified as Rebecca Fitzgerald, Mr. Cobb's granddaughter. The newspaper stated that Rebecca was to be buried in the Cobb family plot located in Lakewood City at the Presbyterian Church on Ethan Avenue the week following the dreadful hit-and-run.

I paused and exhaled heavily. I finally understood why Mr. Robert Cobb Jr. wore a dainty gold chain bracelet. I wiped crestfallen tears from my hot, red cheeks, and then I shut down my computer. Star must have sensed my sadness because she soundlessly came into my office, jumped onto my lap, and licked briny residue from my swollen face.

CHAPTER 9
THE APPEAL

The next morning, I emailed Herschel Marks, *I am appealing Judge McMurray's decision to the Georgia Court of Appeals in Atlanta. Can you email me a copy of your attorney hours and expenses incurred that will substantiate the defendants' $7,222 award of fees and costs.*

The request was perfectly reasonable, and would surely cause no hardship, since Herschel, like any attorney, would without doubt have saved a copy of the information on his computer.

Herschel did not promptly respond, so I phoned him again and left more messages. Eventually, Herschel picked up one of my calls and in an impetuous diatribe laden with unhinged personal attacks, Herschel blew his top. "Stop calling me. I will not provide you with any copies of my hours and expenses. That information is proprietary and protected by the attorney-client privilege. If you weren't so stupid, you would know that!"

"The production of the documents is necessary. The appellate court needs a list of costs incurred by the Association in order to determine whether the award should be upheld."

"No, forget it. File a motion to compel if you need to!" he yelled. "If you don't stop harassing me and my clients, I'll make sure you'll regret it for the rest of your life!"

I hung up the phone, shaken but not stirred, and even though Herschel would not provide me with a certified list of the Association's costs and expenses, I filed my appellate brief in June 2014. I informed the court that Herschel was unwilling to comply with my requests for the production of the expense-related documents.

Herschel sent a pithy email after he had received my appeal, *Will you agree to a continuance allowing me to file my appellate response brief late?*

What? Was he kidding? I was not surprised by his request for a continuance; all attorneys constantly panhandle for continuances believing more time will create some sort of self-serving advantage. I was surprised Herschel asked for the favor after he had screamed at me over the phone a few weeks before he needed my assistance. Unbelievable! He was definitely not going to win a continuance.

I drafted a formal response to the requested continuance and submitted it to the court. I apprised the appellate judges, *With all due respect, I cannot in good conscience agree to a continuance requested for the sole purpose of delay.* Hah!

The court granted Herschel's request for a continuance and expanded his filing deadline to August 1, 2014.

As expected, in response to my appellate brief, Herschel twisted the law and utilized inflammatory, unsubstantiated facts to support his contention that my case was without merit. I dealt with the fictions advanced by Herschel the best way I could; I filed a reply to the response brief wherein I tediously distinguished each case upon which Herschel relied. As opposed to Herschel's zealous advocacy that was predicated on disinformation, I informed the court what law was genuinely applicable. I was honest and straightforward. I was not going to let Herschel's conduct hinder my attempts to successfully win the appeal.

The appellate court clerk called two days after I filed my reply. The friendly female voice on the other end asked, "Are you available for oral argument any time during the month of September?"

"Sure, I will make myself available any date convenient to the court," I said.

The clerk said, "Let me call Mr. Marks and check on his availability." She called back an hour later. "Mr. Marks will not be available until February 2015 for the oral argument."

No surprise . . . delay . . . delay . . . delay.

Two days later, despite Herschel's delay tactics, I received a letter from the clerk's office stating that the oral argument was scheduled for September 15, 2014, during the morning session.

Herschel did not like that too much. He sent me another email and expressed disdain, *I already told the court I was not available for oral argument in September but the court scheduled the case for September over my objections. Now I have to file a formal motion for a continuance. Will you agree to continue the oral argument until February?*

It got really boring—Herschel's begging for continuances, I mean. Of course, I did not give Herschel the satisfaction of agreeing to another continuance and, of course, another continuance was granted. Overall, Herschel was hugely successful in his beggary for additional time. He delayed the case for more than four months. The oral argument was finally scheduled for February 2, 2015, after Herschel exhausted his quota of continuances.

CHAPTER 10
ORAL ARGUMENT

I had not participated in an oral argument for quite some time, and I was quite nervous, to say the least. Years prior, I had argued a case before a federal court of appeals panel that consisted of three of the most knowledgeable judges in the country, and I believed the argument I presented was perhaps one of the best ever made by any attorney—and if it was not the best, it was incontrovertibly the most unique.

A local police department had arrested my client pursuant to a criminal harassment statute for protesting on a sidewalk in front of a local manufacturing business without a permit. My client was protesting the business because the owners utilized foreign-made components in the assemblage of the products they marketed in order to save costs. I was convinced that the statute violated my client's First Amendment right to freedom of speech, so I sued the arresting police department in federal district court and requested that the statute be overturned as unconstitutional. The federal district court initially denied my application for relief, so I filed an appeal with the federal circuit court of appeals and my client was granted an oral argument. I fully understood that my chances of obtaining a reversal of the federal district court's opinion were slim, but in defiance of the odds, I gave an all-out effort. If the federal circuit court ruled in my favor, my client would be completely absolved of guilt, and perhaps be forever hailed a hero and a civil rights protectionist.

On argument day, after the bailiff called my case, I stood at the lectern and opened my presentation with facts that highlighted our nation's patriotic adherence to freedom of speech, the hallmark of our democracy since its inception. I elucidated that James Madison, the fourth president of the United States and author of the US Constitution and the Bill of Rights, did not want to amend the Constitution via ratification of the Bill of Rights because he cohered to the view that the Constitution did not need to provide individual protections to the citizenry because the federal government would never become so powerful. However, at the urging of Thomas Jefferson, Madison reluctantly authored twelve amendments to the US Constitution, ten of which became the Bill of the Rights, the first being the right to freedom of speech.

A few sentences into my introductory discourse, the chief justice asked, "How is the history of the enactment of the first ten amendments to the US Constitution relevant to whether a criminal harassment statute violates the First Amendment right to free speech?"

I stood tall and announced, "Your Honor, it is relevant because it's sooooooo interesting!"

Then it happened. Noiselessness descended upon the courtroom. It was loud and screamingly evident. The deafening quiet lingered for an instant, then an audience member wheezed and barked a cough. After the cough, silence again overtook the room. We all waited for the chief justice to speak, but he did not. He merely expelled a rattled breath and settled back into his chair. I continued with my presentation, reveling in my genius argument. Equating relevancy with being interesting in a federal appeals court had never been done before, at least as far as I was aware.

Nevertheless, despite the novelty of the arguments proffered, I did not win the appeal. The court ruled that the defendant police department did not violate my client's right to free speech because my client had caused a disturbance that inappropriately blocked access to the business he was protesting. Moreover, the court held that the state statute did not violate the Constitution because states possess vested rights to prevent disruptions that impede the free flow of pedestrian and vehicular traffic. I was viciously stung by the verdict's piercing blow. I had tried so hard to win for my deserving client.

My latest oral argument was going to be different—it was going to lead to victory. I did some last minute research just days before the argument to determine if any additional case law had been decided in Georgia since the filing of the appellate briefs that could affect my claims. I found one applicable case that had been decided by the same justices scheduled to hear my appeal. The decision involved a tedious procedural matter, but I felt compelled to argue the salient point because, even though it was not necessarily exciting, it could serve as a basis for a reversal.

In choosing a methodology for delivering my argument, I adjudged that the best approach to take was to write down my entire monologue and read it in open court. I reasoned that if I was pathetically dull, and did not make eye contact with the panel, that would be better than forgetting what to say. The day before the argument, I did a practice read in order to make sure it did not surpass the twenty-minute allotment of time and regrettably, it was too long. As a result, I returned to the drawing board and worked on my argument well into the evening, feverishly editing out the least important points, careful not to minimize the impact of my most important assertions. Near the witching hour, I showered and hopped into bed hoping to catch some sleep, but rejuvenating rest was not my friend that night. I tossed and turned for hours, uncertain whether I was fully prepared to argue before the Georgia Court of Appeals.

I woke prior to dawn and put on a plain black dress and gold stud earrings, then I gathered my legal documents and got into James' vehicle. After he slid in alongside me, he engaged the ignition and his SUV rumbled to life. I looked at James with dreaded anticipation, and in response, he clasped my hand with tender excitement. His touch caused a wave of confidence to swell through my heart as we set off to meet those who would decide my case. I sat silently while James whizzed down the interstate, swerving in and out of purring traffic on our way to Atlanta. I tried to relax by monotonously repeating my argument over and over in my head.

At the halfway mark, James disrupted my anxious concentration and loudly exclaimed, "I forgot to put on my belt. Shit, I'm not wearing a belt." James was not accustomed to wearing a suit. Every day, James donned his uniform, a drab blue scrub suit and comfortable shoes, and he went to work. He was not a snazzy dresser. On my big day, however, my handsome, clean-cut spouse was dressed in a dignified navy wool suit with a light-blue shirt and a silky red-and-blue plaid tie; he had just forgotten to wear the doggone belt.

"Do you need the belt? Will your pants fall down?"

"No, but I'll look like an idiot," he replied self-consciously.

At that point, even though I thought, *Yo, buddy, this day isn't about you, so suck it up and stop complaining,* I held my tongue and said, "Don't worry, you look nice. Nobody will notice, really."

We arrived about a half hour early, so we stopped in the coffee shop across from the courthouse. I ordered a skinny vanilla latte and sat down before a substantial picture window that revealed the entry into the tribunal and the surrounding area. The barista called my name so James picked up my order and politely delivered it to me. While I slowly sipped the piping-hot drink, to my speechless wonder, the board members began to emerge from a nearby parking garage and schlepp into the courthouse. Lavine appeared last. He trudged up the inclining sidewalk clutching an older woman's hand as she protected him from the icy drizzle with an oversized umbrella. Lavine slouched his shoulders and walked with obvious trepidation when he entered the court of justice. My stomach grumbled and my hands twitched as I took one last sip of my latte. It was showtime.

James and I walked across the street and entered the majestic, Renaissance-revival courthouse through an ornate arched entry bounded on each side by matching arched windows. We ascended a stately stairway to the second floor and proceeded through metal detectors. I went to the clerk's office so she could mark me present, and she informed me my case was the only one scheduled for the afternoon. Following the registration formalities, I sat down on a bench adjacent to the courtroom entrance and pulled out my notes to read my argument for the umpteenth time. James stood nearby, checking his messages on his cell phone.

Bill Collins came to the argument with the Wainrights.

"Hi," Bill said as he sidled up beside me on the bench.

The Wainrights simultaneously approached and respectfully bowed their heads in salutation.

"Hi," I said. "I can't talk right now. I need to concentrate."

"Oh, we understand. We will leave you to your work," Ms. June replied.

Bill, James, and the Wainrights began to chatter, so I got up, entered the courtroom, and took a seat in the first row on the left side of the room. Herschel and the board members were congregated inside the courtroom on the right side of the aisle. As soon as they saw me enter, they began boorishly laughing and patting each other on the back, acting as if they were at a party having a wonderful time. Many attorneys had utilized the pretend-party-act against me in the past in order to intimidate me and my clients. The bullying tactic was used to convey the sentiment: I am not at all worried about this case, and I will have a good time annihilating you. It will be fun to see you wither and die. Needless to say, I felt intimidated by Herschel and his cohorts; the fail-safe bullying worked very well. I glanced at James, who had taken a seat behind me, and he similarly displayed an expression of intimidation provoked by the contemptuous behavior exhibited by those against whom I brought suit.

I tried to ignore my adversaries' shenanigans by breathing deep to calm myself. Bill and the Wainrights entered the auditorium and took seats next to James. The bailiff called all to rise, and three justices emerged from a door behind the superlative bench that flanked the wall opposite the entryway. One of the judges called the courtroom to order and asked everyone to be seated; the afternoon session had begun. I was instructed to proceed with my argument.

I recited my name and began. Unfortunately, however, I forgot to reserve time for my counterstatement, even though I had written a reminder in bold capital letters on my notes.

One judge stopped me. "Would you like to reserve any time for rebuttal?"

Damn! "Oh yes, three minutes, Your Honor."

I deeply inhaled, then I steadily exhaled. I grabbed the polished wooden lectern to stabilize my swaying frame and began again. I read two sentences, and then I looked up and made eye contact with each judge. I never looked at my notes again. I argued, answered questions, and cited the pertinent cases right off the top of my head. Miraculously, I did not need any notes. I had studied my case so well, all the information I had stored in my brain poured out of my head straight into the heads of the esteemed judges.

My argument concluded with a reference to the case recently decided by the same panel of justices. "May it please the court, in this case, the lower court did not abide by the proper procedural rules in rendering its verdict. You guys rendered an opinion about two weeks ago reversing a comparable decision, where the lower court also did not heed the same rule of civil procedure. Therefore, I ask that you do the same in this case and reverse the lower court's decision. Thank you."

Herschel's argument was less than compelling. He had little to say, and he did not use all his allotted time. The court seemed incurious and bored. Herschel's voice quaked every time he equivocated, analogous to how Pinocchio's nose grew every time the wooden boy prevaricated. My rebuttal time came at breakneck speed. I needed to correct the record Herschel had attempted to distort, so I methodically listed every misrepresentation and explained why each should not be believed. After my rebuttal, we all rose as the judges exited the courtroom via the door behind the formidable bench. It was over.

I turned and looked at James. He seemed to be in a catatonic state, blindly staring in the direction where the judges had been seated. I walked over to him, Bill, and the Wainrights and asked what they thought of my presentation. Bill was pleased, and so were the Wainrights, but that was not the reaction I received from James.

"Did you call the appellate court justices 'you guys'?" James asked. *Ooooh my God! Did I? I think I did!* I could not believe it! In a pained voice, I softly whispered, "I think I did call the judges 'you guys'!"

A lawyer arguing before a distinguished court should never refer to judges as "you guys." A judge should only be referred to as "Your Honor," or, in the plural, "May it please the court."

James stood and tried to pat me on the back, but I pulled away. He had hurt my feelings, even though he had only made an observation. I felt stupid, and he knew it.

"I'm sorry, you did a great job," he said as his eyes met the floor.

I did not believe him. He was lying. He thought I was an idiot, and so did I.

My feelings of mortification speedily turned into feelings of angry self-loathing for having made such a colossal mistake. I snapped up my coat and purse and marched towards the exit. James, Bill, and the Wainrights tacitly trailed behind. The party animals were leaving the courtroom at the same time, but for some reason, the gaiety had ceased. Herschel and his posse were extraordinarily somber. If I didn't know better, I would have thought Herschel and the board members were leaving the funeral of a beloved friend or family member. The unexpected gloomy behavior of the party people possibly indicated that Herschel and the board members were not pleased with the day's events. Maybe I had done a great job! Maybe the court would see my "you guys" comment as endearing . . . maybe—but maybe not. Regardless, I knew it would be many months before the court issued its written opinion.

CHAPTER 11
THE RED FLAGS

I had an abundance of time on my hands after the oral argument, so I looked into the financial dealings of the Association to determine if its governing members were committing fraud against the Covington Commons community. If there were any red flags signaling some sort of double-dealing, I could submit a formal complaint to the United States Attorney General's Office in Atlanta for a full-blown Racketeer Influenced and Corrupt Organization Act investigation. Identifying red flags, however, had never been my forte. Even overt warning signals often escaped my scrutiny because of my inane desire to avoid suspecting the worst in people. The first federal employment discrimination case I tried underscored my lack of ability in red-flag detection.

I had represented a man named Anurak, a naturalized citizen who had emigrated to the United States from Thailand when he was six years old. After he graduated from high school, he began working for a fine men's Italian clothier located in a metropolitan suburban-area mall. He said he had worked at the same store for eleven years and he was never promoted or given a raise. Anurak told me all he wanted to do was become the store manager, and even though he praised the international company for which he labored, he had become disturbed when a number of young, white male employees with less seniority were promoted to management positions. Anurak was attractive, smart, and articulate. I took his case because I thought he should be the president of the company.

I worked diligently to settle Anurak's case, but since an agreement was not reached, he was subjected to a trial and all the pre-trial discovery that went along with it. During his deposition, opposing counsel asked him to read a document, but rather than look at it, he asked me to read it because he had forgotten his glasses. Months later, on the morning of his trial testimony, before leaving my house, I tucked a pair of reading spectacles into my briefcase, remembering Anurak's need for glasses and his tendency to forget things.

I called Anurak to the stand as my last witness; his direct examination went well. During cross-examination, defense counsel handed Anurak the same document I had read at his deposition and asked him to read it in open court. On cue, I jumped to attention and presented Anurak with the reading glasses I had brought with me. He put on the glasses and fidgeted. He squirmed and fidgeted some more. A bombshell dropped, igniting a courtroom shocker: Anurak could not read the document even while wearing the readers because he did not know how to read.

I should have paid more attention to the red flag that presented itself during Anurak's deposition when he had asked me to read the document for him. Perhaps I could have better dealt with his illiteracy at the trial had I properly identified the subtle yet evident warning signal. Suffice it to say, the jury issued a verdict against Anurak because it was paramount that a manager at a major retail conglomerate be literate.

I resolved not to make the same mistake twice, so I meticulously ascertained as many red flags for Association fraud as possible.

I discovered there were numbers of private security firms that consulted with companies both large and small for the purpose of fraud detection and eradication. Many of the fraud-consulting firms issued annual reports that discussed the applicable state and federal statutes that prohibited fraud; the kinds of fraud schemes perpetrated; the identity of the persons who perpetrated fraud; and the red flags for fraud detection.

The most common types of frauds were skimming (cash stolen before recordation); cash larceny (cash stolen after recordation); billing fraud (invoices drawn up for the payment of fictitious goods or services); payroll fraud (false claims for compensation); cash register disbursements (fraudulent removal of cash from register); fictitious expense reimbursement; check tampering; and misappropriation of cash or assets. Additionally, there were other types of fraud that were more complicated, such as shell company fraud, pass-through schemes, altered shipping records, kickbacks, bribes, pay and return, etc. The list went on and on.

The person who generally committed fraud usually had no prior criminal background. Many had financial problems, or tended to be greedy, seeking personal gain. Men were more likely than women to commit fraud, and just about 40 percent of all criminal fraud cases were committed by people age thirty-six to forty-five years old. Fraudsters loved to brag about their newfound wealth and show off the fruits of their fraud. They all lived above their means and explained their elevated financial status by claiming to have recently come into money through inheritance or good investments. Defrauders could become hostile if asked to account for any financial discrepancies at work or in their positions overseeing a company's finances. Many had a nonchalant wheeler-dealer attitude and believed they were too smart to get caught.

Numerous anti-fraud specialists acknowledged that managers who committed fraud rarely provided accurate financial data to auditors, or others entitled to the accounting information. They further advised that managerial red flags should not be ignored, especially when management decisions were dominated by one person or a select entrenched group. In detecting fraud, one must look for lack of management oversight, numerous bank accounts, changes in banking records, company assets sold below market value, continuous roll-over of loans, accounting personnel lacking proper experience, and management disrespect for company regulations or other state or federal laws. The specialists admonished that successful fraud schemes usually occurred in environments lacking internal controls.

Fraud schemes could go on for years. It was estimated that register disbursement and asset misappropriation schemes lasted about twelve months, whereas more complicated payroll and billing schemes lasted upwards of thirty-six months. Slightly more than one-third of fraud cases were discovered through tips; one fourth of fraud cases were discovered by accident; and one-fifth of fraud cases were discovered through detailed company audits. The security consulting firms suggested companies utilize internal controls to detect and stop fraud, such as fraud tipster hotlines, fraud detection training for employees and management, surprise audits, and rewards for whistleblowers. All the experts agreed that the most common red flags for fraud were missing documents, failure to produce documents to substantiate expenditures, accusations of fraud by others, undue payments to others, unnecessary purchases, and inventory shortages.

CHAPTER 12
THE SHORTCOMINGS

I turned to Bill for assistance after I educated myself about company fraud schemes. He reminded me of the missing utility vans, the event that had sparked his suspicion, then he advised me to look at the most recent tax return posted on the Association's website because state and federal law required the dissemination of a nonprofit's tax returns directly to its members. It was still winter 2015, so the most recently posted return was for the year 2013; the 2014 return was not due for release.

The tax return indicated that the Association had compensated three independent contractors who were owners of local small businesses in 2013. The Carson County Water Maintenance Company received $600,000 for the installation of the water meters, waterlines, and sewer lines for the new homes built in Covington Commons' three neighborhoods. Two building contractors, Lakewood City Construction, Inc. and Georgia Builders, Inc., each received more than $500,000 for community construction projects. The return itemized a number of other payments and write-offs for business expenses and inventory costs, but none of the payments appeared unusual at first blush. In fact, as opposed to raising a red flag, the payments seemed commonplace and predominantly reasonable. In contravention of my first impression, however, when I dug deeper by posing a series of questions to Bill, my first blush reaction turned on its head and the only conclusion that could legitimately be drawn was that the payments were anything but reasonable.

The water company was unquestionably overpaid because just a handful of homes were built in Covington Commons in 2013, not nearly enough to warrant such a disproportionate bill. The building companies were also issued compensation far in excess of what would have been justified because no substantial community amenities were built during the year the overblown deductions were claimed. The construction of the newest amenity, the fitness gymnasium, was completed much earlier, and Covington Commons did not erect or renovate anything in 2013. The only undertaking executed that year was the installation of a paltry gravel equestrian path and it was inconceivable that the path cost a million dollars to commission.

Another suspect renumeration on the tax return was a disbursement of $750,000 to the local oil company for diesel and gas fuel. Gas consumption was at an all-time high in 2013 because the board and committee members reputedly filled up their personal vehicles on a regular basis at the station located on the Covington Commons grounds—a strict violation of the Association's mandated rules. The Association employees were only permitted to use Association gas in Association vehicles while conducting Association business, but many community residents complained otherwise.

I asked Bill if the Association had recently discharged any employees; there was nothing better than an aggrieved former employee who blew the whistle and turned state's evidence. In response, Bill rattled off the names of about ten former employees, one of whom he had personally interviewed, a former maintenance worker named John

Simmons. Bill said John was an important witness to the Association fraud, so he gave me his contact information. Less than an hour after our phone call, Bill faxed me a detailed catalog of the names, positions, and dates of service of all of the board and committee members.

I zealously believed Bill, even though my incurable gullibility had led me to champion many a fabricator in the past. Bill's story was different. His credibility seemed invulnerable because he had been doggedly trying to uncover fraud at Covington Commons for years. Bill's persistence demonstrated that he was either on to something, or he just had variant loose screws, much like any crazy conspiracy theorist.

CHAPTER 13
CONNECTING THE DOTS

I referred to the board/committee-member list drafted by Bill, and I discovered that every board member served in different unpaid Association positions for many years. All of them had begun serving the Association in either 2006 or 2007, with the exception of Lavine, who had begun serving in 2005. Furthermore, each finance committee member also held their positions controlling the purse strings of the Association for prolonged periods of time, in some cases, more than ten years. It was undeniable. I was dealing with an entrenched board that oversaw an entrenched finance committee and that fact naturally led to the question, why would these people seek to remain in uncompensated positions for protracted time spans? Rarely is anyone so selfless.

The answer was, as Bill explained, that in addition to free gas, each board and committee member gorged on a host of other veritable goodies, like free lavish dining at the Association restaurants, waivers of amenity and admission fees, use of the Association credit cards for personal purchases, asset misappropriations, cash payments out of the Association bank accounts, and kickbacks. The corrosively pervasive fraud that was capable of destroying the Association was motivated and corroborated by the lifestyles of the ruling elite. All of the board and committee members lived in splendid lakefront homes, drove expensive cars and boats, and traveled extensively. Their standards of living never declined, not even after the 2008 market collapse. To the contrary, the retired, unemployed Covington Commons oligarchy enjoyed an increased standard of living after the devastating crash that precipitated a recession followed by a sputtering economic recovery.

Lavine had benefitted enormously after volunteering for the Association. He initially lived in an unassuming Peacock Plains home, then upgraded to a custom-built Eagle's Nest mansion after he began serving as an Association finance committee member, then a board member. Lavine openly bragged to the residents, Bill included, that he had come into a considerable inheritance and would be well off for the rest of his life. A number of other board and committee members also publicly spoke of inheriting generous sums of money or boasted about their savvy lucrative investments. Cindy Matthews even claimed she won the lottery after a neighbor complimented her pricey roadster convertible.

Warning signal number one: Entrenchment, wealth, and the explanations for the accumulation of wealth, were vastly important red flags that indicated the Association's governing body was involved in fraudulent activity.

The contractor activity was likewise suspect. Excluding the local oil company, each of the three remaining highest-paid contractors was not only grossly overpaid, but each company openly stated in public records submitted to the Georgia secretary of state's office that they did not employ any staff whatsoever. It was absolutely striking that the independent contractors did not have any regular employees. Moreover, Bill said there was no evidence the Association ever took outside bids for work to be conducted within the community. The building, maintenance, and installation contracts were only given to the same three unstaffed companies year after year. Thus, the building and water maintenance contractors, like the board and finance committee members, were also undoubtedly entrenched and perfectly positioned to commit harmful fraud.

The specific contractor fraud schemes potentially had various components like payroll fraud and kickbacks. For example, suppose the Association paid one of its contractors a sum of money for a job and then the contractor company deposited the sum into its company accounts. The contractor could then write off as part of his expenses transient employee wages since he did not have any permanent personnel. In furtherance of the swindle, the contractor could utilize the Covington Commons employees rather than hire his own employees. Consequently, the money said to have been paid to the contractors' transient employees could be kicked backed to the board with a little left over for the contractor for perpetuating the racket.

Another component of the possible contractor subterfuge involved asset misappropriation and billing fraud. For example, what if Lavine and some other board members wanted to redo their bathrooms and the fitness gymnasium also needed a bathroom rehab. The contractors could order enough product to redo the gymnasium bathrooms and then tack on to the same order extra bathtubs, toilets, sinks, or other fixtures, and install the extra products directly into the homes of the board members. In the alternative, the contractor could write up orders for redoing the gymnasium bathrooms, never upgrade those facilities, and brazenly install the entire product into the homes of board and committee members.

Warning signal number two: Contractor entrenchment, the failure to permit project bidding, the potential for payroll fraud and concealable kickbacks, and possible asset misappropriation and billing fraud were critical red flags, which involved the highest-paid contractors and connected the Association's ruling elite to probable criminal activity.

I hypothesized about Dylan Matthews and his cohort, Haywood Martin, and their roles in the widespread fraud. It was more than plausible that the young men were generously paid more than the amount the Association reported as their income, so both would be motivated to facilitate and conceal the fraud. Dylan was arguably the person who coordinated the fraud between the Association and the contractors. He may have been responsible for executing the contracts and paying for fictitious work that was supposed to have been completed. I assumed Dylan's most important job was to keep the fraud machine soundly running. Martin, on the other hand, worked as Dylan's henchman, helping Dylan carry on the criminal enterprise. Arguably, just as Bill presumed, the obsequious Martin did whatever he was commanded to do: bully a resident, shake down a local official for favors, or merely pick up lunch for Lavine and his comrades.

Herschel Marks, the Association's trusted attorney, and Cedric Holmes, Lavine's trusted attorney friend, had to be in on all the strangulating fraud. There was no way the Association board and committee members could perpetrate such crimes without the help of knowledgeable and duplicitous lawyers. Most of the ruling elite were not well versed in finance, and not one board member had any training in running a business, particularly a business as large as the nonprofit Association.

Warning signal number three: The board needed loyal, dishonest executives and dependable, unprincipled attorneys to shroud the fraud. Dylan Matthews, Haywood Martin, Herschel Marks, and Cedric Holmes dutifully fit the bill, a circumstance that bespoke red flag.

On top of the fraud facilitated by artful attorneys and committed by the board, committee members, contractors, and executive staff, there was the pesky matter of employee theft. Bill speculated that many, if not all, of the Association employees were ostensibly stealing assets as well as money, and he based his assumption on the fact that there was never a reported incident of employee theft, a mind-boggling detail, given the Association employed hundreds of workers. A gas fill-up here, some office supplies there, a free lunch here, a twenty out of the register there, even a nice new set of golf clubs from the pro shop. Ironically, employee theft probably had the effect of insulating the board and committee members from fraud allegations. If low-level employees were stealing, they would be unlikely to complain about theft at the highest levels for fear of exposing their own crimes.

Warning signal number four: Keep the peace and give everyone a little illegal bonus now and then.

To conceal the ubiquitous fraud, the Association board always made a big deal out of the annual audits conducted by the Atlanta accounting firm of Maxwell and Maxwell. The board frequently discussed the audits in monthly newsletters and on social media outlets without addressing any specific accounting issues. The board simply proclaimed that the Association was in terrific financial health, as evidenced by the annual audit reports the board claimed were predicated upon complete reviews of the Association's records and receipts.

The board lied to the community about the audits. The Association audits were not based on complete reviews of its records and receipts. The Association auditors only analyzed numbers and financial data provided to them by the Association board members. The auditors never examined the actual receipts or other accounting records substantiating the expenditures. The audit reports disclosed that fact in devilishly fine print at the bottom of the first page of every audit. Typically, annual audit reports are not designed to expose fraud because they are not based upon reviews of the underlining documents.

Warning signal number five: Failure to acknowledge the flaws in the annual reports was possibly the most conspicuously glaring red flag. Why lie so blatantly to the community residents about the annual reports and the ability of the auditors to detect fraud or financial discrepancies?

The money and assets diverted from the Association coffers through endemic fraud conceivably totaled in the tens of millions of dollars during the duration the entrenched board and finance committee remained in power. I needed more than speculation, hearsay, and uncorroborated evidence in order to go to the United States attorney general. I needed rock-solid physical evidence or unfaltering circumstantial evidence.

CHAPTER 14
CASE RECORDS

I called John Simmons, the former employee Bill had interviewed because I wanted to corroborate as many of Bill's statements as possible. John Simmons agreed to meet me for lunch the next day at the pizza place across the street from the Carson County sheriff's office.

I drove to Lakewood City early in the morning, well before my scheduled meeting with John, in order to look into the case of *State of Georgia v. Theodore Milton* more closely. Cedric Holmes had piqued my curiosity by haunting my daily thoughts and I wanted to determine what role, if any, he had played in the Association fraud. Tapping into the Milton case more thoroughly could provide needed answers about him, his legal practice, his connections, and his enigmatic position within the Association.

The Georgia Administrative Offices of the Courts retained and digitally managed all of the archived court records for the state, but it did not retain the county criminal court records or the county sheriff's office records, so I had to travel to the local offices in order to obtain the information I needed. I visited the Carson County criminal court clerk's office first. It was located in the same gothic courthouse where

I'd had my first run-in with Judge McMurray and the Association representatives he protected. I entered the austere building and found my way to the correct office without the need for assistance. I stopped at an oak-veneered door affixed with a pitted, bronze plaque that read Criminal Court Clerk, then I turned the matching doorknob, and entered the office.

A middle-aged woman with gray hair scooped up in a bun on top of her head was sitting behind a desk, leafing through a copy of a celebrity scandal magazine. I asked her where the archived records were kept, and she directed me to a repository located in the basement. She said the criminal case records since 2000 were stored on the computer. I thanked the clerk, then I proceeded down a flight of stairs at the back of the building and walked toward a closed door with fingerprint-smeared windows. I pulled on the greasy doorknob, but the door was so warped it would not budge. When I tugged at the knob with more force, a bailiff passed and stopped to help. He loosened the door by jiggling the knob upward, then he held the door open as I crept into the room.

The room was inordinately filthy, so filthy in fact, it looked more like a dumping ground rather than a records retention facility. There were shelves filled with large moldy books containing entries that verified each criminal case recorded in Carson County for at least the last hundred years, and there was a computer on a small worktable with long legs and wheels. The computer was at least twenty years old and it had no mouse. The Milton case had been brought to trial in 2008, so I booted up the computer and waited until the screen popped on to plug in my query.

Milton had been arrested on Thursday, February 21, 2008, and he was brought before a magistrate judge for his initial appearance via closed circuit TV two hours later. The judge apprised Milton that he was charged with first-degree murder, then he denied Milton bail and ordered him to obtain counsel. The following morning, Friday, February 22, 2008, Milton was formally arraigned in the Carson County superior court by the same magistrate judge who oversaw his initial appearance. The judge assigned Milton to a public defender named Lisa McGuire at the commencement of the proceeding because Milton still had not retained an attorney. On the advice of Lisa McGuire, Milton entered a plea of not guilty to the charge of aggravated first-degree murder. Cedric Holmes entered his appearance as Milton's attorney on Monday, February 25, 2008. Lisa McGuire withdrew as Milton's counsel on Friday, February 29, 2008. Cedric filed a motion for a speedy trial and the case was fast-tracked to commence five months after the murder. The trial lasted from Monday, July 14, 2008, to Friday, July 18, 2008. On July 18, 2008, the trial was terminated, and the jury was released.

Copies of Milton's autopsy and toxicology reports were attached to the computer file. The autopsy report stated that Milton was found deceased in his jail cell on July 18, 2008, and it indicated that no toxic substances were found in Milton's system. The coroner deduced that Theodore Milton died due to a massive coronary heart attack brought on by natural causes prior to the conclusion of the trial.

I did not leave right away. I decided to look up the Dylan Matthews case; again, curiosity got the better of me. Bill had told me that Dylan was arrested for DUI in March 2010, so I entered another query into the computer relic and it flashed back that Dylan had been arrested just before midnight on March 17, 2010, for DUI. The next morning, Dylan was brought before a magistrate for his initial appearance and granted bail. Cindy Matthews immediately posted bond and Dylan was released to her custody that afternoon. Dylan was arraigned on Monday, March 22, 2010, and he pled not guilty to the crime. The court records confirmed that Robert Cobb Jr. represented Dylan at the arraignment and at the subsequent plea-agreement hearing. Dylan was convicted of misdemeanor reckless driving and issued a $500 fine on Monday, January 24, 2011.

I left the courthouse and headed north to the Carson County sheriff's office, another formidable old structure built in the same gothic style as the courthouse.

A frizzy blond girl with noticeably dark roots sat behind a glass enclosure in the reception area, filing her nails. She slid the glass door open when I advanced toward her. "Hello, how can I help you?" she asked with a smile that exposed red lipstick smeared on her teeth.

I pointed with my finger to my teeth before speaking.

The girl cracked opened a mirrored compact resting on her desk, peered into it with opened lips, rubbed her teeth with her fingers, and removed all traces of the lipstick.

"Thank you for telling me. I hate when that happens."

"No problem. I was wondering if I could look at the files on two closed cases."

"Sure. What are the names of the cases?"

"State of Georgia v. Theodore Milton" and *"State of Georgia v. Dylan Matthews."*

"I'm not familiar with those cases."

"They occurred years ago."

"Right. I've only been working here for two years."

"Oh, really?"

"I got the job right after I graduated from high school. My husband is training to become a sheriff's deputy. Hopefully, he'll pass his test next month."

"I wish him luck. I heard those tests are difficult."

"Come on back. I'll show you to the records room," she said as she hit a buzzer that opened an adjacent door.

I followed the receptionist to a locked back room that she opened with a brass key. "The sheriff's office didn't start storing records in digital format until 2013, so any records before that year are contained in the big books in the bookcases."

"I'm surprised it took so long to change over to computer records."

"The county didn't have enough money to upgrade its system until then."

"Oh, I see."

"You can take your time in here. If you need me, I'll be at my desk."

"Thank you," I said as I scanned a much neater repository filled with a half-dozen old microfiche machines and loads of oversized books, each imprinted with a year on the binding.

I picked up the 2008 book; I figured I would start with the Milton case.

The sheriff's office report revealed that seventy-eight-year-old Ed Weatherly was found dead in his Covington Commons home at approximately 4:45 p.m. on Wednesday, February 20, 2008. Weatherly was discovered by his seventy-four-year-old wife, Edith Weatherly, after she returned from a luncheon and shopping trip with a friend. Ed Weatherly was brutally beaten. He had been knocked out of his wheelchair, smacked to the ground, and bludgeoned to death. A cast-iron frying pan was the suspected murder weapon because it was found covered in blood near the victim. The police did not recover any identifiable fingerprints on the suspected murder weapon and the scene was devoid of any incriminating DNA evidence.

Detectives interviewed numerous neighbors, and two remembered seeing Theodore Milton at the Weatherly home late in the afternoon on February 20, 2008. Theodore Milton was described as a fifty-four-year-old man, approximately five feet ten and weighing approximately 225 pounds, with no identifying scars or tattoos. The neighbors knew Milton well. He often visited Ed Weatherly; they were friends and business associates. The witnesses informed officials that Milton had worked for Weatherly's building firm, Weatherly Building Contractors, as a supervising manager for the last twenty years.

At the time of his death, Ed Weatherly still owned the company. Edith told deputies that Ed initially contracted to sell the firm to Milton, but Ed wanted to cancel the agreement when he was offered more money by the Covington Commons Homeowners Association. She revealed that the Association wanted to purchase the building contractor firm so it could build patio spec homes on Association-owned lots for resale to buyers wishing to downsize. Edith told deputies that Ed had planned on meeting with Milton on the afternoon of February 20, 2008 to notify Milton that Ed was canceling the contract.

An intriguing, unsourced, handwritten notation was scribbled on Edith Weatherly's statement to the sheriff's office. *Secretary heard Ed Weatherly argue with somebody the day before Weatherly murder at Ed Weatherly's.* The statement did not identify the witness secretary, disclose with whom Ed Weatherly argued, or report what was said. I assumed from the statement, however, that the secretary must have overheard the argument while working at the offices of Weatherly Building Contractors because an employer generally does not have his secretary work from his private residence.

I returned to the receptionist's desk after I perused the Milton case documents and asked the young woman if I could make copies of the sheriff's office records. In response, she jumped up and exclaimed, "I don't care to make the copies!" The first time I heard the southern phrase, "I don't care to," I thought it meant, "I won't do that," but I later learned that the correct translation is actually, "I'd be happy to do that." Therefore, I handed the book to the secretary designating what pages I wanted copied, then I reentered the archives room to find out what I could about Dylan.

I picked up the 2010 record book and opened it to the month of March. Dylan Matthews had been stopped for suspected DUI on March 17, 2010, at approximately 11:35 p.m. He was detained near the Stony Pony Pub and Grill on US Route 27, a biker bar situated one mile away from the Carson County line, heading toward Atlanta. Dylan failed a field sobriety test and the ensuing breathalyzer test, both of which were administered at the scene of the DUI stop. Dylan admitted he was at the bar celebrating Saint Patrick's Day, and he confessed to drinking approximately nine gin and tonics before he left to drive home. Resultantly, Dylan was arrested and taken to the county jail, where he spent the night.

The entry that pertained to Dylan was so short, I decided to snap a photo of it with my phone rather than have the provision copied. Thereafter, I closed the book and lifted it off the table to put it away. As I did so, a small piece of paper fell from its pages and slowly floated through the air. I picked it up after it landed near my right foot. At the top of the paper, inscribed in formal typewritten black print, were the words, *Carson County Daily Times, From the Desk of Michael Ketron*. A handwritten note was scrawled in blue ink below the type that read: *Dylan Matthews—murder.* I placed the paper in my handbag and left the room. Retrieving copies of the Weatherly murder documents on the way out, I briskly exited the sheriff's office and dashed to my car. I Googled Michael Ketron and discovered he was a veteran reporter for the Carson County Daily Times. I called his direct line at the newspaper, but he did not answer, so I left a message, then I set out to meet my lunch date.

John Simmons was standing outside near the front entrance of the pizza place when I arrived. He was a twenty-something skinny man, with cropped brown hair and a pronounced southern accent. His attire consisted of a faded gray jumpsuit adorned with an embroidered patch on the upper-left corner advertising the name of his bottling company employer. On the whole, he did not give off a stellar first impression, which worried me because his credibility could be an issue; neat and tidy people tended to be better believed. Nonetheless, the longer I considered him, the better I thought of him because I was sure he could be cleaned up before providing official testimony.

John relayed that he often witnessed board members, committee members, and other employees steal Association food, property, and gas. He admitted that he had not immediately reported the thefts because he feared reprisal. It was only when he saw Lavine fill up his car, his wife's car and his daughter's car on the same morning, that he sprung into action and filed a complaint with the local district attorney's office. Two weeks after John filed the complaint, he was summoned to the district attorney's office to discuss his allegations in further detail.

On the appointed date at the appointed time, to John's chagrin, he was met with Andrew Wilson, Gerald Lavine, Dylan Matthews, and Herschel Marks. Wilson informed John that Lavine and Dylan had filed sworn statements disputing his claims. In addition, Wilson apprised John that filing a false police report was a crime punishable by up to one year in prison, but he was willing to forgo prosecution if John would withdraw his complaint. Herschel Marks said filing a false police report was grounds for immediate termination from the Association. John agreed to withdraw his complaint in lieu of prosecution but he was still discharged from his well-paid Association position.

John walked me to my car after lunch. The skies had become cloudy and the frigid air was motionless. I saw John's breath crystalize right before my eyes when he stated, "I don't want to get involved with the members of the Association anymore."

"But maybe we could stop the board from stealing from the people who live in Covington Commons," I said, pulling my coat collar close around my neck.

"Those board members are a bunch of nasty people and I think they might try to hurt my family if I talk anymore."

"I definitely think we can stop them if we try."

"Miss, I'm a young guy; I'm not even thirty. I don't want to be blackballed anymore. Sorry I can't help you."

"Thank you, I do appreciate your help," I said as I looked into the young man's sorrowful blue eyes while he held my car door open.

I did not say anything when I slipped into my vehicle. The seat was so cold, my bare legs instantly froze and stuck to the hardened leather. John hesitated as if to speak, but instead, he shut my car door. I engaged the ignition and the engine revved, spewed fumes and stalled; the icy air controlled the day. I tried again, and the engine hummed after momentarily warming up. I slowly pulled away. John remained standing in the parking lot without a coat, forlornly watching me. He disappeared when I turned out of the parking lot onto the street.

I weighed my options during my drive home to Champaign and I concluded that my options had dwindled significantly. Maybe the Association's ruling class was untouchable. With no apparent recourse available, a fortuitous circumstance needed to present itself in order for my fraud investigation to move forward.

CHAPTER 15
THE INVESTIGATORS

The next day, I received a phone call from Robert Cobb Jr., a stunning event, because I did not remember giving him my contact information when I had last seen him.

Mr. Cobb was supremely jovial. "Hello, young lady, this is Robert Cobb Jr., the attorney. We met months ago at the clerk's office in Lakewood City. I enjoyed meeting you that day."

"Thank you, Mr. Cobb. I enjoyed meeting you, too."

"I have been hearing good things about you and what you are trying to do to help the residents of Covington Commons. I heard an appeal has been filed. How is that going?"

"Oh, very well, sir."

We discussed my case in detail. Mr. Cobb thought my claims were original questions of first impression the appellate court would be interested in ruling on, and he was convinced I had a good chance of winning. I felt excited he was interested in my case. I thought he might make a good confidant since he was so well respected in Lakewood City; his integrity was without doubt beyond reproach.

I informed Mr. Cobb I wanted to pursue another angle and determine whether the Association board members, committee members, or any employees were embezzling Covington Commons treasury money or misappropriating assets. I listed the litany of red flags and the reasons I believed the red flags indicated criminality. At the close of my exposé, Mr. Cobb agreed the information I uncovered, although merely circumstantial, warranted further investigation into the Association's financial activities.

"I use two former police officers as private investigators when I need to conduct surreptitious surveillance, and I would be happy to offer up their services to you anytime you need them."

"Investigators are expensive. I'm not sure about the costs," I hedged.

"Don't worry about that, my dear. I pay them on a salaried basis, so there would be no cost to you."

"Really?"

"How about we meet on Friday morning at my offices here in Lakewood City and I can introduce you to the investigators?" Mr. Cobb suggested.

"Sure, what time?"

"How about at ten?"

"Thank you, Mr. Cobb. I'll be there."

"Good day, young lady."

I drove over an hour to reach Mr. Cobb's law firm, which was located in an old bank building on the first floor, four easy to walk blocks from the courthouse. Mr. Cobb greeted me warmly in the waiting room and ushered me into his private office, where the lingering smell of oaky cigar smoke scented the dense air.

"Please have a seat. Can I get you anything?"

"I'll have a glass of water. Thank you for your help."

Mr. Cobb's dainty gold chain bracelet shimmered in the fluorescent light when he poured water from a pitcher that sat on a credenza beneath a bay window accented with ruby drapes. "Oh, I am happy to help. The investigators will be here soon. I thought we could have a little talk before they arrive."

"Is this your wife?" I asked, pointing to a photograph of a silver-haired woman about sixty years old that rested on his chestnut desk.

"Yes, sadly she died almost three years ago in June 2012, just a day before our forty-first wedding anniversary. She was a lovely woman. We were high school sweethearts. We married right after graduation," he said as he handed me a tepid glass of iceless water.

"I am sorry for your loss." I did not mention the loss of his granddaughter, which had occurred six months later, in December of the same year.

Mr. Cobb's eyes glassed over. "It's okay. Things happen."

"I love your offices. They are beautiful," I said, trying to change the subject.

"Thank you. My wife decorated all of the rooms. She loves—I mean loved, dark earthy colors."

I inspected the knotty-wood paneled walls, the fringed paprika rug, and the sepia barrister bookcases filled with old law reporters. "Are you the only attorney here?" I tried once again to change the subject.

"Yes, my daughter practiced with me for a number of years, but her husband was transferred to California for a new job in Silicon Valley last year. So now I am here by myself."

"Maybe you can hire another associate," I said after I placed my water glass on a coaster on the grand desk.

"Yes, I would like to hire an associate and eventually sell my practice."

"I'm sure you'll find the right attorney."

Our discussion then turned to the purpose of our meeting, my introduction to the investigators, retired Atlanta Police Chief Randall

Wise and retired Nashville Police Detective Claude McCrackin. Mr. Cobb advised me that Wise was the congenial, upbeat member of the duo who had a knack for getting people to confide in him. McCrackin, on the other hand, was the secretive, analytical one who quietly observed what was going on and made mental notes of each interaction. The two men worked well together as a team.

Several minutes into our conversation, a secretary peeked into the office and advised us that the investigators were present and waiting in the conference room. Mr. Cobb hastily rose from his crimson leather swivel chair and escorted me to meet the investigators.

The okra-painted conference room was well lit by an elk-horn chandelier that hung over a walnut pedestal table surrounded by eight armchairs upholstered in green leather. The deep pile, sage carpet was a bit tricky to navigate in high heels; I twisted my ankle a little when I stepped into the room. After I steadied myself, Mr. Cobb introduced me to the investigators. Wise was a portly man with a full head of wavy white hair. I guessed he was in his late fifties, maybe early sixties. He was amiable and bubbly, somewhat like Santa but with a clean-shaven face. McCrackin was bald, tall, and pencil thin, about the same age as Wise. He wore gold-rimmed aviator glasses, a manicured goatee, and a constantly pursed lip, which made him look a tad angry.

During our meeting, which lasted just over an hour, I explained why I believed the Association board and finance committee members might have committed fraud. At the adjournment, the investigators suggested we have lunch at the Covington Commons yacht club so we could better orient ourselves to the community. Mr. Cobb begged off; he said he had a lot of work to do, but I eagerly agreed since I had not yet been to the yacht club. The investigators offered to drive, so I followed them to a four-door sedan that resembled a government-issued vehicle because it was indistinctive and stripped of all upgraded options. It arguably was the perfect vehicle for private investigators; the car's blandness rendered it relatively inconspicuous.

The yacht club foyer was decorated with white wallpaper embossed with golden fleur de lis, complementing crown molding, and flaxen carpets. The hostess station was unmanned when we arrived, so we waited briefly for someone to appear, but when that did not happen, McCrackin said, "I guess they're not serving lunch right now. We should probably go."

As we turned to leave, a run-down woman with curly, cinnamon-dyed hair burst through a door that led from the kitchen into the vestibule where we stood. "I'm sorry, our hostess is out sick, so I'm pulling double duty today. How are y'all today?"

Wise smiled at the woman. "Oh, we're all doing well. How about you?"

"I'm fine. Thanks for asking. Will y'all be having lunch?"

"Yes, three for lunch," McCrackin said.

"We're not serving lunch in the main ballroom for a couple of weeks because it's being renovated. But we're serving lunch in the bar, if that's okay."

"That will be fine," Wise said.

I trailed closely behind our waitress as she led us to our table. She smelled faintly of cigarette smoke and distilled spirits. Somber circles and cavernous crow's feet framed her lifeless eyes. Her hands were rough, red, and cracked and her skin was sallow. She moved slowly, shuffling her feet as she walked. Her haggard appearance betrayed the probability she was living a hard, unfulfilling life.

"I'm Millie and I'll be taking care of you today. Let me leave you with these menus. What can I get you to drink?" she said as we all sat down.

"Just a glass of water, please," I replied.

Wise ordered for himself and McCrackin. "We'll both have black coffee."

Our waitress returned quickly with our drinks. "The coffee is fresh. I made a pot right before you walked in."

"How do you like working here? Seems like a mighty fine restaurant," Wise asked.

"Oh yes, I love working here. I've been working here for almost fifteen years. This is my last day, though. My mother needs an operation, so I'm going to take a leave of absence to take care of her."

"Are you from around here?" McCrackin asked.

"No, I moved here close to twenty years ago. I'm from Nashville; that's where my mother lives."

"How long will you stay in Nashville?" Wise asked.

"The doctors say she'll need to recuperate for about six months or more, so at least through the end of the summer . . . maybe I'll like it better back home and move there for good. Who knows?"

"I hope your mother gets well soon," McCrackin said as both Wise and I nodded with sympathy.

"It's quiet today. No one is here," I observed.

"It's still the off season, being late February. In March, throughout the spring, business picks up, but the best time to visit the yacht club is in the summer and fall. That's when the oleander is in bloom," gushed Millie.

Wise glimpsed at his menu and asked, "How is the lobster roll sandwich?"

"I'm sorry, sir. We're out of lobster right now. There was a dinner party here last night and so many people ordered lobster, we ran out. That happens every time the board members eat at the yacht club. We should have more tomorrow."

"What board members?" McCrackin inquired.

"Oh, the homeowners association board members, they run Covington Commons."

Wise continued. "Do the board members frequently eat at the yacht club?

"Oh yes," Millie exclaimed. "Mr. Lavine and his friends love eating here."

Wise delved further. "Who is Mr. Lavine?"

"He's the board president," Millie responded.

"How often do Mr. Lavine and his friends eat at the yacht club?" Wise asked.

"Mr. Lavine likes to come and eat on Friday and Saturday nights with his wife. Almost all the board members eat here on Friday and Saturday nights with their wives, or boyfriends, too; the board vice president is Ms. Matthews, and she isn't married. On Friday and Saturday nights, the cook always prepares a lobster special for the menu. Mr. Lavine and his friends love lobster. We usually have lobster for lunch on Friday, too, but last night Mr. Lavine celebrated his seventy-third birthday with a lot of his friends. That's why we ran out," Millie unwittingly testified.

"Sounds like a fun party," McCrackin commented.

"Yes, it was, it really was. Sorry, I'm talking so much. What would you all like for lunch?"

We looked at the menus.

McCrackin ordered first. "I'll have the steak special."

Wise agreed. "Put me down for the same and add a side of onion rings, please."

"I'll have the grilled chicken sandwich with fries," I said softly.

The table conversation during lunch was dull. Wise and McCrackin discussed baseball's spring-training lineup while I picked at an overcooked sandwich and soggy fries.

As we left the restaurant, Cedric Holmes popped into my mind. I had forgotten to mention the instance when Bill was brushed off as inconsequential when he had sought legal advice from him.

I explained the connection between Bill Richards and Cedric Holmes after we were seated in Wise's car.

"I know of Cedric Holmes," Wise said as he pulled out of the yacht club parking lot. "Many in the community, and people as far south as Valdosta, thought it was strange that a family law attorney would be the defense attorney in a highly publicized first-degree murder case."

"That is strange," I concurred.

"Wise and I will both be taking your case, and we hope to help you determine if there's ongoing fraud at the Association," McCrackin declared.

"I thought you had to take the case because you're Mr. Cobb's employees."

"Noooooo, we are not Mr. Cobb's employees. Mr. Cobb hired our Atlanta firm, which is headed by both me and Claude here to take on this matter."

"So Mr. Cobb is paying your wages and expenses to take on this case?"

"Yes," McCrackin answered.

"But why?"

"We are not at liberty to say," Wise replied.

I asked the men how they undertook undercover operations in the context of having an independent firm. "How do you preserve your anonymity in the face of social media? Couldn't anybody Google your name and find out who you are and that you own a private investigation firm?"

"Each investigator's identity is kept secret to preserve their ability to go undercover. No identifying information is ever listed on any document or digital internet transmission about any individual who works at our firm," Wise said.

All at once, I began to feel uncomfortably warm. I was unsure about the two investigators. I speculated Wise and McCrackin were pseudonyms and the men were not who they pretended to be.

When Wise pulled up near my car, McCrackin jumped out of the back seat and opened the door. "Let us know if you come across any additional information that might pertain to the investigation."

"Okay, no problem."

McCrackin shook my hand. "We'll be in touch."

"Goodbye," Wise said.

The weather had become gloomy and so had my spirits. I drove home in the pouring rain, doubtful that Mr. Cobb trusted me or my motives.

CHAPTER 16
THE DINNER PARTY

In order to infiltrate the Association's ruling class, the investigators posed as executives working for a Florida real estate investment firm, instructed by their company's CEO to travel to various Appalachian mountain lake communities to purchase lots for resale to wealthy Florida retirees. Wise and McCrackin believed the Covington Commons board would never pass up a chance to unload thousands of Association-held lots to gain additional assessment fee income. Selling hundreds or even thousands of lots would mean a turnaround for the Association's budgetary deficiencies and a bump to the bottom lines of the board and committee members' financial portfolios because they would have a larger pot from which to steal.

Wise contacted a former colleague who had retired to Florida after serving as an Atlanta police detective under Wise's authority for many years. Wise's buddy, Henry Calhoun, agreed to act as the CEO for the illusory Florida real estate investment firm, Sunrise Real Estate Investment, Inc. McCrackin set up a phony website and the scheme was off to the races. The unsuspecting Lakewood City realtor they retained was a woman by the name of Trisha Jenkins.

Calhoun instructed Ms. Jenkins to inform Lavine that his Florida firm, Sunrise Real Estate Investment, Inc. might be interested in possibly purchasing 1500 - 2000 lots. Ms. Jenkins gave the information to Lavine and she informed Calhoun that Lavine was ecstatic. If the Florida investment firm purchased 1500 quarter-acre lots at the tax-assessed value of $30,000 per lot, the Association would realize $45 million, plus more than $9 million in extra annual assessment fee income.

Lavine phoned Calhoun right after he spoke with Ms. Jenkins. Calhoun informed Lavine there was a huge market for Georgia mountain real estate in Florida because the retired elite did not like to summer in the Sunshine State's oppressive heat. Lavine invited the CEO to Covington Commons for a private tour of the community and dinner at the yacht club. Calhoun said he would send his top two executives to scout the luxurious lakefront community. The date was set for Wednesday, April 1, 2015.

Lavine met with Wise and McCrackin at approximately four in the afternoon on All Fools' Day and treated them to a first-class tour of Covington Commons in his pristine Italian automobile. He was careful not to take the men to the neglected neighborhoods in states of dilapidation. Instead, he drove them through the classy, populated, lakefront neighborhood of Eagle's Nest, the Upper East Side of Covington Commons, so to speak. The men explored the golf courses, the fitness gymnasium, the tennis courts, the equestrian trails, and the marina. Lavine raved that the best Covington Commons had to offer was certainly the breathtaking views and the mild weather.

The trio's last stop was the yacht club. They arrived about a half hour early, which provided the men with time to freshen up before the big dinner event. Wise and McCrackin were both dressed casually in polo shirts and dark-colored slacks. Neither was aware that the event they were about to attend was set to be a lavish night full of extreme indulgence. The guests began to arrive about six thirty, and all were clothed in elegant evening wear, with the exception of the grand marshals of the parade, Wise and McCrackin, who were not forewarned to bring their Sunday best. The women wore full-length gowns and the men wore white dinner jackets with white shirts, black bowties, and black trousers. The servers were also impeccably dressed, in what looked to be brand-new tuxedo-style uniforms.

It was too chilly to serve the before-dinner drinks on the outdoor decks as planned, so the aperitifs were served in the ritzy private lounge, decorated with Louis XIV marble and gilt furnishings. After imbibing cocktails with the Association's VIPs, the investigators were seated at the finest table in the club's elaborate ballroom, which was also decorated in the Sun King's garish style of shimmer and shine. Wise and McCrackin's dinner companions were Mr. and Mrs. Gerald Lavine, Mr. and Mrs. Cedric Holmes, Cindy and Dylan Matthews, and Herschel Marks and his date, Trisha Jenkins, the realtor. The tables were divine. Each was draped in luscious gold silk and set with fine silver and exquisite china centered around an extravagant floral bouquet that emanated a redolent aroma that permeated the entire ballroom.

The fragrance emitted from the flowers was so powerful, Wise asked Lavine, "What kind of flowers are on the tables? My wife would love the smell. The flowers smell like bubble gum."

"Oleander. We had to order the arrangements on the tables tonight because the oleander doesn't start blooming in Covington Commons until late spring. In June, the yacht club will be covered in oleander blooms and the flowers last through the fall. The oleander is one of the biggest attractions around the yacht club. Our gardening club planted the shrubs more than ten years ago," Lavine replied.

"The oleander is beautiful. I think it smells like orange soda pop," McCrackin added.

"I'm disappointed that Millie, our head waitress, could not be here tonight. She's caring for her ill mother. Millie loves the oleander, and if she were here tonight, she would get an earlier-than-expected dose of it," Lavine ruefully pined.

The evening's menu included four different types of rare caviar, premier Russian vodka, fine Kobe steaks, succulent Maine lobsters, and exquisite French Champagne that did not stop flowing. The chefs had prepared six courses in the formal French manner, which required service of a salad and a cheese plate after the main course. Specialty chocolate soufflé was served at the end of the delectable meal with whiskey-laden Irish coffee. A chamber-music quartet serenaded the diners to classical music while they ate under glimmering chandeliers that diffused low light and created an intimate atmosphere in the vast ballroom.

Herschel seemed uncomfortable and said nearly nothing during dinner. Cedric, however, was another story. He was happy, laughing, and joking throughout the course of the meal. All the attendees found him amusing except his wife, who seemed agitated and refused to look at him. Wise kept the conversations going; he was a master at making sure there was never a boring lull. He asked about the community, the extracurricular activities, and the level of enjoyment each person experienced as a resident of Covington Commons, but he did not ask about any financial specifics concerning the payment of fees or the running of the Association.

Following the scrumptious dinner, a cover band played fun music from the '60s, '70s, and '80s. Many people got up and danced. Everyone was having such a marvelous time, no one noticed the bleak clouds that crept across the skies above the yacht club and concealed the luminous full moon and glistening stars. The band played upbeat music for about an hour, and then it quietly transitioned to crooning a country-themed ballad. Couples were swaying to the sedate tune, holding each other close, when thunderous rumblings struck so loud all of the windows at the yacht club began to shake. The shaking was so pronounced, for a split second, many attendees thought Covington Commons was experiencing a cataclysmic earthquake. Tumultuous thunder clapped again and then some exceedingly bright light lit up the inky sky. Icy rain pounded the ground, causing billowy steam to rise from the warm spring earth.

The band continued to play, but the musicians had lost the attention of the partygoers. All eyes were fixated on the windows, peering out, waiting for a break in the extreme weather. The violent storm lasted a quarter hour. When the rain ceased, many people raced to their cars, fearing another round of storms would commence yet again. During the mass exodus, Lavine was seen looking down, shaking his head in disbelief. The local meteorologist had predicted ideal evening weather earlier that morning, but Mother Nature had defied the forecasts and played the perfect April fool's trick on the Association that night.

As the last guests left, Lavine approached Wise and McCrackin, who were waiting for the valet to retrieve the glitzy sedan they had rented for the investigation.

Lavine asked, "Do either of you play any golf?"

"Sure, we both play a round now and then," Wise responded.

Delighted, Lavine asked, "Well, why don't you two join me for a game tomorrow morning for an eight o'clock tee time? I believe the weather will be nice and calm with low winds."

"Sorry, Gerald, tomorrow's no good. Both McCrackin and I are flying back to Florida to report to our CEO. He wants to find out what we think of all the Appalachian mountain lake communities we visited. He wants to know what community we think Sunrise Real Estate Investment should invest in," Wise replied.

Lavine anxiously asked, "How about one day next week?"

Wise glanced at McCrackin, who bobbed his head in agreement. "Sure, Gerald. How about next Friday morning?" Wise asked as he shook Lavine's hand.

"Fantastic, we'll see you two next Friday," Lavine said.

CHAPTER 17
THE MEETINGS

The day after Wise and McCrackin provided me with a precision debriefing about the Association's lavish dinner party, I woke up early to make some phone calls. First, I spoke with Lisa McGuire, Theodore Milton's original court-appointed attorney; she agreed to meet with me on April 13 after the criminal court's morning calendar call. Thereafter, I left another message for Michael Ketron. I had left numerous messages for him over the course of several preceding weeks, but he had not replied. At last, however, moments after I left the message, Michael Ketron returned my call and I picked up on the first ring. We discussed his note and he agreed to meet me in the afternoon on the same day I was scheduled to meet Ms. McGuire.

Ms. McGuire's offices were located in the basement of the courthouse near the holding cells, down the hall, and around the corner from the room where the criminal records were archived. A receptionist led me to a small unwindowed office with a gunmetal desk, a matching bookshelf, and three wooden chairs. Nothing hung on the walls. The receptionist left me alone and summoned Ms. McGuire. A minute later, the public defender entered, introduced herself, and sat down in a wooden chair positioned behind the steely desk.

Ms. McGuire was a young woman, who had probably been practicing law for about ten years. She had messy light-brown hair and oversized tortoise-shell eyeglasses. She was dressed in a crisp white blouse and a freshly pressed black suit. She was cordial, and she made it abundantly clear that the sole reason she agreed to speak with me about the Milton case was because the attorney-client relationship had expired at the time of Milton's death. She did not want to give the impression she willy-nilly talked about former clients freely in derogation of their rights to the attorney-client privilege. I thanked Ms. McGuire for her graciousness and she proceeded to discuss her relationship with Theodore Milton.

Ms. McGuire explained that the court had appointed her to Theodore Milton's case because he had not selected an attorney prior to his arraignment. The first time she met Milton was just before the proceeding, when the bailiffs brought him upstairs from the basement courthouse holding cells. Ms. McGuire advised Milton he would not obtain bail because he was charged with first-degree murder. She said Milton seemed dazed and confused when she instructed him to plead not guilty to the charges leveled against him. The only words Ms. McGuire recalled Milton say were, "Okay, thank you." That was the only time she spoke with Theodore Milton.

Subsequent to the arraignment, Ms. McGuire received a call from Cedric Holmes informing her he would be taking over the representation of Theodore Milton. Knowing Cedric well, she asked why he would represent Milton, since he was not a skilled criminal defense attorney—which was exactly what Milton needed. In response, Cedric declared that the case would never go to trial, and he further claimed that he possessed all the skills necessary to properly conclude the matter. Ms. McGuire countered Cedric and advised him that the prosecutor would never plea-bargain a case like Milton's because he was charged with murder one. Cedric ordered her to prepare her motion to withdraw as counsel for immediate submission to the court. That was all she knew about the inner workings of the Milton murder trial.

"What did you think when you heard that Theodore Milton was found dead in his jail cell hours before he was supposed to testify in his own defense?" I asked.

Ms. McGuire scratched her head in apparent puzzlement. "I thought there was more going on than met the eye. That's why I agreed to meet with you. Maybe someone should be investigating the matter. My office refuses to have any continued involvement in the Milton case."

I left Ms. McGuire's office with more questions than answers.

Michael Ketron did not want to rendezvous at his offices at the Carson County Daily Times. Instead, we decided to meet at the community park in the historic district of Lakewood City near the amphitheater that served as a venue for the weekly farmers' market and the Saturday-evening summer concerts. I got to the park about thirty minutes early. It was crowded with people eating brown-bag lunches, celebrating the pleasant sunny day. I seated myself on a bench beneath a shady sassafras tree near a small fountain.

Michael advised me he would be wearing a Dodgers baseball cap because he had gone to college in Los Angeles and remained a devoted fan. I conscientiously searched the crowd, looking for my appointment. Soon, I spotted a man wearing a Dodgers cap at the opposite end of the park. I waved to him, and when he saw me, he pulled his hat's visor further over his eyes. As he stealthily approached, I realized I should not attract too much attention. The mystery man took a seat beside me on the park bench and removed his cap.

Michael was a stocky man of average height who looked to be about thirty-five years old. He was completely bald and hugely muscular, similar to a steroid-taking bodybuilder. The only hair discernable on the exposed areas of his body was bushy, dirt-brown eyebrows and a tuft beneath his lower lip that was groomed and dyed blonde. His eyes were cloudy and his sizable nose must have been broken at one time because it was cocked to one side. He was wearing jeans and a red t-shirt that exposed tattoo sleeves on both arms. His knuckle-ink spelled out the phrase "true grit."

Michael spoke in a shrill, soprano voice. "Why do you want information about Dylan Matthews?"

I could not answer directly because spontaneous giggles suppressed my speech. I hadn't expected his voice to be so high-pitched; it had sounded much deeper over the phone. I held my hand over my mouth until I regained my composure while Michael displayed perturbed annoyance. Despite my reaction, Michael did not seem personally insulted, probably because that was not the first time someone had giggled in response to initially hearing his voice. Eventually, I pulled the paper with his name and the hand-inscribed phrase from my purse.

Michael turned to me with a slight look of dread and cryptically advised, "Everything I'm going to tell you needs to be kept completely confidential."

"Why?"

"Both for your safety and for mine."

A frosty shiver shot down my spine. "Okay."

"Dylan was arrested and charged with DUI in March 2010, and Dylan was represented by Robert Cobb, Jr."

"Let me stop you there. I know all of this. I even know Mr. Cobb; he's helping me with a civil case against the Covington Commons Homeowners Association."

Michael continued. "I've been secretly looking into Dylan Matthews for a number of years. Dylan's first DUI was nothing more than a routine stop after a Saint Patrick's Day party at the Stony Pony. The result was not extraordinary. He obtained competent counsel and pled guilty to the lesser offense of reckless driving. It was a desirable result for all involved, including Dylan's attorney, Mr. Robert Cobb."

"Why are you interested in Dylan Matthews?"

"Please let me finish," Michael scolded.

"Sorry, go on," I mumbled.

"On December 22, 2012, Dylan was involved in another horrific accident right after he returned home after getting his MBA. Yes, he was drinking and driving, and possibly under the influence of amphetamines. Dylan was driving north on Georgia Route 132 when he crossed the median and struck a blue car, driven by a woman who was accompanied by her young daughter."

I gasped loudly and covered my mouth with my hand.

Michael persisted. "The officers used the Jaws of Life to extricate the occupants from the vehicle. The mother was unconscious and severely injured, so the paramedics airlifted her to the nearest hospital. The child wasn't so lucky. The officers said she didn't appear to be injured when they removed her from the vehicle, but she was pronounced dead at the scene. The coroner later determined that the child had suffered from acute internal bleeding, and that, coupled with asphyxiation, had caused her death. The car was filled with Christmas presents, some wrapped and some unwrapped. The little girl's doll was buckled up in the seat alongside her. The mother was Susan Fitzgerald, the daughter of local attorney, Robert Cobb Jr. The child was Rebecca Fitzgerald, Mr. Cobb's eight-year-old granddaughter."

"How do you know all of this?" I whispered, choking back a sob.

"I spoke with the sheriff's deputies who were called to the scene. I was assigned to cover the story for the Carson County Daily Times."

"Oh my God!" I cried.

"The editor of the Carson County Daily Times later killed my story about the accident, and the article never went to print. The editor published a statement about the event that only named the victims and not the perpetrator."

I thought Michael must have been referring to the article I had read on the internet.

"The official records pertaining to the accident were wiped off the books in Lakewood City and Carson County. Dylan was never charged with a crime."

"Oh my God," I repeated.

Michael stood and curtly declared, "I have to leave. Here's my cell phone number. Never contact me at the newspaper."

"Okay," I said, taking his business card.

I did not know what to do after Michael left. My mind began racing. It was difficult to fathom such a horrific chain of events. I was flabbergasted. Robert Cobb Jr. had gotten a sweet plea deal for the drunkard, Dylan Matthews, who later injured his daughter and killed his granddaughter. The tragic circumstances surrounding the death of Mr. Cobb's granddaughter were utterly unthinkable. Nobody should have to live with that kind of guilt.

I pulled my phone from my purse and called Mr. Cobb. "Hello," I said to his secretary. "Is Mr. Cobb available?"

"No, he won't be available for the rest of the afternoon. You could try him on his cell phone."

"That's okay. Please tell him I called. Thank you, bye."

"Bye," the secretary returned.

I sat on the park bench for a long time before I was ready to make the trek home.

On the way to my car, I stopped at a newsstand to purchase a copy of the Carson County Daily Times. I figured I should better acquaint myself with the publication.

My cell phone rang while I was at the newsstand, so I stepped away from the counter and let the person behind me pay for his items.

"Hi, this is Robert Cobb."

"Hello," I said in a commiserative tone.

"I wanted to know when we could get together to meet with the investigators. Evidently, they have obtained additional information. They want us to meet at their offices in Atlanta."

"How about the day after tomorrow? Wednesday," I said.

"Fine. Would you like to drive with me? I can pick you up on the way."

"Oh no, that's okay. I can drive myself. Since I'll be in Atlanta, I want to stop by and visit a friend after our meeting," I lied.

"Sure, I understand. If you change your mind, let me know. The address is 60 Forsyth Street, Suite 200. See you then."

As the call ended, I stepped up to the counter and handed the newsstand cashier my payment, then I left with my paper.

I paged through the Carson County Daily Times when I arrived home later that night. I read a story on the second-to-last page written by Michael Ketron. The article stated that a woman's body had recently been found washed up on the banks of Carson Lake. The Carson County sheriff's office said the woman was approximately twenty to twenty-five years old and five and a half feet tall, with purple hair and numerous tattoos and piercings. Law enforcement was unable to make a positive identification, so they asked for help from the public to determine the woman's identity.

James came home while I was reading the newspaper in my office and petting Star on my lap. He greeted me with a kiss and asked, "What are you reading?"

"The Carson County Daily Times."

"Anything interesting?"

"No."

I called Bill the next morning.

"What do you know about the Ed Weatherly murder?" I asked.

"Well, my wife is friends with Vicki, and I knew Theodore pretty well. But I didn't know too much about the case other than what was written in the newspapers. Vicki didn't speak about the case because

Theodore's attorney, Cedric Holmes, instructed her not to talk to anyone in order to protect Theodore's chances of an acquittal."

"Did Vicki ever speak about the case after Theodore's death?"

"Not to me, and Eva told me Vicki never brought the topic up between them. Eva thinks Theodore's arrest and death are too painful for Vicki to discuss."

"Were Weatherly or Milton close to any of the board members? Or to Dylan Matthews or Haywood Martin?"

"The murder had nothing to do with any board member or Covington Commons employee," Bill emphatically stated.

"Do you think Vicki Milton would mind speaking with me?"

"I'm not sure, but I'll give you her number . . . it's 555-5437."

I got the feeling Bill thought I was a run-of-the-mill conspiracy theorist with no facts to back up my unsubstantiated claims, so I moved on to another topic. "Do you think Dylan is qualified to be the operations manager at Covington Commons?"

"Dylan has an MBA, which he obtained after he settled his DUI charges, so I imagine that would provide sufficient qualification, but he doesn't have any actual work experience that I'm aware of."

"Do you think Dylan is a good operations manager?"

"That's hard to say, no one sees much of Dylan, or watches him work, since his offices are located in an obscure building behind the Eagle's Nest fitness gymnasium. He rarely attends any board meetings or community events. No one knows much about him."

"When Dylan was hired, were community members upset? Maybe because of his DUI conviction or lack of experience?"

"When Dylan was hired to be the Association's operations manager, the board held a meeting and discussed his hire with the community members who wanted information about the decision. Some community members were upset. I attended the meeting to protest his hiring, not because of Dylan's prior arrest or his lack of qualifications, but because the board engaged in impermissible nepotism when Cindy Matthews' son was hired."

"Is Dylan a nice person?"

"Dylan seems like a nice enough man, clean cut and polite, though maybe a little shy and awkward."

"When Dylan was arrested outside the Stony Pony on Saint Patrick's Day night in 2010, was that the only time Dylan was charged with a crime?"

"Yes, Dylan was only arrested and charged with a crime that one time," Bill affirmed.

"Wasn't Dylan charged with another DUI or some sort of vehicular crime involving injured victims?"

"Absolutely not," replied Bill.

"How can you be sure?"

"Because if Dylan had been charged with committing another crime, it would have been in all the papers."

After I spoke with Bill, I dialed Vicki Milton's number and the phone rang maybe ten times. I was about to hang up when a breathless woman answered. "Hello?"

"Hello," I replied. "I'm an attorney and I came across your husband's case while I was researching a different matter. I was wondering if it would be okay if I asked you a few questions about your husband's tragic death."

"I'm shocked anyone cares about Theodore and how he died."

"Maybe we could meet and talk about Mr. Milton."

"Sure, but I'll be away for three weeks. I'm going to visit my sister in Minneapolis. Why don't you call me after I get back and we can set something up?"

"Okay, I'll call you when you get back from your trip. Thank you very much," I said, encouraged she hadn't refused to meet with me.

CHAPTER 18
TEE TIME

Wise and McCrackin's offices were located in the upscale section of Atlanta near the state capitol, across the street from the high-rise federal building. The building itself was a brick-and-mortar Victorian structure erected during the first quarter of the twentieth century. There was no firm name or other distinguishing designation on the exterior of the building other than the street name and number. Inside the lobby was a list of named tenants on a wall opposite the doorway. The office I was directed to visit was identified solely by a suite number and no firm name.

I took a crowded elevator to the fourth floor, and I found the investigators' offices situated at the far end of an unadorned, beige-carpeted hallway. The receptionist showed me to a conference room adjacent to the entryway. She offered me coffee and a Danish, and I eagerly accepted both. I waited for about a half hour because I had arrived a half hour early. Arriving early had become a nasty habit, so in the interim, I chewed my Danish and drank my coffee in the sundrenched conference room, furnished with caramel-shaded oak furniture, bronze overhead pendant lanterns, cream walls, and tan marble floors.

Just after I gobbled the last morsel of my snack, the doorknob twisted and the squeaky hinge began its rotation. I swiftly grabbed a tissue from a box on the table and wiped crumbs from my lips. Mr. Cobb and the investigators entered and soberly observed me. McCrackin furtively shut the door. My eyes examined the face of each man. I did not get up. I felt glued to my chair. I was surprised at the cloak-and-dagger attitude they displayed. Wise broke the silence and offered me more coffee, which I respectfully declined, I was already quite jacked up on caffeine. Wise and McCrackin then delineated the events that had occurred during their golf outing. I was literally awestruck at the investigators' fastidious descriptions of the incidents they recounted.

Nine days after the ruined party, Wise and McCrackin showed up at Covington Commons' Turtle Dove golf course for the scheduled game. They arrived before Lavine, so they carefully examined the high-end merchandise displayed for sale in the exceptional pro shop. The store sold top-of-the-line golf equipment, unusual golf-themed gifts, and deluxe sportswear for both men and women. Wise heard a soft thump moments after he had started to browse the shop, then he saw Lavine enter through a side door at the far end of the store. Not noticing Wise or McCrackin, Lavine began examining men's sportswear hanging on an expensive clothing carousel.

Wise made himself known and yelled across the room, "Hi, Gerald! Glad you could make it! Are you ready to lose a game of golf today?"

Lavine moved toward the men and laughed. "No way, but I'm ready to beat you two in a game of golf today."

The men shook hands, and then Cedric entered and joined the group.

"Hello, people. The fifth wheel, Herschel, should be here soon," Cedric said as he patted Wise's back while shaking hands with McCrackin. Thereafter, Cedric turned to Wise and firmly grasped his hand. "I think we'll have a great game today. The weather is perfect and the best two caddies in Covington Commons are outside waiting for us."

"I'll meet you all outside by the golf carts. I need to change before the game," Lavine said, walking toward a dressing room near the cash register at the front of the store.

Outside, Cedric, Wise, and McCrackin retrieved their clubs, and the caddies loaded them into an equipment cart just as Herschel pulled into the parking lot. Hershel unpacked his clubs, deposited them with the caddies, and joined the golfers near a six-passenger cart. Lavine came outside carrying his clubs and wearing the green shirt he had examined in the pro shop right before he noticed Wise and McCrackin. One of the caddies rushed to Lavine's aid and relieved him of his burdensome weight. Lavine took control and sat behind the wheel of the six-seater, then he invited the men into the vehicle. Wise sat beside Lavine, and Cedric sat behind Lavine, next to McCrackin. Herschel was forced to sit on the back bench that faced away from everyone. Wise and McCrackin both noted that Lavine and Cedric each had a set of Honary clubs, the most prized of all golf clubs; one Honary club had a price tag upwards of $5,000.

Cedric played a superlative game. He displayed excellent balance and a keen backswing, which caused him to birdie eleven out of the eighteen holes. Lavine was also a consummate golfer. He exhibited consistent alignment and an uncanny ability to hit the ball with a perfect angle of attack. It was clear Cedric and Lavine knew the course well and played often. Herschel did not play well. He hit a ball into a bunker, bogeyed too many holes, and hit a fat shot into a tree, which caused the ball to sink into a pond. Wise and McCrackin did not say much about their games. They merely said they earned respectable scores, and easily kept up with Cedric and Lavine.

Throughout the entire course of the game, Lavine raved about the quality of a Covington Commons lifestyle and extolled the virtues of its residents. When the men reached the fourteenth hole, Lavine asked Wise and McCrackin, "I was wondering if either of you would consider buying property in Covington Commons. I've noticed you both seem quite smitten with the community and the beauty of the southern tip of the Appalachian Mountains."

McCrackin said, "I would love to purchase a lot on the lake for me and my wife and build a home. I think my wife would prefer to live here, as opposed to Florida, since our children are grown. Our youngest is getting ready to graduate with her master's degree from Florida State University in May."

"This is a remarkable community and there are many activities to keep empty nesters occupied!" cried Lavine.

Wise chimed in, "I would love to relocate to Georgia. I was thinking of bringing my wife this weekend to have a look, but she had a charity dinner to attend."

"Charity is a wonderful thing. We believe here at Covington Commons that serving on the board or on a committee is an important contribution to the community. We're always looking for new volunteers. Would either of you be interested in serving as a committee member?" Lavine asked.

"Yes, of course," Wise replied, while McCrackin expressed his assent with a nod.

"There are fabulous benefits for Covington Commons residents who volunteer and join the committees," Lavine said with a chuckle.

"What kind of benefits?" McCrackin inquired.

"Well, if we secure a promise by Sunrise Real Estate Investment to purchase at least fifteen hundred undeveloped lots, and you each purchase Covington Commons property, we could arrange for waivers of all obligations to pay annual assessment fees. In addition, we can offer you free admission into all of the amenities, including free use of all Covington Commons golf and equestrian facilities. You'll also be eligible for free unlimited gas for personal consumption. We have a gas station on the premises," Lavine said.

"Sounds like an awesome opportunity," Wise responded, aghast.

Lavine was ebullient. "That's not all, gentlemen. If you become committee members, then you can attend all the meetings at the yacht club and enjoy the lavish complimentary meals served during those meetings. You would also be entitled to free vacations at enticing locations to attend property owners' association conventions all over the United States."

McCrackin observed Herschel's brow dampen when Herschel declared, "Certain benefits are offered to board and committee members to encourage residents to work for and support their community. The benefits are legal in all regards and should not be interpreted in any way that might seem as though Mr. Lavine is trying to goad Sunrise Real Estate Investment—and you two in particular—into investing in Covington Commons based on any untoward motivations. It's an honor to be asked to become a committee member at Covington Commons and it's a privilege only afforded to intelligent, motivated individuals. The board and committee members make numerous sacrifices volunteering their services because the work is difficult and oftentimes tedious. It's not so glamorous pouring over books, records, and other financial data for the benefit of the community. It's very time consuming."

Herschel failed to inform the investigators that the Covington Commons declarations and bylaws strictly prohibited board and committee members from accepting any payments or in-kind benefits for serving on the board or in a committee.

The investigators had recorded every incriminating conversation during the golf game. They gave me a copy of the audiotape and they also provided me with stakeout photographs taken by their staff associate, which showed Covington Commons board and committee members filling up their personal vehicles with Covington Commons gas.

Bill was absolutely right; I had finally procured the physical and testimonial evidence necessary to substantiate his allegations. I believed I had enough information to give to the United States attorney general. The information gathered could provide the attorney general with enough evidence to subpoena additional financial records from the Association and its contractors, sparking a larger investigation that could lead to the execution of search warrants and the issuance of indictments.

I knew it would take weeks to draft the complaint for the attorney general, so I asked Wise and McCrackin to stay on the case and continue to string the Association board along so they wouldn't become suspicious. The men agreed. They informed me they would set up additional get-togethers and tell the board they were in the process of convincing Sunrise Real Estate Investment to invest in Covington Commons.

Mr. Cobb accompanied me to the parking garage after the conclusion of our meeting. I decided not to speak to him about his granddaughter; the time didn't feel right. How does one bring up such a gut-wrenching subject? Besides, was Michael Ketron's version of events even true?

When we reached my car, he asked, "In what part of Atlanta does your friend live?"

"What?" I said as I climbed in. I had no idea what he was talking about.

"Remember, you said you were going to visit a friend and that was why we could not drive together?"

"Oh yes! She's a friend from law school. She lives in the south part of the city. I'm heading over there right now."

"Have fun," Mr. Cobb said as he shut my car door.

The ill-fated man turned and confidently walked away with broad, firm shoulders. His body intercepted the light, and an imposing image appeared on the floor of the parking garage. The arresting shadow tracked its leader until it ceased to exist. I sat in my car for half an hour before leaving; I did not want to pass Mr. Cobb on the only highway leading to my house and to Lakewood City.

CHAPTER 19
THE BODY

I revisited the Carson County sheriff's office to check the archived records again. Michael Ketron had to be wrong. There had to be records of Dylan's second arrest, where he was charged with injuring Mr. Cobb's daughter and killing his granddaughter—if that had, in fact, occurred.

I walked into the waiting room and the young receptionist happily greeted me with clean white teeth. I explained I needed to review more archived files, so she escorted me to the records room and opened it using the same brass key she used before. I checked the 2012 records book; no recordation of any crimes committed by Dylan Matthews. I quickly left and headed to the courthouse to search the criminal court records for any arraignment or other court dates involving Dylan for the year 2012—once again, nothing. In addition, since the collision had happened at the end of 2012, I also checked the records for 2013 just to be on the safe side; Dylan was not mentioned. I called Michael Ketron and he picked up on the first ring.

"Maybe you're wrong about Dylan's involvement in the Fitzgerald case," I said. "I couldn't find any court records. I looked again today."

"No way! I told you the records were erased or removed. However you want to put it, somebody destroyed all of the records."

"That can't be possible," I argued.

"Anyone can access the records rooms. They're a mess. I could walk into them today and steal whatever I want."

"I guess you're right," I admitted. "But how do you even know there was a crime committed?"

"When I arrived at the scene on the night of the accident, the mother had already been flown to the hospital and Dylan was leaning on the squad car in handcuffs."

I was surprised to discover Michael had actually been at the crime scene. "Did Dylan see you at the scene?"

"No, I don't believe so. He was completely drunk, as far as I could tell."

"Did you ever discuss this matter with Robert Cobb Jr.?" I asked.

"No," was all I heard, and then the call dropped.

Michael called back. "We need to meet as soon as possible."

"I'm in Lakewood City right now."

"Meet me at the pizza place across the street from the courthouse."

"I know the place. I can get there in ten minutes."

Michael was seated at a table in the middle of the restaurant waiting for me when I arrived.

"Ever since the terrible collision that killed Mr. Cobb's granddaughter, I tried to determine why my news story was killed, and why Dylan was never charged and brought to trial."

"What did you do?"

"Well, I befriended Dylan. I knew him as an acquaintance, but I needed to get closer to him, so I started going to the Stony Pony hoping our paths would cross. Sure enough, after a couple weeks, I ran into Dylan at the club and we became friends."

"Wow, smart thinking."

"Dylan loves to go to Vegas whenever he has time off from work. He enjoys wining and dining the prostitutes, and he loves gambling. About six months ago, I went to Vegas with Dylan for a weekend trip. One night, which night turned into morning, after I'd gambled for a while at the blackjack table, I went back to our room around two o'clock and I found Dylan raping a young female prostitute. Dylan was drunk and combative, but I was able to get control of him so the girl could escape."

"Oh my God," I heaved.

"Dylan didn't remember any of the events that took place that night, and I never spoke about what I saw."

"You should have reported Dylan to the authorities."

"I didn't want to do that because it might have impeded my investigation into Rebecca Fitzgerald's murder."

"Oh, right. Murder is punishable by a much harsher sentence. I understand."

"Based on what I saw in Vegas, I think Dylan may have committed acts even more sinister than the murder of Rebecca Fitzgerald," Michael remarked.

"I read the article you wrote about a Jane Doe who was found washed up on the banks of Carson Lake last week."

"I think I may be on the trail of the perpetrator. But I need more facts. That's why I don't want you to say anything about what I told you about Dylan."

"Do you think Dylan is the killer of the unidentified woman?"

Michael dolefully hung his head between his hands and quietly replied yes.

The last thing I asked Michael was whether he had any information about any of the Covington Commons board members. He said it was rumored that the board was crooked, and stole money from the Covington Commons treasury, but he had no proof. Michael wrote an article when Bill and Alfred sued the board, and he quoted Bill, who accused the board of giving the community members the runaround for years. Resultantly, when the article went to print, Gerald Lavine went nuts.

Lavine called Michael's editor and demanded a retraction. The editor, Sam Evanson, gave Lavine the opportunity to write a response to the article in the op-ed section the next day, essentially providing Lavine with a bully pulpit to unfairly castigate two men who had attempted to stand up for the community. Thereafter, Evanson only published press releases and stories about the Association that were authorized by Lavine, and he forever banned Michael from covering any matter that involved Covington Commons. Evanson was the same editor who had axed Michael's story about Dylan killing Rebecca Fitzgerald.

I traveled back to the sheriff's office after my impromptu date with Michael.

The young receptionist greeted me. "Hi, you're back so soon."

"Hello again. Do you think I could speak with the detective assigned to the case of the Jane Doe found on the banks of Carson Lake?" I felt sorry for the nameless victim. Maybe she had family who cared what happened to her, or maybe not. Nevertheless, the Jane Doe needed to be identified and humanely laid to rest.

The receptionist whispered, "Which Jane Doe are you referring to? Three female bodies were discovered in Carson Lake in the last year. And a fourth body was found on the shores of Middleton Lake in Green County."

"I guess the case from last week," I said.

"Detective Brady is assigned to the cases. I'll go get him for you."

"Thank you so much," I replied as she left her desk and walked to a back office.

Detective Justin Brady came out to meet me. "Please come into my office."

"I'm an attorney doing some legal work in Lakewood City and I read the article about the woman who was found in Carson Lake recently," I said sitting in a chair opposite the good-looking detective's desk.

"Can you write down your name, address, and phone number for me on this piece of paper? I need to make a record of this interview," Detective Brady said as he handed me a pen.

"Sure, no problem."

"I can't comment on the case in detail, but I can say we've linked the murder to several others in the local vicinity."

"Who else was murdered?" I asked.

"We have a total of four females who were murdered and thrown into nearby lakes. The Jane Does were surely involved in prostitution, but we don't know who they were, where they came from, or where they worked. They weren't local residents, though."

"How do you know they weren't locals?"

"Well, if they were local, then someone would have reported them missing, or someone would have recognized them from the descriptions we posted in the local newspapers."

"Does the public know there's a possible serial murderer on the loose?"

"No, we haven't made our theory public. We don't want to cause alarm, should our hunch be wrong."

"Well, that's disturbing," I reflected.

"What information can you tell me that could help with the investigation?"

"I don't have any information, just curiosity . . . sorry I can't help . . . but thank you for meeting with me. If I come across anything helpful, I'll let you know."

Detective Brady did not hide his exasperated disappointment when he walked me to the exit with dragging feet and groaning sighs. He did not shake my hand after I outstretched mine. Instead, he retreated to his office, leaving me feeling awkward with embarrassment. In time, Detective Brady would become privy to the fact we were members of the same team with the same goal of justice. The sweet blonde receptionist waved sympathetically as I departed.

CHAPTER 20
SOME FUN

Too many uneventful days languidly lapsed with no developments in my case against the Association, so James, sensing my apathetic boredom, proposed we take a weekend trip somewhere fun.

"How about Nashville or Greenville, South Carolina? Maybe Washington, DC? We loved going to Washington when we were in school."

"Let's go to New York City, then we can meet Sandy and her husband, Connor. Sandy loves New York City and she never passes up a chance to visit."

"Sure, springtime in New York City will be fun."

James booked the plane tickets and a room at a posh boutique hotel. I was so excited; I searched the internet for tickets to a Broadway show. I was ready to disassociate myself from the Association for a few days.

We flew into New York City on a Thursday night. It was a remarkable descent into the metropolis. The plane glided over Manhattan about eight o'clock, and the entire skyline was aglow in blue light, which bathed the Statute of Liberty and the Empire State Building in such a way the iconic landmarks appeared ethereal. I snapped pictures from my window seat, hoping to forever capture the captivating vista. James leaned toward me, kissed my cheek, and peeked out the window right before our pilot landed the aircraft smoothly.

After exiting the plane and collecting our luggage, James hailed a cab to our hotel. Our driver was a young man named Miguel, who had immigrated to New York City from Cuba when he was a child. He recommended we visit the Empire State Building after we checked in because evenings were the best time to visit since there were no crowds. During the day, the wait could last upwards of three hours just to take the elevator to the first viewing level. I asked Miguel what was his favorite pizza place and he proposed two options: one near the theater district and one in Soho.

The hotel was gorgeous, and it was still happy hour when we arrived, which meant the hotel bartender was serving free Champagne . . . no kidding. That was an offer I could not refuse—free Champagne? Yes, please. After partaking in some bubbly, it was still early, so James suggested we heed Miguel's advice and walk to the Empire State Building. I jumped to attention, excited to participate in the adventure, and James took my hand and led me out of the hotel lobby onto the cobbled city streets. We followed the glowing blue light that beamed from the skyscraper and soon found our feet at the entrance to the world's most emblematic building, a symbol of American pride and ingenuity. I was amazed at the magical energy the Empire State Building projected on that profoundly romantic evening.

James and I climbed numerous steps, rode several elevators, and were finally rewarded with the most breathtaking city views on the planet. At the apex of the spired monument, outside on the spectacular observation deck, James enveloped me in his warm, strong arms and pulled me close to his athletic, firm body. I tousled his silky golden hair as I looked deep into his hazel eyes that gleamed with love and affection. I studied his oval face and his rugged jawline; I never tired of gazing upon his chiseled features. James passionately kissed my neck and face. The evening spring breeze felt refreshing as we embraced. We had come to terms with what had happened in our marriage. We were finally happy, both individually and with each other, after a dubious struggle to save us as a couple.

Sandy and Connor arranged to meet us the next day for lunch at a cute Irish restaurant situated across the street from the hotel. James and I arrived first, so we sat down on two high-backed stools at a dimly lit mahogany bar to wait for them. An old man with a strong Irish brogue took our drink orders. James ordered a pint of Guinness and I ordered Irish red lemonade. I was enthused to see Sandy and Connor. The last time we had met was when I embarked on my self-imposed sabbatical. Times had greatly improved since then. The bartender served our drinks, then James and I toasted to happiness just before Sandy and Connor entered the restaurant.

Sandy looked ravishing. She wore a bright-red dress with pink pearls that exquisitely accentuated her cascading auburn hair. Her green eyes sparkled when she greeted me with a tight hug and European kisses on my cheeks. Connor looked heavier than when I had last seen him, and he had definitely lost quite a lot of hair, despite his young age. Nonetheless, he was still a sturdy, handsome Irish man in his prime. Connor gave me the same tight hug with European kisses I had received from Sandy.

We had a lot to catch up on. Sandy discussed her recent promotion to partner at her law firm and Connor proudly updated us about his construction company and the new buildings he was erecting. James spoke about his rural medical practice and his love of small-town America. I did not speak about anything for a while. As I listened to my friends and husband boast about their achievements, I sank into my thoughts; an intense sensation of self-worthlessness pervaded my being.

Sandy noticed my despondency, and in an attempt to alleviate it, she asked about my endeavors, not realizing I was sad because it had been a while since I had occasioned any accomplishments. In response, I spoke with self-doubt about my singular case against the Association in a stammering almost inaudible voice. Sandy warmly consoled me. She emphasized that one seemingly insignificant lawsuit can have an effect that facilitates monumental change for many ancillary beneficiaries of the litigation. I perked up a little after her inspirational advice; Sandy had a way of making people feel better about themselves.

James was ready to leave after the bill was paid. It was a nice day and he wanted to take a walk. Sandy and Connor decided to return to the room they had reserved at our hotel to unpack. We confirmed a double date for that night to see a Broadway show, followed by a late-night dinner.

James and I proceeded on a desultory course toward the chaos of Times Square. Taxis roared passed and herds of people brushed by us as we walked hand in hand. There was a blockade at the intersection of Eighth Avenue and Forty-Fifth Street due to a boisterous group demonstrating against the unfair treatment of animals, so we skirted around the protesters and took a left on Forty-Fourth Street to avoid the mob. We quietly continued our walk through Hell's Kitchen. It was soothing to be with James, strolling along the rambunctious streets of New York City.

We stopped for coffee, and while James placed our orders, I sat at a table and checked my phone. I received an email from the appellate court clerk; it was the opinion the court issued in my appeal. I rapidly scrolled through the digital copy of the decision and read the last line first because the last line codifies the final outcome. A broad smile erupted on my face, evincing hard-fought vindication.

James handed me a latte and asked, "What has you so happy?"

"I won. I won the appeal. The appellate court agrees with me, the superior court erroneously dismissed my complaint."

James hugged me with tremendous joy. "I'm so proud of you."

I forwarded the copy of the opinion to the Wainrights, Bill Collins, and Mr. Cobb.

Later, we met Sandy and Connor in the hotel lobby and I shared the news about my big win against the Association. "I won the appeal. Can you believe it?!"

"Congratulations," Sandy responded with concern in her voice.

"What's wrong? You don't seem excited about my win," I bewailed.

"Doesn't your win put a target on your back?" she theorized.

I paused, knowing she was right. "Maybe," I answered. "There's no question I angered a powerful group of people who thought they had vanquished me. But what can they do to me now?"

James jumped in. "You two are hypersensitive. Nothing is going to happen and there are no targets. Hey, since you two ladies are distinguished attorneys, I have some legal humor that might lighten the mood. Are you ready?"

"Sure, lay on the jokes," Sandy replied.

"What did the judge say to the dentist?"

"I don't know," I said as Sandy and Conner shrugged their shoulders.

James laughed. "Pull my tooth—my whole tooth and nothing but my tooth."

"That was really bad," Conner winced.

James continued. "Wait . . . I have another. Why is an English teacher like a judge?"

"No more silly jokes, please," Sandy teased.

"Because they both give out sentences."

"Ugh," Conner groaned as Sandy and I giggled like schoolgirls.

James was smooth; he had effectively brightened everyone's spirits.

When we finished our happy-hour cocktails, we fetched a cab to Broadway.

The show we had chosen was awe-inspiring and duly entertaining; it did not disappoint. During intermission, Sandy and I left James and

Connor in their seats and retreated to the concession stand to order drinks. Since I was alone with Sandy, I confided that I had been unofficially researching several matters.

First, I described how Ed Weatherly was savagely murdered in his Eagle's Nest home, and the alleged perpetrator was later found dead in his jail cell. Sandy agreed the facts raised suspicion, but she believed stress elicited from being charged with first-degree murder could have easily caused the accused to have a heart attack.

Second, I discussed the Rebecca Fitzgerald case and divulged that the girl's drunk-driver killer was likely a serial murderer. I revealed the relevant facts that indicated Dylan Matthews, the Association's operations manager, had murdered four women. Sandy was appalled there was a potential serial murderer on the loose near Carson Lake. More importantly, she was worried that I had voluntarily involved myself in the investigation.

Sandy admonished me to be careful and she advised me not to take any unnecessary risks. As a former federal public defender and an attorney who had represented a serial killer, Sandy claimed serial murderers were master manipulators, who disguised their predatory behavior in ways that made them seem charming. She said they would stop at nothing to defend their actions and continue killing. I assured Sandy her fears were completely unfounded. Since I knew the identity of the serial killer, which was undoubtably Dylan Matthews, it would be easy for me to avoid him.

We walked back to our seats with drinks in hand, and on the way, I asked Sandy to keep our conversation confidential because James had no idea I was looking into the Weatherly case or matters relating to Rebecca Fitzgerald and Dylan Matthews. Sandy reluctantly consented.

I returned home on Sunday evening and listened to messages from the Wainrights, Bill Collins, and Mr. Cobb before I jumped into bed alongside James.

CHAPTER 21
THE SLIP UP

I phoned the Wainrights and Bill Collins the first thing Monday morning, and I was not surprised to hear they were all exceedingly pleased. Bill planned to bring up the case at the next community board meeting scheduled for the following week. He had many ideas he wanted to impart to the board with regard to repairing the roads and amenities in Peacock Plains and Mockingbird Heights. I cautioned Bill that the board still had the opportunity to appeal the case to the Georgia Supreme Court, and if the board appealed, there was a chance the supreme court could overturn the appellate decision. I advised him that the board would surely appeal, if for no other reason than to cook the books a little longer. As a consequence, Bill agreed to wait until the appellate process was concluded before he discussed the case at any board meetings.

I called Mr. Cobb last.

His voice sounded anxious after I told him about the appellate court decision. "Oh yeah, that. I heard. Can we meet in person today? I have some disturbing news."

"Sure, I can be at your office this afternoon."

"No, how about I come to meet you in Champaign this afternoon? I have family nearby I was planning on seeing tonight, so it would be no trouble for me to come to you."

"Sure, that'll be fine," I replied as Star swirled around my feet.

After a pause, I asked, "Should I be worried?"

There was no response—Mr. Cobb had already hung up.

I spent the interim hours mopping the floors, dusting the furniture, vacuuming the rugs, and scrubbing the bathrooms, waiting for the disturbing news.

Mr. Cobb arrived at my home slightly later than expected. "I apologize for being late. There was a lot of traffic today. The highway between Lakewood City and Champaign is still being repaired."

I showed my guest to the den and motioned him to take a seat in one of the two armchairs flanking the fireplace. "Can I get you a cup of coffee?"

"No thank you, I cannot stay. My sister is waiting for me."

"Can I get you anything else?" I asked as I sat across from Mr. Cobb on the sofa.

"No thank you. Let me get right to the point. I regret to inform you that your identity may have been compromised, and the disclosure could present difficulties for you."

"What are you talking about? I don't understand!" I exclaimed in an agitated voice.

"Relax. Do not worry, young lady."

I wrapped my arms around my body and slouched forward. Star came into the room and sat at my feet, then Mr. Cobb moved to a spot on the sofa and cozied toward me. He put his arm around my shoulder and pulled me in close. I felt repulsed by his bad breath and his unprofessional behavior, but I was afraid to move away from him. Holding his left arm tightly around my shoulders, he reached into his pocket with his right hand and produced a thumb drive.

"What's that?"

"This is an audio copy of the latest meeting Wise and McCrackin had with the Association board members. Wise emailed the audio feed to me this morning, so I made a copy for you."

Unexpectedly, the back door popped open.

I jumped up and yelled, "James, is that you?"

James walked into the living room and I nervously introduced him to my guest. "James, this is Mr. Robert Cobb Jr., and Mr. Cobb, this, this is my husband, James."

"You caught us, young man!" Mr. Cobb joked as he offered his hand to James, which was grudgingly accepted. "It is very nice to meet you. I was in town and I needed to discuss a legal matter with your lovely wife."

I could tell James was not pleased to see me alone with another man in our home. Mr. Cobb did not know that implying in a humorous manner that he was my lover was not funny to either James or myself, considering what we had been through.

James' displeasure rapidly turned into anger. "What's going on here? I think this discussion is over. Can I show you to the door, Mr.— Mr. Cobb, is it?"

"Oh yes, young man, I was on my way out. Sorry to cause any inconvenience to either you or your wife."

I led Mr. Cobb to the front door and James tagged close behind. "Goodbye," Mr. Cobb said as he left.

When I shut the door, James raised his voice and again asked, "What's going on here?"

I placed my hand over James' mouth and whispered, "Shhh, be quiet."

We peered out the foyer window and observed Mr. Cobb coolly walk away with lingering hesitation, but rather than proceed directly to his car, he began to carefully survey our property. He looked up, down, and around our house, and he even peeked into the backyard for a quick look. Startled by his behavior, James reached for the door handle to shoo Mr. Cobb away, but I stopped him. I suggested Mr. Cobb was merely admiring our flower gardens that were in full bloom that sunny May day.

After Mr. Cobb sped off, I asked James to sit on the sofa, then I sat beside him and spilled my guts. I told him about Ed Weatherly, Theodore Milton, Rebecca Fitzgerald, Dylan Matthews, the Association fraud, the investigators, the complaint to the United States attorney general, the prostitutes, everything—I told him everything. At the completion of my confession, several seconds of disconcerting silence ensued then James stood up and paced the living room with an unsettling, jumpy gait. He wrung his hands, inattentive to his surroundings, and nearly tripped over Star when she darted across the floor and leapt into my lap. Eventually, James reseated himself close to me, and when he did so, he clasped my right hand with his left hand and remarked, "That Cobb guy seems really creepy."

"Do you want to listen to the audio recording Mr. Cobb gave me today?"

"Of course, sweetheart."

Wise and McCrackin had lunched with Lavine and the other board members at the Covington Commons yacht club three days before. The meeting was scheduled by Lavine so the board could pressure Sunrise Real Estate Investment, Inc. to purchase the Covington Commons lots. The board wanted to complete a mass sale of lots as soon as possible. Wise and McCrackin attended the meeting to provide me with additional time to complete the United States attorney general complaint.

The luncheon was benign enough at the beginning; a young waitress served drinks and lunch to the attendees. However, after about an hour, there was a shift change and a different waitress served the final course.

Millie recognized the investigators immediately.

"Hello, how are you two? It's been a while since I last saw you both."

Wise professed ignorance. "Pardon me, I don't believe we've ever met. You must have us confused with other customers, which is understandable, since you have so many customers each day."

"Oh no, I remember you two exactly. You came for lunch with a pretty tall woman who had a strawberry-blonde ponytail. You asked how I liked working here and you wanted to know how often the board members eat at the yacht club," Millie asserted.

"You are mistaken, miss. We've never met," McCrackin affirmed.

"Yes, I'm sure we've never met," Wise agreed.

"I know that we've met. You must remember," Millie said.

"Millie, if the men say they never met you, they never met you," Lavine said.

"Oh . . . I guess you're both right. I apologize for the mistake," Millie said.

Millie took the dessert orders and then left the table.

"I'll be right back," Lavine said as he excused himself from the table.

An instant later, McCrackin said, "Please excuse me also. I need to make a phone call."

The audiotape conveyed the clanking of pots and pans and cooks yelling to servers to pick up their orders. McCrackin had somehow positioned himself outside of the kitchen and recorded an exchange between Millie and Lavine.

"Millie, have you seen those two gentlemen before?"

"Yes, Mr. Lavine, they were both here with a tall woman who was pretty, and she had strawberry-blonde hair. I'm certain."

"When were they here at the yacht club?"

"In the middle of February. I served them lunch here at the club."

"Millie, could you identify the woman again?"

"Oh sure, I never forget a face, sir."

"Did you ever see the woman lawyer who brought that lawsuit against me and the other board members?"

"No, why?"

"Because your description of the woman who had lunch with our two guests could describe that nasty, meddling lawyer," Lavine scoffed.

"Oh, I'm sorry, sir."

"If that lawyer was here with the representatives from Sunrise Real Estate Investment in February, then something's up. I didn't meet the men until April first."

"Remember, Mr. Lavine, I left before April to take care of my mother."

"Yes, I do remember. You weren't at the party we held in honor of Sunrise. I can't talk anymore. I have to get back to the table right now. We'll discuss this matter later."

"Yes, sir. Anything you need."

When the party reconvened at the table, Lavine asked Wise, "When will you be able to confirm that Sunrise Real Estate Investment will be purchasing Covington Commons lots?"

"Our CEO is on the verge of making a decision, and I believe the decision will probably be forthcoming within the next two weeks."

I completed the fraud complaint and submitted it to the United States attorney general shortly after my visit from Mr. Cobb. I received acknowledgment from the attorney general's office that my complaint was docketed the day after Mother's Day. Two weeks later, a formal inquest based on my allegations and supporting evidence was opened to investigate the Association. The day after the state opened its inquiry into the Association, I received notification that the Association appealed the decision rendered in favor of the Wainrights' breach of fiduciary duty claims. The Wainright case was scheduled to be argued before the Georgia Supreme Court on Monday, August 31, 2015.

CHAPTER 22
VICKI MILTON

The sultry month of June 2015 came to a close with extremely hot temperatures that reached into the triple digits. Evelyn's pink oleander shrubs were flourishing, and I could smell the sweet-scented blossoms when the wind blew softly from a northeasterly direction. It had not rained in Georgia for many weeks; the local television stations cautioned residents to reserve water fearing an impending draught. Notwithstanding the warnings, Evelyn faithfully watered her oleander every day with loving care.

Late one weekday morning, just days before the Fourth of July holiday, I sat in my backyard drinking ice tea with Star nestled in my lap when the phone rang inside my house. I gently nudged Star to the ground and moved toward the screened backdoor. Star followed close at my heels. We both entered the kitchen and I checked the caller ID. Unfamiliar with the number, I turned to go back outside, but a gnawing impulse restrained my movement and forced me to answer.

"Hello, this is Vicki Milton. I didn't hear from you after you first called, and I wanted to speak with you."

Oh! I had totally forgotten to call Vicki Milton after she returned from her trip. I had originally phoned her more than two months before, in April.

"Hello, I'm sorry I didn't call you back, but I've been busy."

"Oh, that's okay. I was hoping maybe you still wanted to talk to me about Theodore." It sounded like Mrs. Milton might have been crying.

"Definitely. When can we meet?"

"Well, you can come to my house anytime you want."

"Where do you live?"

"In Covington Commons, in Lakewood City. I live in the Eagle's Nest subdivision."

Taken aback, I proposed an alternate location. "How about if I take you out for lunch?"

"That would be fine. Where should we go?"

"Well, I live in Champaign. Would it be a problem to meet halfway?"

"No, not at all."

"There's a cute restaurant in Canton called the Vidalia Café. If we meet after the lunch crowd leaves, we could sit and talk for a while because we'll have the place to ourselves." I remembered Bill's thoughtful advice about the comings and goings at the Vidalia Café.

"Sure, I know the place. That will be nice."

On the appointed day, close to the scheduled time, Mrs. Milton texted, *At Vidalia Café.*

I texted back, *In the parking lot, where are you?*

At table next to the windows.

Moments later, the hostess showed me to Mrs. Milton's table and asked for our drink orders. I chose strawberry lemonade and Mrs. Milton asked for a coffee refill.

My lunch companion was a frail, unremarkable woman in her late fifties. Her coarse gray hair was pulled back into a bun at the nape of her neck, and she wore a floral brocade jacket over a white jersey top and white pants. Mrs. Milton's drooping eyes conveyed sorrowful confusion that did not fully mask repressed anger.

"How are you, Mrs. Milton?"

She clutched my hand across the table and warmly replied, "Please call me Vicki."

"Vicki, do you feel comfortable talking about your husband's case and his death?" I asked tenderly.

She leaned in and whispered, "He didn't kill Ed Weatherly, and he was murdered in his jail cell."

"I'm familiar with Mr. Milton's case. I read the court records. It is my understanding that Mr. Milton was at the scene of Mr. Weatherly's murder and that Mr. Milton had motive to kill Mr. Weatherly after Mr. Weatherly breached his agreement to sell his business to Mr. Milton."

Vicki jerked back and snapped, "Lies, lies. It is all lies. Theodore didn't kill anyone. They killed Theodore."

The hostess again approached our table, set our drinks down, and said, "We're understaffed this afternoon, so I'll put your orders in so I can help your waitress. What would you like for lunch?"

"I'll have the chicken and dumplings with green beans and corn," Vicki said.

"Chicken salad on wheat toast for me, please."

"Would you like fries with your sandwich?"

"No thanks, do you have a fruit cup?" I replied.

"Yep, I'll put that order in for ya'll."

When the hostess hurried off, we continued our conversation.

"Vicki, the official records clearly state that Mr. Milton died of a heart attack while he was incarcerated."

"Let me tell you what actually happened."

Ed Weatherly was an aging man and he decided to sell his general contracting firm to his veteran associate, Theodore Milton. On the morning of February 20, 2008, six weeks after the sales contract was finalized but prior to the closing, Weatherly called Milton and invited him to his home to discuss their agreement at four o'clock that afternoon. During their discussion, Weatherly informed Milton that the deal was off because he had decided to sell his business to the Association so it could turn his company into a subsidiary and develop patio homes on the lots it held. The men argued. Weatherly admitted the Association offered him double the amount of money for his business in cash after hearing about the prospective sale to Milton. Weatherly did not change his mind, even after Milton threatened to sue for breach of contract.

Milton returned home right after the argument and told Vicki what had transpired. Milton did not have any blood on his clothes or scratches on his body. Moreover, although he was agitated, he was not nervous or scared. Vicki and Milton discussed their options. Milton talked about opening his own contractor firm and they agreed to visit the community bank the next day to see about procuring a loan. The couple went to bed in high spirits believing there was indeed a silver lining to the deal that had fallen through.

A little after five in the morning, they arose to heart-jolting, clamorous pounding on their front door. The deputy sheriffs announced their presence and commanded, "Open the door! We have a warrant for the arrest of Theodore Milton for the murder of Edward Weatherly!"

Milton was altogether shocked. He whispered to Vicki in incredulous disbelief, "Ed is dead?!" That was when Vicki knew her husband was not the killer because he would never have been able to feign convincing shock; she knew his expressions of emotions all too well after twenty-eight years of marriage.

Milton alighted from his upstairs bedroom and opened his front door to armed gunmen and wildly barking canines. The deputies grabbed him, threw him to the ground, and slapped handcuffs on his wrists, which were twisted behind his back, and then they aggressively jerked him into a standing position. On his way out the door, Milton said to Vicki, "I love you. This'll be cleared up soon." Vicki put on a coat without changing her pajamas, jumped into in her vehicle, and followed the sheriff's office motorcade to the local station.

At the station, the deputies paraded Milton before a band of waiting journalists and shoved him into the back door of the sheriff's office. Vicki dashed to the front entrance, and when she reached for the door handle, she saw Mrs. Weatherly coming toward her with a young sheriff's officer. Vicki held the door open for them as they exited the building; she did not say anything to the crying Mrs. Weatherly. The officer helped Mrs. Weatherly into a waiting squad car that drove off in a flash.

Vicki tried to stay calm. She patiently waited in the lobby to post bail for her husband. After a number of hours, another young officer entered the lobby and advised Vicki her husband was charged with first-degree murder and denied bail during his initial appearance that was conducted via closed-circuit TV after his arrival to the sheriff's department. The officer said Milton's arraignment was scheduled to take place at the courthouse the next morning. Vicki left the sheriff's office and walked out to a bright sunlit morning. No one asked her for a statement. Vicki went home and sobbed.

The next time Vicki saw her husband was at his arraignment. He looked haggard and unshowered in his orange jumpsuit. The bailiff uncuffed Milton and forced him into a seat next to a well-dressed woman in a gray suit sitting at defense counsel's table. Vicki was seated directly behind her husband, but he never turned to look at her during the brief proceeding. After the judge accepted Milton's plea of not guilty, verbalized to the court by the well-dressed woman, Milton was rounded up, placed once again in cuffs, and ushered out of the courtroom.

Vicki left the courthouse and returned home after stopping to fill up her vehicle with gas. As soon as she pulled into her driveway, her cell phone rang. It was Cedric Holmes, a man with whom she was somewhat familiar as a neighbor and local attorney. Cedric informed Vicki he would be representing her husband. She was relieved her husband had selected an attorney for his representation. Vicki inquired about the attorney fees and Cedric revealed there would be no charge; he agreed to take the case pro bono. Vicki was elated. She felt hope her husband's precarious situation would be speedily rectified.

Vicki's narrative was interrupted when our food was delivered. The woman who delivered our food was not the hostess. It was the waitress assigned to our table, a woman I readily recognized. There was no disputing it; I'd had a prior encounter with her.

The waitress turned to me and said, "Hi! Remember me? I also work at the Covington Commons yacht club restaurant. I waited on you when you were at the yacht club with two older men. Remember? The two friendly men?"

"No, you must be thinking of someone else."

She persisted. "Remember? I'm Millie."

"No, we haven't met before."

"Yes, yes, we have."

Vicki broke in. "Hi, Millie. I forgot you also work at the Vidalia Café."

"Hi, Mrs. Milton, I can use the extra money. My daughter's having another baby and I'd sure like to help her out since her boyfriend took off."

"Millie, my friend doesn't know you. She said she never met you."

"I thought you were someone else. Sorry," Millie apologized.

I nodded and tried to look away as Millie returned to the kitchen. I peeked at my phone and pretended to read a message. "I need to leave. My husband, James, has car problems and he needs help."

"You go on. We can talk later."

"I'll call you as soon as I can and we'll meet again."

I knocked over my lemonade making a mess when I stood to leave, but thankfully, Vicki said, "Go on! I'll have this cleaned up. Your husband needs you."

The fact was I needed James to help me straightaway. Lavine would know for sure I had met with the investigators at the yacht club several months before because Millie would undoubtedly be capable of positively identifying me after seeing me for a second time. I decided to go to James' office. I hoped that by the time I got there he would be seeing his last patients of the day.

I sat in the waiting room until James emerged.

He was surprised to see me. "Hello, nice to see you here after a hard day at the office."

I did not say anything.

James sensed my distress. "Are you okay?"

Again, I said nothing; I did not want the receptionist to hear my words.

James brought me into his private office after he dismissed his staff.

I told James I had met Mrs. Milton for lunch and Millie had waited on us because she also worked at the Vidalia Café.

I felt his fear, and then I experienced his nonchalant way of casting doubt on my overblown concerns.

"Everything will be fine," he said. "She probably didn't even recognize you."

"But she did recognize me. She said so."

"Don't worry about it. How about if I take you out for a nice dinner?"

"I guess that would be good."

We ate at our favorite restaurant in downtown Champaign.

"Now wasn't dinner delicious?" James asked as we drove home.

"Yes, thank you. You're right, everything'll be fine. I think I worry too much."

James pulled into our driveway just as the pink summer sun set behind our house, scattering lustrous rays across the blue sky. Twilight eased in right before nine o'clock. We entered our house through the backdoor, as we always did, and found the door ajar and its window smashed. I walked through the threshold. My body became motionless, but my mind raced with bewilderment. The kitchen was torn apart; debris containing broken dishes and destroyed glassware dirtied the floor. The countertops were strewn with remnants of the Champagne glasses we had toasted with at our wedding.

James' steady-under-pressure trait kicked in. He pulled out his cell phone and called 911. I began to move through our home. James grasped my arm and whispered, "Don't move. Somebody might still be here."

James tried to pull me backward out of the house, but I wriggled from his grip and screamed, "Star!" Star scampered across the kitchen and sprang into my receiving arms. The 911 operator advised us to leave the premises at once and retreat to a safe place. My mind continued to race. Millie probably told Lavine she had seen me with Vicki Milton—but that could not be the reason for the intrusion. The timing was off. The burglary could not have been scheduled radically, in rapid response to Millie's revelation that I had lunch with Vicki Milton hours beforehand.

We knocked on Evelyn's door and reported what happened. She frantically welcomed us in and waited with us for the police to arrive. Evelyn said she did not hear any loud noises or observe any strange occurrences at or near our home during the afternoon or early evening. The police arrived minutes later and began to cordon off our house. Our home, our sanctuary, had become a crime scene. The police questioned us, but neither James nor I disclosed any information about the intrigue surrounding those affiliated with the Association, the Weatherly murder, or Dylan Matthews. After an hour or so passed,

James and I were permitted entry into our home to collect necessary items, before we were directed to leave so the police could conduct a thorough criminal investigation.

James asked Evelyn to watch Star, then we left town and traveled south toward the Florida border. We drove aimlessly in silence, subjugated by an unknown intruder over whom we had no control. We stopped driving when exhaustion took over and replaced our fear with sleepiness. We stayed in an obscure hotel located in a remote south Georgia town.

CHAPTER 23
THE AFTERMATH

The hotel we chose was not actually a hotel; rather, it was a seedy motel off the interstate with room doors facing a parking lot. I waited in the car while James entered the office, illuminated by a muted light viewable through a smudged transom window atop the entry door. James swiftly returned, carrying an old key hanging from a wooden block and two dingy white towels. He gave me a glum look. "This won't be too bad. It's only for the night."

Our room was not inviting and it was barely utilitarian. The bathroom was dirty, the bed was lumpy, and the sheets exuded a faint smell of mildew. I wanted to cry when I rifled through my suitcase looking for my pajamas, but despair coupled with overbearing fatigue prevented me from developing tears. Nevertheless, although the manifestation of my feelings remained cloaked, I was still able to complete my nightly rituals, even though lethargy resulted in me taking more time than usual to do so. As soon as I finished, I climbed into the wretched bed beside James, who was already fast asleep and fretfully snoring. Most of that night I lay awake, wide-eyed and thinking. I thought about prison and those who deserved to be sent there.

At one time, I had been an idealist. I truly presumed each and every incarcerated individual was either innocent of the crime of which they were convicted, or they suffered from some kind of mental illness that excused their actions. Hence, after graduating from law school with an eye toward rehabilitating those unjustly imprisoned, I volunteered for a three-day educational program held at a maximum-security men's prison that was organized to teach volunteers how to help inmates acclimate to the outside world once they were released.

I showed up ten minutes late on the first day of the program, and after a brief orientation held in the prison lobby, the program volunteers, me included, exited through a hallway dead-ended by massive overhead steel garage doors that were chained and bolted shut. A guard came out of a room next to the doors, unlocked the chains and released the bolts, then he pressed a button on the wall. The mammoth doors grinded open. A different guard on the other side guided us through another hallway to another set of monstrous overhead steel garage doors. The guard unchained and unbolted those doors as well, then he likewise pushed a button on the wall that caused the doors to open onto an outside yard covered in winter brown grass. The yard was surrounded by impenetrable, brick walls and when we stepped into it, the guard waved to us, he did not escort us any further. He remained in the building from which we had emerged and pushed the button once again. The doors forcefully crashed to the ground with a blasting boom.

In the yard, many men were attractively dressed in fleece-lined denim jackets and navy chino pants. Some were laughing, some were mulling about, some were shooting hoops, some were sitting on picnic tables, and some were smoking, but all seemed at ease, just as if they were taking a break from their classes on a college campus.

I asked one of the volunteers, "Are these the maintenance workers for the prison?"

"No, these are the prisoners. We're in the main prison yard."

"Where are the guards?" I asked.

"I don't see any," the volunteer replied, shrugging his shoulders.

I slogged through the yard as the prisoners leered, trailing the group to the area of the prison referred to as the library. I was anxious to get to a more secure location; the prisoners scared me, I was sure there would be guards in the library. Unfortunately, when we reached our destination, it was devoid of any security detail; instead of armed guards, we were greeted by fifteen men, all dressed like the rubberneck men in the yard. Their denim jackets were piled on a table in one corner and they all wore dark-blue, button-down shirts that matched their chinos. We were told the inmates in attendance were participants in the program because they had the same desire to educate soon-to-be-released prisoners about the world in which they would live after securing their freedom.

"Hello," a young inmate said as he extended his hand. He could not have been much past his teenage years.

I cautiously shook his hand, and after exchanging prefatory pleasantries, I inquired, "When are you going to be released?"

"Never. I was convicted of first-degree murder and sentenced to life without parole," he replied without emotion.

Another prisoner approached me. "Hi, how are you?"

"Fine, thank you. Why are you here?" I hastily asked.

"Murder one and arson."

A third inmate introduced himself, and incredibly, I knew who he was, not by direct contact, but because I had read his case in law school. The inmate had savagely mauled and brutally raped a woman in a wooded area near the restaurant in which they had earlier dined. The woman did not die, however, even though she was left for dead. The brave woman miraculously survived and told her story to the police. The sadistic rapist was sentenced to life without parole for especially aggravated rape and kidnapping. I trembled as I stealthily looked around and reaffirmed there were no guards protecting us.

In all, I was held captive for approximately sixteen hours in that prison. I did not leave until a guard came to retrieve our group right before midnight. As I rose from my chair to leave that odious place, the rapist with whom I was familiar leapt across the room, thrust himself on me, and delivered a breath-stealing hug. I involuntarily capitulated. I was scared and disgusted by my submission; feelings of self-hatred slithered into my psyche.

I was struck by an inimical revelation, adverse to my deep-rooted convictions, when I left the prison and sprinted to my escape vehicle parked in a lot surveilled by armed snipers ready to shoot. Not one of the inmates I had met appeared to be innocent or mentally challenged. To the contrary, they were highly intelligent and personable, clearly capable of luring people into situations where they could victimize them.

My experience in that supermax left permanent tattoos etched on my memory. When I recalled being there while I lay awake far from home in a dumpy room staring at a brown stained ceiling, revolting sensations sprang to life. I saw wasted lives, I tasted bitter air, I felt desperate tension, and I smelled rotting odors. One strange stench I will always remember conjures images of sweat dripping from a coward fearful of retaliation for actions committed but not regretted. I never went back to that prison. I dropped out of the program.

I looked out of the grimy motel window as the yellow sun rose over a hill across the road and I came to a trinity of conclusions. The Association board and committee members deserved to be jailed for deceiving an entire community of elderly people. In addition, the nameless women whose bodies washed up on the shores of Carson Lake and Middleton Lake needed to tell their stories, so it was vital that Dylan be punished and contained. Finally, it was imperative that the murders of Ed Weatherly and Theodore Milton be solved.

I bestirred myself from the mildew-scented bed, took a cold shower, and tried my best to put on a brave face. Then I phoned Michael Ketron. He had heard about the break in. It was all over the local news. I told him we had left town because we could not return home due to the police investigation. Michael suggested we meet in Atlanta. James agreed; he wanted answers and he wanted them from Michael Ketron.

On our way to Atlanta, when James was gassing up our car during a stop, I phoned Vicki Milton. She had heard about the burglary. She asked to meet with me again. She had more information. I said I was headed to Atlanta and she agreed to travel there to see me.

CHAPTER 24
THE BIG PEACH

James booked a room at a five-star luxury hotel during our so-journ in Atlanta. We both required pampering after our intrusive burglary and our stay in an unforgettably crummy flophouse, so we checked into Atlanta's finest hotel about four in the afternoon. Michael Ketron met us at the lavish hotel bar a short time later.

Michael seemed annoyed when James got down to business and demanded answers to a number of questions. James wanted to know if Michael had any idea who would break into our home, and he wanted to know why. Did it have anything to do with the members of the Association I was suing and reporting to the United States attorney general?

Michael believed my actions against the Association occasioned the burglary because the Association board members had a motive to quiet me, or possibly just scare me. Michael opined, however, that my investigations into Dylan Matthews, the dead prostitutes, the Weatherly murder, and the Milton death had not triggered the burglary because no one knew I was looking into those matters.

Michael's annoyance appeared to dissipate when he changed the subject and eagerly discussed a new lead. He disclosed that he had interviewed the guard who stood watch over Milton on the night Milton died in his jail cell. The jailor relayed that Milton was served dinner early in the evening, then later, right about ten o'clock, he met with his attorney, Cedric Holmes, for an hour, likely discussing the testimony he would give the next day in court. Cedric brought Milton ice tea and homemade cookies, which Cedric said were prepared by his wife. Cedric left Milton's cell just before eleven o'clock.

Around three in the morning, Milton began vomiting, so the guard had gone to Milton's cell to ask if he was okay. Milton explained that he had drunk too much ice tea and he was nervous about his upcoming trial testimony. He declined the offer to have a doctor called. The jailor left Milton in his cell and returned to his desk. The guard looked at the camera that surveilled Milton's cell numerous times throughout the night and all he saw was Milton sleeping on his bunk. Nothing out of the ordinary. On the morning of his anticipated testimony, Milton could not be awoken. The paramedics declared Milton dead minutes after they examined him in his cell.

"What was the name of the night-shift guard?" I asked.

"David Clifton," Michael replied.

"He's Herschel Marks' tenant!" I cried.

"Yes, I know," Michael said.

"So what if the Weatherly murder wasn't about Milton killing Weatherly because Weatherly backed out of a deal to sell his property to Milton?" I asked.

"What do you mean?" James asked.

"Michael, have you ever spoken with Vicki Milton?" I asked.

"No, why should I have?"

"I guess not. I was wondering, that's all."

"During my coverage of the Milton trial I tried to speak with her a couple times, but she never returned my calls and she wouldn't speak with me at the courthouse."

I was ready to tell both James and Michael about my past and future meetings with Vicki, but I refrained; I feared if she found out I had told anyone about us meeting, she would no longer trust my ability to keep her confidences.

"Perhaps the Association was involved in the selection of Cedric Holmes as the substituted attorney for Milton. After all, the reason why the contract between Weatherly and Milton was breached was because the Association wanted Weatherly's business," I speculated.

Michael hedged but then he began to shake his head in agreement. "Yes, they're all quite chummy, Herschel Marks, Cedric Holmes, and Gerald Lavine. Cedric is Lavine's regular golfing buddy. Most weekends, they play on one of the Association's courses. Herschel joins the two occasionally. That's what Cedric Holmes told me when I covered a celebrity golf tournament at Covington Commons years ago."

"Cedric representing Milton would have given Lavine and his Association buddies control over the trial and the potential negative publicity that might have impacted lot and home sales in Covington Commons if the community was deemed unsafe," James commented.

"I agree," I said.

"So do I," Michael said.

"Michael, is it normal for an attorney to visit a client in their jail cell at ten o'clock at night? Don't county jails have specified visiting hours?" I asked.

"I asked Clifton if there were designated visiting hours and he said an attorney could visit his client up until seven at night, but he allowed Cedric Holmes to meet with Milton after receiving a specific request to permit the afterhours meeting from Andrew Wilson, a lawyer from the district attorney's office. Andrew Wilson is now the district attorney. He replaced Roger Blessures."

"Oh yes, I know," I said.

"At the time of the Weatherly trial, Roger Blessures was lead counsel in the prosecution of Weatherly and Andrew Wilson sat second chair. He was Blessures' trial assistant," Michael said.

"Was Blessures aware of the afterhours meeting?" I asked.

"David Clifton said Andrew Wilson told him Mr. Blessures agreed to the afterhours meeting between Cedric Holmes and Theodore Milton."

"Why would Cedric need an afterhours meeting? Why didn't he meet with Milton during regular visiting hours?" I pondered in a rhetorical way.

James added, "Why would Andrew Wilson call Clifton to arrange a meeting? It sounds strange to me. Shouldn't Cedric Holmes have been the one to call and make the arrangements for the meeting?"

"Legally speaking, if both parties agree to a matter, then a judge would not have to intervene. Wilson probably called to establish that the prosecution didn't have a problem with an afterhours meeting. But why would the prosecution allow an afterhours meeting?" I asked.

"Maybe Andrew Wilson and Cedric Holmes had other motives," Michael said.

"What motives are you talking about?" I asked.

"I don't know, but maybe Andrew Wilson and Cedric Holmes didn't want anyone to see Cedric at the jailhouse. Afterhours, only a skeleton staff remained on duty, so there would be fewer witnesses to a meeting between Cedric and Milton," Michael replied.

"Why would it matter if there were fewer witnesses? They were all being recorded," I said.

"Right, but they weren't recorded in the jail cell. Remember, attorney-client privilege?" Michael reminded me.

"Oh yeah, you're right. If there weren't as many witnesses, the chances were better that their conversation wouldn't be overheard."

"Were there other prisoners in neighboring cells?" James asked.

"No, Milton was kept in a secure location with no neighboring cells. David Clifton showed me Milton's cell. The only people who could have conceivably overheard any conversations Milton had in his jail cell were the employees."

After what seemed to be hours drinking cocktails and eating bar food, our thinking became exceedingly dull, so we decided to adjourn for the night. Michael said he would be in town for the next two days for a seminar and we agreed to meet for dinner the following evening.

The next morning, I woke up early feeling unrefreshed and groggy. I needed a strong cup of coffee and an excuse to get away from James so I could meet with Vicki. She texted me the day before and asked if we could have lunch. James was not a fan of fictional literature, so, being in Atlanta, I suggested we visit the Margaret Mitchell House and Museum. I knew he would never go for it. He would have preferred sitting in a room blindfolded and handcuffed to a chair rather than visit the *Gone with the Wind* museum.

I slipped out of the shower and shouted to James through the closed bathroom door, "How about if we visit the *Gone with the Wind* Museum today?"

James busted into the bathroom. "What? I couldn't hear you."

"I thought it would be fun to visit the *Gone with the Wind* Museum today. Do you want to go?"

"Well, I don't want you to miss the museum, so why don't you go? I have to dictate some notes over the internet to my office and I can use the hotel club room to do that."

Score! Hiding my gloating sense of success, I unhappily whined, "Okay, how about we eat breakfast and then take a walk in the park by the hotel where all the locals play chess? I can go to the museum by myself after that."

"Sure, that'll be fine. Then I can get a little work done in the afternoon."

Vicki and I met at a local diner known for its fantastic burgers. Vicki arrived first, and I found her waiting in a booth near the rear of the restaurant. She seemed relieved I appeared to be doing fine after the burglary. "How are you? Are you okay?"

"Yes, I'm fine. It was scary, but I'm better now," I assured Vicki.

"Do you think the burglary of your home has anything to do with Theodore or Ed Weatherly?"

"I don't know, but that may be a possibility. So to be on the safe side, we should keep all of our communications secret."

"Of course. No one knows we have spoken."

I then thought of Millie, but Vicki must have forgotten about that chance meeting.

"I think the last time we met you told me you had just been notified that Cedric Holmes agreed to represent your husband pro bono."

"That's right."

"Before you begin, can you tell me if your husband was ever offered a plea deal?"

"No, he was not."

Cedric counseled Vicki and Milton that a speedy trial was preferable to delaying the legal proceedings for many months because Milton would not be provided with bail, given he was charged with first-degree murder. The couple did not mull over the decision to seek a speedy trial; they readily took Cedric's advice because the quicker the acquittal, the quicker Milton would be released. Therefore, Cedric filed a motion requesting the case be fast-tracked and expeditiously placed on the court's docket for the selection of a jury and a subsequent trial. The prosecutor was more than happy to comply. Mr. Blessures thought the case was an easy win for the State of Georgia: dead body, simplistic motive, premeditation, and presto—Milton would be convicted and put to death.

Milton remained in jail for approximately five brief months before his trial. On July 14, 2008, an oppressively steamy day, Vicki filed into a packed courtroom followed by local news journalists and their parasitic camera crews. Judge Doyle McMurray called the room to order after the Invocation. Thereafter, Mr. Roger Blessures commenced the state's case at nine o'clock that morning with a compelling opening statement given in a resounding authoritative voice. In contrast, Cedric's opening statement was fleeting, and delivered in an apathetic undertone that amplified Vicki's apprehension.

Mr. Blessures called Mrs. Weatherly as his first witness, and she vividly described finding her dead husband lying near his wheelchair after being mercilessly beaten. She testified that the sole person with whom Ed had any problems was Theodore Milton. Mrs. Weatherly explained that Milton was likely furious with Ed because Ed had reneged on the deal to sell his construction company to Milton. She averred that Ed was a man beloved by all his friends, and she testified that he attended church regularly. The witnesses that followed were the investigating sheriff's deputies, the coroner, and friends of the deceased who stated Weatherly had no enemies with a motive to kill. Vicki said Cedric Holmes barely cross-examined any of the witnesses, and when he did, the cross-examinations were weak, yielding virtually no exculpatory information. After four days of testimony, the prosecution rested its case late in the afternoon on a rainy, dismal Thursday, July 17, 2008.

Seconds later, Cedric rose and informed the court he was only going to call one witness, the defendant, Theodore Milton. That maneuver prompted the judge to adjourn for the day so the parties could start fresh in the morning without an overnight interruption during the testimony of the accused.

I intervened. "What happened that night in the jail cell where Theodore was being detained?"

"I have no idea what occurred that night in Theodore's jail cell."

"Did Cedric visit Theodore?"

"I don't know," Vicki said as she rapidly blinked, trying to prevent tears from forming.

"I'm sorry, I know this is hard."

Vicki reached into her handbag, pulled out an envelope, and handed it to me. "Theodore wrote this letter to me in his cell before he died."

"Where did you get this?"

"The guard on duty at the jail the night Theodore died gave it to me."

"David Clifton?!" I cried.

"Yes, that's his name."

Vicki explained that David Clifton had come to her house the day after Milton died and told her Milton requested he give her the letter. David Clifton expressed his condolences and then he left.

I looked at the letter, and when I turned it over, I noticed it was still sealed. Vicki had never opened it. She had never opened it because she had fallen into a state of clinical depression after the passing of her husband. Reading his last words was a task too tragic to endure. In addition, she was convinced that she would be reunited in the afterlife with the man she loved so dearly, so she did not read his last letter because reading it might portent no reunification.

Even though I found Vicki's motivations incredible, I did not question her superstitions. I certainly had more than enough of my own crazy notions.

"Can I read it?"

"Of course. That's why I gave it to you. I thought it might be helpful."

I asked one last question. "Do you remember who the secretaries were who worked at Weatherly Building Contractors the day before Ed Weatherly was killed?"

"Oh yes. At that time Ed had downsized, so the only secretary who remained employed by Ed was a woman by the name of Marjorie Schwartz. I believe she may have moved to Knoxville, Tennessee after Ed was killed."

I left the restaurant after lunch and walked across the street to the Margaret Mitchell House and Museum because I did not want to lie to James about actually having visited the place. The Victorian house had been subdivided into apartments when Mitchell lived there with her husband while she wrote *Gone with the Wind*. Mitchell lived in tiny apartment number one, the first stop on the tour. It was curated with various artifacts, including the typewriter she used to write the controversial literary classic. The remainder of the tour included numerous exhibits showcasing the making of the movie and the travesties the minority actors suffered under the Jim Crow laws that prevented their entrance into the movie premier.

James met me at the Coca-Cola museum after my visit to the Margaret Mitchell house. He seemed well-rested, and I guessed correctly that he hadn't dictated his notes over the internet earlier that day, but rather, he had taken a well-deserved nap. We forgot about the precariousness of our situation while we sipped an array of different flavored colas in the vibrantly colored tasting room. Hours later, in the hotel elevator on our way to our room to change for dinner, James received a call from the Champaign police department requesting we return pronto because there was an additional development unrelated to the burglary.

James hung up and yelled, "What the hell is going on?"

"I'm sure they just want to discuss what evidence they uncovered at the scene of the break-in of our home."

"No, they said there was a new development."

"Please don't get upset."

I texted Michael Ketron, *We can't meet you for dinner tonight. We have to return to Champaign.*

I'll contact you soon, Michael replied.

CHAPTER 25
THE ATTEMPT

We arrived at the Champaign police station at approximately eight o'clock that night. The police chief, Barney Sullivan, was waiting for us in his drab office decorated with a photograph of the governor of Georgia on the wall. The burly man started the conversation after we seated ourselves on rigid chairs positioned in front of his desk

"Folks, we have a problem. A man by the name of John Simmons came to the Champaign police department today and met with one of our detectives."

"John, who?" I asked.

"John Simmons—S-I-M-M-O-N-S. John Simmons reported he was offered a sum of money to kill an individual, but rather than agreeing to the hit, he thankfully reported the alleged attempted crime."

"Who was the target?" James inquired.

"Your lovely wife," Chief Sullivan disclosed.

"Who wants me dead?" I gasped.

"I cannot divulge that information because frankly, I can't be sure if it's true. We'll be conducting a thorough investigation."

"Is John Simmons a former employee of the Covington Commons Homeowners Association?" I asked.

Chief Sullivan squinted and looked at me askance. "Why yes, yes, he is."

Chief Sullivan shifted in his chair, then he asked about my dealings with anyone who might want to cause me harm. I discussed my interactions with the Association and the board members, even though I had initially kept that information from the police after our house had been ransacked. When the interview concluded, Chief Sullivan advised us to keep the details pertaining to the possible murder-for-hire secret because John Simmons had agreed to wear a wire and expose the person who had requested the hit.

"Do you have a possible motive for the burglary of our home?" I asked.

"Not yet, although it does appear nothing was stolen. Your jewelry in the bedroom wasn't touched and all the electronics were in place. The investigators said things were merely pushed off tables and counters. Your files were searched in the home office."

"I see," I meekly replied.

"You two can return to your home tonight. I'll provide additional security in the areas surrounding your residence."

"Do you think the attempted murder-for-hire is in anyway connected to the burglary of our home?" James asked.

"If there was in fact a request made to kill your wife, then yes, I do believe the two criminal acts may be connected."

James and I returned home and found our house surrounded by caution tape, which we pulled down as we entered our property; then we hesitantly roamed our house assessing the damage. The room picked through the most was my office. It looked like all my files had been tampered with, so I sat in the middle of the floor and organized my documents. I tried to discern if anything was missing. I had a feeling something had been taken, even though the police did not believe that was the case. After a brief time, I knew what the intruders had swiped.

The intruders absconded with every bit of information I had compiled that pertained to Dylan Matthews, the Weatherly murder, and Milton's jailhouse death. As I tried to make sense of the theft, I remembered the letter Vicki had given me, so I tiptoed past James, who was tidying up the den, and furtively hastened to my car to retrieve my purse. I sat on the patio porch swing and read the letter under the midsummer moonlight that was so bright, I did not need additional illumination.

Dear Vicki:

> *I am sorry about everything that has happened. I didn't kill Ed Weatherly. On the day Ed died, we had an argument which started off being about the broken sales contract but we also had another argument that I did not tell you about. I told Ed if he didn't agree to sell me his business I would tell the police he gave illegal kickbacks to the Association board members when he was overpaid for construction projects. Ed was always overpaid by the board members for the construction work he did for the Association. Ed would keep half of the money for himself then he would give back the rest of the money to the Association board members. The kickbacks were first put into an Association accounts receivable bank account as legitimate overpayments then the money was put into a board expense account. The board members were reimbursed for the phony expenses they submitted then they gave out the money to themselves and other committee members or anybody they wanted to. The scam has been going on for years. There were many other scams Ed helped the Association board members with but I won't get into them right now. Many people became very rich stealing from Covington Commons. Don't be upset,*

but I was part of the racket and I also stole from Covington Commons. I am very sorry. But I didn't kill Ed. I was angry when I left Ed's house after we argued. I was so angry that my hands kept shaking and I couldn't drive so I had to sit in Ed's driveway for a while to calm down. I thought about going directly to the police but I didn't. I am a coward. When I drove away from Ed's house I saw Gerald Lavine's car pull into Ed's driveway in my rearview mirror. I think Gerald may have saw something that day. Cedric and me argued many times because he didn't want me to testify about the kickbacks and other scams and that I saw Gerald at Ed's house. Cedric didn't want me to testify at all at the beginning but then he agreed I could testify as long as I did not testify about stealing from the Association. He said if I testified about the stealing and admitted I stole too then the jurors would never believe anything I said. Cedric just wants me to testify I saw Gerald Lavine. Cedric was here tonight after 10 o'clock preparing me for my testimony tomorrow. Cedric even brought me cookies and sweet tea that his wife made. I was so thirsty I drank all the tea. I am going to ask the guard here at the jail to have someone give you this letter in the courtroom tomorrow morning because I want you to know the truth before my testimony. I love you sweetheart. I need to rest. I feel sick. I think I drank too much sweet tea. I am sorry. Please forgive me. See you soon.

Love, Theo

I heard James calling, so I jammed the letter into my purse and went inside. James was in the kitchen picking up broken dishes and discarding them in the trashcan.

"The damage isn't too bad. It's really just a matter of cleaning things up," he said.

I walked toward him and squeezed his hand. I softly whispered in his ear, "Thank you. I love you."

He leaned toward me and kissed my cheek. "I love you, too."

We stayed up late, sorting through the mess and restoring order to our home.

Subsequently, John Simmons wore a wire, but he could not get the alleged culprit to state that he or she would pay to have me murdered. That being the case, Chief Sullivan would not divulge the name of the person of interest in the alleged murder-for-hire plot because the person had privacy rights since no actual evidence of a crime had been definitively substantiated. Even so, despite the lack of evidence, Chief Sullivan cautioned that I was still a target based on my fraud complaint against the Association board members.

CHAPTER 26
SUPREME JUSTICE

I had not talked to Wise or McCrackin for weeks, and I realized I had not notified them that the United States attorney general had accepted my complaint for investigation, or that the Association had appealed the appellate decision in the Wainright case to the Georgia Supreme Court. I called them one morning when I needed a break from researching and writing the appeal. A sweet-voiced secretary transferred my call to Wise because McCrackin was not available.

"Hello, how have you been?" Wise greeted me amiably.

"I'm doing fine and I hope you are, too."

"Oh yes, I'm fine. What can I do for your today?"

"I wanted to let you know the United States attorney general accepted my complaint against the Association for investigation."

"Wonderful," Wise praised.

"Also, the Association board members have appealed my win in the appellate court to the Georgia Supreme Court, so the case is still going on. I'm hoping the supreme court will affirm the appellate court's decision to reverse Judge McMurray's decision."

"I hope so, too," Wise said.

"I don't know if you heard but my home was broken into and vandalized recently."

"Oh no, I hadn't heard. We don't routinely receive Champaign local news here in Atlanta. What happened?"

"Nothing was taken but the perpetrators emptied drawers and looked through papers in my office." I did not mention the stolen documents.

"Maybe the break-in was related to our investigation into the Association?"

"Maybe."

"I feel terrible I compromised your identity when we ate lunch at the yacht club the first time we met."

"Don't even think about it. It's okay. There's something else . . . a former Association employee, John Simmons, filed a police report with the Champaign police department and he alleged that someone solicited him to murder me."

"What? That's very serious."

"I know, but John Simmons wore a wire and went back to the solicitor of the crime and the person did not make the offer again. I don't know who wanted to have me killed, and Chief Sullivan, of the Champaign police department, said he can't be sure John Simmons was telling the truth without any evidence."

"Did you speak with Mr. Cobb about the burglary or the alleged attempt on your life?"

"No, I was going to call him today."

"I think it would be best not to tell Mr. Cobb since he isn't personally involved."

"Yes, I think you're right. He's done so much for me already, he doesn't need to be burdened with my problems."

"Maybe I could help and look further into the matters."

"No, don't worry, the Champaign police are on the job, but thank you anyway. I'll let you know when I hear back from the United States attorney general."

I resumed my research for the Wainright appeal over the ensuing weeks. The pure tedium of legal research and writing could be obfuscating at times, but I persisted and finally submitted my first brief to the Georgia Supreme Court in a timely manner, a week before the due date. I phoned Bill Collins, Alfred Mertz, and the Wainrights after the completion of the brief to inform them they need not attend the oral argument since it would be a transient event and it did not make sense for them to waste time driving to Atlanta. I continued to edit my oral argument right up to the moment it was delivered on August 31, 2015.

The night before my Georgia Supreme Court debut, I drove to Atlanta and stayed in a hotel near the courthouse. James did not accompany me because he had an excessive amount of backlogged work to complete. I arrived at the hotel right before seven, ordered room service, and then called James. He wished me good night and good luck. Ms. June also called to wish me luck. She professed faith in my abilities as a lawyer, and although her words were intended to boost my confidence, I felt insecure. I did not want to let the Wainrights down—again. The Wainright case was more than an ordinary lawsuit; it had morphed into doing the right thing for an entire community. In other words, it had blossomed into a full-blown cause. After eating, I settled down to rest, even though I knew I would never have the good fortune of actually sleeping on the eve before a state supreme court oral argument.

The Wainright appeal was the first case of the day, scheduled to begin at nine in the morning. I arrived a half hour early, entered the empty courtroom, and seated myself at appellees' counsel table. I waited alone until the parade of Association disciples walked in and looked for places to sit. Herschel strolled in chatting with Lavine, then Herschel sat at appellants' counsel table and Lavine took an audience seat directly behind him. Haywood Martin walked in solo and secured a seat rearward of Lavine. Cindy Matthews entered, accompanied by Dylan, who was given the job of carrying his mother's purse and umbrella; it was a tremendously stormy morning. The mother sat beside Martin and the son slouched in the seat behind the woman who had given him life. The other Association board members trotted in on the heels of the Matthews and took seats near their comrades. Yes, every Association elite member was present and accounted for.

Surprisingly, when the clock was about to strike nine, the courtroom door gradually squeaked open and Michael Ketron and Mr. Cobb snuck into the room and slid into the last row. Michael had told me he would be attending the argument, but I did not expect to see Mr. Cobb. I hadn't talked to Mr. Cobb all summer; the last time we had spoken was when he had come to my house in the spring and we had a rather uncomfortable conversation. I gave the men a wave. Michael waved back and Mr. Cobb gave me the old thumbs up for encouragement.

Herschel took the lectern first, dressed in what looked to be a brand-new, quite expensive, chocolate-brown suit with a subtle yellow tie and a white shirt. Herschel was by no means good-looking, but that day he looked polished, and even somewhat attractive. He used all of the time allotted for his argument, right up to the last nanosecond. To an unknowing observer, he might have sounded believable. I, however, did not buy his act; he was not forthright with his claims, which were self-serving at best. Herschel returned to his seat after he completed his address to the court seemingly pleased with his performance.

Once again, it was my turn to defend the Covington Commons residents. At the onset, I reminded myself that I was actually in the driver's seat because the chances of getting a reversal of an appellate court decision were quite slim, so I at least had that factor going for me. I did the best I could and I did not call the supreme court justices "you guys," probably because one woman sat in judgment on the panel. Herschel rebutted my assertions then the chief justice slammed his gavel on the bench and ordered the hearing adjourned. Thereafter, I placidly gathered my things and made my way to the exit.

I felt the blazing stares of the Association elites as I walked down the center aisle to leave, but I did not look at them because I dreaded their condescending scowls. Instead, I fixed my eyes on the double leaf doors I intended to pass through alone. As I got closer to the exit, James unexpectantly stood from his aisle seat, clasped my clammy hand, and led me to the doorway. I smiled at Michael and Mr. Cobb on my way out.

"I stayed up late last night. I felt disappointed I didn't come with you to see the culmination of your case against the Association," James said as we exited the courtroom.

I squeezed his hand and snuggled up to him.

James went on. "I saw some patients this morning but I rescheduled most of them so I could get to the courthouse on time."

"Thanks for coming," I murmured.

"You did a great job. Herschel's going to lose. He was not convincing. He seemed disingenuous."

I was glad to hear a knowingly subjective opinion.

Right after we left the building, I realized I had forgotten my umbrella, so James offered to get his car and wait for me at the building's entrance while I retrieved it. I took the steps two at a time to the second floor and bolted down the hall to the courtroom. Many of the Association members were still loitering around the antechamber talking with each other and Herschel. I found my umbrella in the crowded courtroom filled with attorneys waiting for the justices to return from a recess. When I exited the courtroom, I looked to my right and witnessed Mr. Cobb in an intimate conversation with Michael Ketron about a hundred feet down the hallway.

CHAPTER 27
THAT WHICH WAS KNOWN

During the days succeeding my supreme court oral argument, I made a mental list of that which was known. I knew the Association board and committee members and the operations manager, Dylan Matthews, embezzled money, stole supplies, waived admission fees, and even misappropriated utility vehicles and other goods from the Covington Commons homeowners through the Association. Theodore Milton outlined the kickback scheme between Ed Weatherly's firm and the Association board members. Haywood Martin was without doubt the patsy who acted at the behest of the Association's ruling elite. Gerald Lavine was the ringleader overseeing the entire operation. Wise and McCrackin procured unassailable evidence of fraud.

But what more was going on?

I believed Theodore Milton had seen Gerald Lavine pull into Ed Weatherly's driveway after Milton left Ed's house on the day of Ed's murder. Could Lavine have been the one who murdered Ed Weatherly? Why? Lavine had made a lucrative deal with Ed Weatherly on behalf of the Association concerning the purchase of the building contractor company just hours before the murder. The Association stood to make millions building the anticipated patio homes and that meant there would be more Association money available for the board members to purloin.

And what about Marjorie Schwartz, Ed Weatherly's secretary? Mrs. Weatherly's official statement to the sheriff concerning her husband's death included a handwritten notation indicating a secretary heard Ed Weatherly argue with somebody the day preceding his murder. Vicki revealed Marjorie Schwartz was the sole secretary employed by Ed Weatherly at the time of his death. Who was Marjorie Schwartz and what did she know?

One morning after I returned from a trip to the grocery store, I noticed a voice message on my cell phone. "Hi, my name is Marjorie Schwartz and I received a call from Vicki Milton. She said my name came up in a conversation between you and her about the deaths of both Ed Weatherly and Theodore Milton. Can you please contact me?"

I saved the message and tapped on my phone to return Marjorie Schwartz's call. I hung up, however, before the call was transmitted. I decided to activate my phone's recording app so I could secretly tape what Marjorie would say, then I called again.

Marjorie had worked for Ed Weatherly as his office manager for years. The morning following Ed's murder, Marjorie showed up for work not knowing Ed had been killed. The offices were cordoned off and she was not allowed inside. Marjorie answered every question posed to her by the deputies assigned to the investigation but she was not asked to provide a formal statement. Afterward, she returned to her rented apartment, boxed up her things, and moved away from Lakewood City that same day, never to return. She relocated to Knoxville, Tennessee to be near her daughter and grandchildren.

I explained to Marjorie that I had seen a notation in the Weatherly case file that indicated a secretary at Weatherly's firm reported Weatherly argued with someone at his office the day before the murder.

Marjorie acknowledged she made the statement. She told investigators she did not know with whom Weatherly had argued and she told them she did not hear what was said.

Marjorie began sobbing softly between words as she spoke. "I know it was wrong not to tell the truth, and not tell the police everything I knew, but I was scared. I thought about my grandchildren, too. What if they were threatened?"

"Do you want to tell me what actually happened?"

"Yes, yes, I do. Vicki deserves to know and so does everyone else," Marjorie said, continuing to choke back tears.

Marjorie had left Ed alone in the office five minutes before noon on the day before his murder to make banking deposits and grab a lunch. She told Ed she would only be out for an hour, but she returned about twenty minutes sooner than expected. Upon her return, Marjorie heard Ed and Gerald Lavine speaking in Ed's office with the door closed; they were apparently unaware of her presence in the office. Marjorie knew Lavine's voice well. He and Ed were friends and business associates. Marjorie explained that the conversation seemed nice enough at the onset but then it devolved into an angry shouting match.

"I recorded most of the conversation I heard with my cell phone," Marjorie divulged. "Do you want me to play it for you?"

I gulped loudly. "Yeah, sure."

"Give me a minute to find the conversation."

Before long, Marjorie accessed the audio recording and played it for me.

"Gerald, I'll get the asking price for the company and I want double the amount already offered by Theo."

"No way, Ed. That's far more than the company is worth."

Ed and Lavine went back and forth over the price, then Ed yelled, "Damn it, Gerald! I'll get my money, or I'll call the sheriff and tell them about the prostitution you've been involved in all these years. You used my offices and my secretary to carry out the whole operation. Hell, you even solicited me to help funnel the girls into Carson County from Memphis, Nashville, and New Orleans."

Lavine went ballistic. "You're an idiot! The disclosure of the prostitution operation will implicate you as well. Like you said, we used your offices and your secretary to operate the ring. You were complicit at every step."

"I'll seek immunity before I disclose what I know and I'll get it," Ed claimed.

"What about the kickback scheme between the Weatherly firm and the Association? That was your project; you own that. Can't get immunity for something you orchestrated. I'll tell the authorities about your corruption!" Lavine cried.

"Look, disclosure of the kickback scheme won't help either of us," Ed calmly said in an effort to diffuse the rage.

"I guess you're right, Ed."

"Look, Gerald, there's no reason to get angry. You're not spending your money on the purchase of my business. It's Association money, remember?"

"I know, but I hate to agree to a bad deal. If I give all the money to you, then no one else gets any."

"The Association will make a lot more money once the building of the patio homes begins. There'll be plenty to go around for everyone."

"You're right, I guess. The Association will pay twice the amount offered by Milton. Satisfied?" Lavine capitulated.

"Yes. I'll tell Theo and then I'll have the papers drawn up for the sale of my business to the Association soon after."

"Give me a call right after you speak with Milton and let me know how it went."

"Sure, Gerald."

"You should tell Milton in person about the broken agreement. It wouldn't be very nice to do it over the phone."

"Yes, you're right. I'll call and invite him over to the house tomorrow, then I'll tell him."

Sensing the confrontation was coming to a close, Marjorie had hurried outside and hid behind the building. Fortunately, she had parked her car in the rear lot where it would remain unnoticed by Lavine as he left the offices.

Marjorie admitted there was a small-scale prostitution ring in Carson County, ostensibly run by Gerald Lavine. Lavine would bring the women in from various impoverished cities located throughout the south. Oftentimes they were runaway teenagers trying to escape a life of abuse and torment. At first, Lavine would be the one to venture out to the various locations and select the women himself, but after he had become increasingly busy with Association business, he had employed Dylan Matthews to do more and more of the scouting. The prostitutes were brought to Carson County and given housing in secluded cabins near the lake. The cabins were also used for the sex trysts in which the prostitutes engaged. Marjorie believed the sex ring continued on well after she had left town, and she believed it probably continued to exist on the day we spoke.

"What was your role in the ring?"

"I was the person who scheduled the rendezvouses while I worked at Weatherly's firm. There was a private line I used to schedule the appointments. Lavine was the only one who was permitted to give out the number. Even I didn't know the unlisted number."

"So in other words, only Lavine could authorize a person to be a customer?" I asked.

"Yes, that's correct. In addition, each customer was given a code number by which they were identified so they could remain anonymous. But I recognized some of the voices."

"Who were the standouts?"

"Cedric Holmes and Haywood Martin," Marjorie stated without hesitation.

"Was Theodore Milton involved in any way in the prostitution operation?"

"No, absolutely not. Although, I do believe he took questionable bonuses from Ed when they completed a project for the Covington Commons Homeowners Association. He was definitely not involved in the prostitution—I am sure of that."

"Are you willing to disclose the facts about which you are aware and hand over the evidence you control to law enforcement? Like the tape recording I just heard?"

"Yes, I think it's time."

"You need to hire a criminal defense attorney who can possibly obtain immunity for you to protect you from criminal charges. I'll wait until you find legal representation before I go to the prosecutors."

I hung up the phone and brainstormed based on the new information. Lavine had argued with Ed Weatherly, and perhaps Lavine wanted Ed dead because Ed was a loose cannon. Who cared about an accusation of financial fraud? Even if convicted for white-collar crimes, Lavine would merely be placed on probation or given a light prison term in a federal country club facility. Exposure of the prostitution ring, however, would mean a prolonged prison sentence served in a dangerous state penitentiary; Lavine would never let that happen. Killing Ed would not only benefit Lavine, it would also benefit all the Association board and committee members because Ed would be rendered incapable of snitching about the financial fraud and the theft of Association property. Milton was the perfect fall guy for the Weatherly murder because Milton had motive and opportunity.

Arguably, Lavine had known exactly when to arrive at Ed's house to perpetrate the murder and frame Milton because Lavine had told Ed to call him after he had spoken with Milton in person. But why hadn't any of Ed's neighbors told the sheriff's deputies they saw Lavine at Ed's house on the afternoon of the murder? The police reports stated that the neighbors had only seen Milton at the Weatherly residence that day. Was it possible no one actually saw Lavine at the Weatherly home on February 20? Suddenly, I remembered that Lavine and the Association had funded the campaign of the district attorney who'd sat second chair during Milton's trial, Andrew Wilson. Maybe Wilson was in cahoots with the Association well before he had become district attorney. Perhaps, Wilson purged important facts from the record in order to secure future favors from Lavine in the form of campaign donations.

Cedric surely told Lavine that Milton saw him arrive at the Weatherly home on the day of the murder and that Milton wanted to testify under oath to that fact in open court. Maybe Milton was murdered, just like Vicki believed. The circumstances surrounding Cedric's afterhours jailhouse visit to Milton were clearly suspect. Notwithstanding, the coroner had determined that Milton died of a heart attack. Could a deadly heart attack be induced through the administration of a poison or other drug? I did not know, but I knew James would know.

That night during dinner, James educated me about the various drugs that could cause death when taken in large amounts. He said the singular medication capable of producing a heart attack was potassium chloride. James quickly concluded, however, that Milton was not administered potassium chloride in his cell the night before his scheduled testimony because the only way the drug could have triggered a fatal heart attack would have been via intravenous transmission and that would have killed him instantaneously. The facts did not match up; Milton died hours after meeting with Cedric.

James was not as well versed in the use of poisons, so we did an internet search. We found that most ingested poisons produced respiratory and central nervous system distress that resulted in paralysis and failure to breathe, ending in death. We did not discover any poison that could produce a delayed massive heart attack that would precipitate a victim's demise. Moreover, James was unconvinced Milton was drugged or poisoned because any drug or poison in Milton's system would have been detected by the toxicology tests conducted during the autopsy. I read Milton's toxicology report and the toxicologist had deduced that Milton had not ingested any toxins prior to his death. The coroner determined Milton died of a run-of-the-mill, commonplace heart attack. Therefore, based on a lack of evidence, I was forced to abandon my poisoning theories.

One morning in early September, Evelyn knocked on my door holding Star.

"Hi, Evelyn," I said. "Please come in. Would you like a fresh cup of coffee?"

"No thank you, mija. I'm on my way out to do some errands. I came to bring back Star. She's been getting too close to my oleander flowers," Evelyn tattled.

"I'm so sorry Star's bothering you. I'll keep her inside."

"Well, it's not my flowers I'm worried about, it's Star. Oleander is poisonous and can kill our beloved Star. I don't want her to get hurt," Evelyn said as she placed Star in my arms.

I was puzzled. "Oleander is poisonous?"

"Oh yes, it's deadly, especially the yellow oleander. I love the fragrant smell and the beautiful blooms that last all summer into the fall, but it's dangerous for animals. Years before you moved in, I had a cute Yorkshire terrier named Flo. Flo ate the oleander flowers and she died a few hours later. Flo's heart just stopped."

I stood there dumbfounded.

"Are you okay, mija?" Evelyn said with concern. "You look a little peaked."

I perked up and smiled. "Oh, yes, I'm fine. Thank you for protecting Star."

"I'll take a raincheck on that coffee," Evelyn said as she scurried off.

After I shut the door, Star jumped out of my arms, scampered into my office, and settled herself on the rug beneath my desk. I followed behind and turned on the computer, as I waited for it to boot up, I picked up Star and kissed her nose. Star helped me in an important way that day.

I ascertained that oleander was a common ornamental garden plant found in most locales in the southern portion of the United States. Though not indigenous to the United States, it was brought here from places like Morocco, Portugal, the Arabian Peninsula, and southern Asia. Historically, it was thought that consuming oleander would promote fertility in women. Galveston was often called "Oleander City" because the dazzling, fragrant shrubs grew in abundance in the warm Texas climate.

Evelyn was right; oleander was patently poisonous. I discovered there were at least four harmful toxins present in the flowers, leaves, and even the woody stems. Yellow oleander was the most virulent of the variations. In addition to ingestion, burning oleander wood could similarly poison an individual after inhalation of fumes. All of the experts agreed, oleander poisoning mimicked the symptoms of a heart attack. Oleander poisoning could affect the gastrointestinal system, causing nausea and vomiting; the heart, causing a racing sensation or irregular beat, ultimately slowing the heart rate to below normal levels; and the central nervous system, causing drowsiness, seizures, and coma, leading to death. The experts universally agreed that initial symptomatic reactions like nausea and vomiting occurred rapidly after ingestion of the poison, and if enough of the poison were taken, death would certainly occur between one to two hours, and up to twenty-four hours later.

There had only been a scant number of human deaths in the United States directly linked to oleander poisoning. Each death was apparently caused by accidental self-ingestion of the plant material. One study confirmed a woman had died after drinking oleander tea to boost her fertility, not knowing the potentially lethal qualities of the plant. Two toddler brothers had died in their beds one night after ingesting oleander leaves hours before their bedtime. Accordingly, since death by oleander poisoning in humans was so rare, coroners did not test for its presence as part of routine autopsy procedures. One report stated that toxicologists never tested for the presence of oleander as part of official cause of death inquests anywhere in the United States. Oleander poisoning was unquestionably the perfect murder weapon. It mimicked death by heart attack and coroners did not test for the poison during autopsy procedures.

Cedric brought Milton iced tea hours before Milton had died, and Milton recounted in his letter to Vicki that he had drunk every drop. Milton even said the reason he felt sick was because he drank too much tea. Oleander bloomed during the summer, well into the fall, and Milton's trial had taken place in July 2008 during the oleander blooming season. Oleander grew in abundance in both Lakewood City and Champaign. The Covington Commons gardening club planted scads of the plants all around the yacht club years before Milton's death. It would have been easy for Cedric and Lavine to pick it without suspicion or detection, and later prepare and dispense a deadly elixir to Milton.

There was motive, opportunity, and the perfect murder weapon. I was completely convinced Cedric Holmes and Gerald Lavine had conspired and killed Theodore Milton. The body of Theodore Milton needed to be exhumed and tested for oleander.

CHAPTER 28
THAT WHICH WAS NOT KNOWN

Who was trying to have me killed? Since the police would not provide me with that information, I decided to take it upon myself and determine the identity of my would-be murderer, so I called John Simmons.

"Hi, I hope you remember me," I said after I identified myself.

John stammered, "The, the Champaign police instructed me not to communicate with, with anyone who may be connected to the case."

"What case?" I asked.

"I think you should call my attorney if you have any questions. His name is Roger Blessures."

"Okay, I'll look up his number. He's in Webster, right?"

"Yeah, yeah, that's right."

I phoned Mr. Blessures and he invited me to his office the next day.

Minutes after, I received a call from Chief Sullivan. He said his department had interviewed a number of people regarding the break-in and the attempted solicitation of John Simmons. Sadly, the interviews were fruitless and Chief Sullivan concluded there was not ample evidence to warrant keeping either case open. As a result, he could not continue to use any additional county resources to provide police protection in and around my home. Hanging up the phone, I fearfully acknowledged that James remained my sole protector against enemies who likely harbored homicidal intentions against me because I could catalyze their mortifying financial downfalls, lengthy incarcerations, and possible executions, should murder one be charged and ordered.

The day was overcast and unseasonably brisk when I ventured out to visit Mr. Blessures. His office was located in a strip mall, anchored by a nationally recognizable dollar store sandwiched between a local pharmacy and a Chinese restaurant. The tacky signage above the front door depicted an oversized photo of a man wearing a crisp suit and a fedora, underscored by the slogan The Attorney Who Always Listens. I peeked at my watch while I sat in the parking lot observing my surroundings, and without surprise, I noticed I was half an hour early. I thought about waiting in my car until the appointment was scheduled to commence, but the cool air from the misting rain began to fog my windows, so I proceeded toward Mr. Blessures office to seek shelter in his reception area.

Mr. Blessures' youngish, attractive male secretary asked me to be seated in the tiny waiting room. I sat in an inexpensive wooden chair upholstered in vinyl and studied the diplomas on the wall. Roger Blessures had graduated from the Georgia Institute of Technology with a degree in chemistry and from the Georgia State University College of Law with a juris doctorate. Other diplomas indicated that he had taken continuing legal education in both criminal and civil law. One certificate confirmed that Mr. Blessures had taken an obscure course in identifying various poisons used as weapons in first-degree murder cases.

The man depicted on the sign was indeed Mr. Blessures, a friendly, robust African-American man in his middle fifties, who greeted me in his waiting room with a solid handshake, direct eye contact, and an authentic smile. He escorted me to his private office and reintroduced me to John Simmons, who stood and offered me his hand. Although I had not expected to see John, I did not hesitate to shake his hand.

"Thank you for coming," I said.

Mr. Blessures opened the meeting. "Are you aware John went to the Champaign police department and reported that someone requested he kill you?"

"Yes, I know. Who asked John to kill me? Maybe I could figure out the motive and prevent my intended murder."

"I wholeheartedly agree with you," Mr. Blessures replied.

John Simmons turned to me and said, "I met with Haywood Martin at a restaurant in Lakewood City and he asked me to have you killed. He offered me ten thousand dollars and the job of maintenance director at Covington Commons at triple the pay I received before I was fired. I told him I would think about it, and that was when I went to the police department in Champaign and reported the crime."

I felt cheaply disappointed Martin had only offered a mere $10,000 to have me killed. "Why didn't you report the case in Lakewood City since that's where you were approached by Haywood Martin?"

"I don't trust district attorney Andrew Wilson. He didn't do anything when I filed a complaint against the Covington Commons board members for stealing. He turned the whole case against me and I lost a good-paying job."

"Did Haywood Martin say why he wanted me dead?"

"No, not really, he just said you were causing the board members a lot of problems, and you weren't playing by the rules, so he asked me if I could make you permanently disappear. I took that to mean he wanted me to kill you."

Mr. Blessures broke in. "John later wore a wire and told Haywood Martin he wanted the job and all the perks that went along with it, but Haywood Martin pretended he didn't know what was going on.

He stated on the audio recording he had never offered John a job and there was no deal. That was why the police dropped the investigation into the murder-for-hire plot."

"Chief Sullivan called me yesterday to tell me he was closing the case."

"I have to get back to work," John said.

"Thank you for doing the right thing. I know how hard this is for you," I said to John.

"I feel like I haven't done enough. Those people over there at Covington Commons are really bad people, even though they try to act better than everyone else."

Mr. Blessures got up to show me to the door after John's departure, then I spontaneously asked him about Bill Collins and the case he had brought against the Covington Commons Homeowners Association. Mr. Blessures seemed reluctant to discuss the matter, so I assured him I was friends with Bill.

Mr. Blessures inquired, "What is it that you want to know?"

"Why did you take the case?" I asked.

"I always felt like Bill did, actually, like something was going on at the Association, but I was never able to put my finger on the pulse of the problem. I thought if the Association was forced to produce important financial records to the homeowners, then the people could judge for themselves whether or not the board members were acting in the best interest of the community. The case did not produce a productive outcome. Even to this day, no one can be sure how the board members are spending Association funds. I regret that I failed."

I felt sorry for Mr. Blessures, and rather than ask any more questions that might further undermine his self-worth, I collected my things and attempted to leave, but when I stood, Mr. Blessures asked, "Do you know Vicki Milton?"

"Oh, yes I do," I declared.

"I ran into Vicki last night at the Vidalia Café when I was having dinner with my wife. Vicki mentioned that she had an attorney looking into the Weatherly case and Theodore's untimely death. When Vicki brought up your name, I was familiar with it because I'd recently agreed to represent John Simmons with regard to his murder-for-hire claims."

I was stunned. I imagined Vicki would hold a grudge against the man who had prosecuted her husband and would not have spoken to him when she saw him at a restaurant. It was impressive yet confounding that Vicki had the ability to graciously turn the other cheek in defiance of generally expected principles of human nature. After a brief interlude, I cleared my mind and looked into the eyes of the "attorney who always listens," and responded with a broader question: "Mr. Blessures, why did you permit an afterhours visit by Cedric Holmes to Theodore Milton on the night before Theodore Milton died?"

"I never permitted an afterhours meeting. What are you talking about?"

"David Clifton, the guard on duty the night Theodore Milton died, told a newspaper reporter that Andrew Wilson phoned the jail on the eve of Milton's death requesting that Cedric Holmes be permitted to visit his client. Cedric showed up around ten o'clock and met with Theodore Milton in his jail cell."

"I never knew Cedric Holmes visited the jail that night. Does David Clifton still stand by that statement?"

"Yes, I believe so."

Mr. Blessures seemed lost in thought. "That's crazy."

"Maybe Cedric Holmes had something to do with Theodore Milton's death. And maybe David Clifton grew a conscience. Maybe David Clifton doesn't want to protect Herschel Marks or the Association anymore."

Mr. Blessures seemed unnerved by my revelations, so unnerved that I felt he was a man who could be trusted. "How easy would it be to have Theodore Milton's body exhumed for further testing?"

"That would be difficult, absent some pretty believable proof. What kind of testing do you think should be done?"

"I believe Theodore Milton may have been poisoned with oleander."

"On what do you base your theory?"

"Well, according to David Clifton, Cedric Holmes brought Theodore Milton iced tea and cookies when he visited Theodore's cell. Theodore drank all of the tea and ate all of the cookies, then hours later, Theodore died."

"Is that all you have?"

"No, I have more."

"Oh, sorry for interrupting."

"The autopsy report said Theodore Milton died of a heart attack, but oleander poisoning produces the exact symptoms of a heart attack, and causes death hours after ingestion of the poison. Toxicologists almost never test for oleander poisoning in the United States. I think we should try and have Theodore's body exhumed and tested for the oleander."

Mr. Blessures believed my theory, incredulity aside. "I've studied oleander poisoning and its deadly effects. Is there any evidence to corroborate David Clifton's testimony regarding Cedric Holmes bringing tea and cookies to Theodore Milton?"

"Take a look at this," I said as I pulled Vicki's letter out of my handbag and handed it to Mr. Blessures. "It's a copy. I put the original in a bank safety deposit box."

I thought Mr. Blessures was going to fall off his chair after he read the letter. Then he confided, "As you may be aware, my contacts in Lakewood City and Carson County have dried up. I don't believe I could convince Andrew Wilson to file a motion with the local court requesting the exhumation of Theodore Milton."

"Bill told me about the rumors involving Cindy Matthews requesting that you drop all DUI charges against Dylan in 2010. Are they true?"

"Yes, the rumors are true, which is why I relocated to Webster."

We racked our brains to come up with a way to get someone involved who could help us. I, too, had few contacts in the legal profession in Georgia. I thought about contacting Mr. Cobb but then decided not to. Mr. Cobb had been extremely helpful in assisting me with the investigation into the Association and I did not want to take advantage of his generosity. Besides, Mr. Cobb did not know anything about Ed Weatherly or Theodore Milton.

"I know, I can call my friend from law school, Sandy. She was a federal public defender for years. She must know someone, or she knows someone who knows someone else, who can help us."

Mr. Blessures returned Vicki's letter to me. "Good idea. I don't think you can turn the letter over to district attorney, Andrew Wilson because he evidently has a motive to destroy the document."

"Yes, I believe you're correct."

As I left, Mr. Blessures said, "Thank you, I never felt like the Weatherly case was properly brought to a close. I wish I could've helped Bill Collins the way he should have been helped."

"Maybe this time we can rectify both cases and rid the Association of corruption."

On the way to my car, I pulled out my phone and dialed Sandy's number. She picked up and I explained my dilemma. She promised to put me in touch with her contacts that could help.

CHAPTER 29
FAIR WEATHERLY

I called Edith Weatherly the day after I met with Mr. Blessures and John Simmons. I introduced myself and explained I was researching her husband's murder case because I wanted to include the unusual case history in the curriculum for a criminal justice class I wanted to teach at the local Champaign community college. I hated lying to Mrs. Weatherly but I did not think she would have been willing to speak to me if I had told her the truth.

Mrs. Weatherly paused before responding. "Would you like to come to my home for tea?"

"How about if I take you to lunch? Anywhere you want to go."

"I'd love to eat at the Vidalia Café."

"The one in Canton?"

"Oh yes! The Vidalia Café is in Canton. The food there is delicious!"

"Sure, I'd love to go to the Vidalia Café."

Mrs. Weatherly advised, "I can't drive due to my vision difficulties."

"Don't worry, I can pick you up and we can drive together."

"Thank you. Can we meet on Monday for lunch?"

"Sure, that'll be fine."

I jotted down Mrs. Weatherly's address and told her I would pick her up Monday at noon.

I was afraid to drive my own car to Eagle's Nest to pick up Mrs. Weatherly; I didn't want anyone to recognize me or my car, so I borrowed Evelyn's. I told Evelyn I was having car trouble and I had to go to an important meeting in Canton. Again, I lied! I had to! Evelyn impetuously agreed; she was always so accommodating. The chilly fall weather had arrived, so I wrapped a scarf around my head and put on a heavy sweater and dark glasses to disguise myself before collecting my lunch date.

Mrs. Weatherly must have heard me pull into her driveway because she promptly exited her house and approached my car window.

I opened the window and introduced myself. She warmly shook my hand and I asked, "Do you still want to go to the Vidalia Café?"

The petite, attractive elder, dressed in a handsome camel-hair coat said, "Oh yes! I can't wait to go! I think I'll order the biscuits and gravy!"

"Great," I responded. "On y va!"

"What?" Mrs. Weatherly asked.

"Oh, that means 'let's go' in French," I explained.

Mrs. Weatherly smiled and got into Evelyn's immaculate early model white hatchback. We spoke about Ed on the drive to the Vidalia Café.

"Ed and I had been married for more than forty years at the time of his death."

"It must be difficult to suffer such an awful loss after so many years of marriage."

"My marriage to Ed was unfulfilling. I stayed in the marriage for financial security. I had my friends, and Ed had his friends and business associates."

"I'm sorry to hear that."

She continued. "I believe Ed had many girlfriends during our marriage, but I didn't mind. Ed would leave me alone and let me do my own thing. My life is much better since Ed died."

I took my eyes off the road for a second and glanced at Mrs. Weatherly. She was looking out of the passenger-side window and I was unable to discern her expression. I was obliged to swerve slightly to properly stay in my lane after refocusing on my driving.

"I hope you don't think I'm heartless, but Ed wasn't a good husband and he wasn't a good father to our two children."

I was so startled by Mrs. Weatherly's revelations; I missed the exit and had to backtrack to the restaurant.

When we entered the Vidalia Café, I remembered Millie worked there. How could I have possibly forgotten that fact? Fortunately, Mrs. Weatherly excused herself to use the ladies room before we were seated, so I approached the hostess and asked if Millie was working. The young hostess informed me Millie no longer worked at the Vidalia Café. She had quit two weeks earlier.

Feeling quite lucky I had dodged a bullet, I smiled thoughtfully. Mrs. Weatherly returned and asked, "What's put that smile on your face?"

"Oh, getting to eat at the Vidalia Café."

Mrs. Weatherly smiled in return. "That makes me happy, too."

The hostess seated us at a table in front of the window facing the front parking lot and our waitress came to take our order. Mrs. Weatherly ordered the fried chicken with a side of biscuits and gravy and a glass of lemonade. I, on the other hand, did not feel as though I knew Mrs. Weatherly well enough to eat fried chicken in front of her, so I ordered a glass of water and the less-messy chicken Caesar salad I could easily eat with a knife and fork.

Mrs. Weatherly was friendly and engaging. She said she enjoyed living in Eagle's Nest, and she disclosed that Ed had built many of the homes in Covington Commons since it was established. Moreover, she revealed that Ed had served in various volunteer positions for the Association over the years, including past president, treasurer, board member, and committee member. Mrs. Weatherly believed Ed's constant involvement with the Association caused the disintegration of their marriage because he never had time for her.

"Why do you think Mr. Weatherly was unfaithful to you?"

"I don't believe Ed had a regular girlfriend at any time. No. I think Ed engaged in one-night events, maybe even with prostitutes."

"Where would someone obtain a prostitute in Lakewood City?"

"Maybe Ed went to Atlanta. I don't know. But Ed didn't stay out overnight. He always came home."

Our waitress brought our lunch after a short time. My meal looked unappetizing; the lettuce was brown and the chicken looked dry. In comparison, Mrs. Weatherly's lunch looked deliciously decadent. As we ate, I asked my companion, "Did you ever volunteer at Covington Commons and work for the board or any of the committees?"

"I didn't work specifically for any committee but I did volunteer many times helping with a number of social events, like summer barbecues by the pool, or fall and winter dinner parties. The last dinner event I helped organize was held to honor two gentlemen who represented a Florida company that wanted to invest in Covington Commons."

"That's interesting."

"Oh yes, it was interesting. The company wanted to purchase numerous lots for resale to Floridians seeking to escape from the oppressive summer heat and relocate to the cool Georgia Mountains."

"What happened?"

"The dinner was held last April 1, 2015, and a terribly violent storm ended the party early. I also heard the Florida company didn't choose Covington Commons as the community in which to invest. They went with another lake community somewhere north of Covington Commons. So, all and all, the party was not a success, to say the least. Gerald Lavine, the board president, was extremely upset about the disastrous event."

"I'm sorry," I said before I took a sip of water. "I heard there are a lot of clubs at Covington Commons. Have you joined any?"

"Oh yes, I love gardening. I'm a founding member of the gardening club. I helped plant the oleander around the yacht club."

"I heard the flowers are lovely during the blooming season."

"Oh yes, that's true. When we decided on a landscape design for the yacht club, we imported all of the best oleander shrubs from Texas because Texas has the most unique varieties."

The waitress cleared our plates and that gave me the opportunity to change the subject. "Whatever happened to Ed's business after he died?"

"After Ed's death, I sold it to a local contractor and he renamed the company Lakewood City Builders. The company's still around. They do business with the Association."

"I thought Ed agreed to sell the company to the Association."

"Yes, that's right, but there wasn't a formal contract. I offered the company to the Association under the terms of the proposed verbal agreement, but Gerald Lavine only offered half of the original price, so I sold it to someone else."

Mrs. Weatherly prattled on about nonsense for another half hour, then, just when I'd chugged the last gulp of water from my glass, she said, "I think there are prostitutes in Carson County, and some of them were murdered and washed up on the shores of Carson Lake."

I nearly spewed the water from my mouth onto to the table, but prior to that happening, I squeezed my lips shut and swallowed hard. "What are you talking about?"

"It's common knowledge, but no one speaks of it because everyone's scared. I think Ed was involved."

"Why do you think that?" I asked in a soft, breathless voice.

"One day, many years ago, I overheard one of Ed's phone conversations. He was scheduling an appointment to meet with 'Sugar.' He used vulgar terms to describe her and what she was going to do for him. There were other incidents as well, at least up until the time he became infirm."

"Do you think anyone else was involved?"

"Well, I do think Ed and Gerald Lavine became close after Gerald moved to Eagle's Nest and began volunteering for the Association. I thought they spent too much time together on the phone, making what Ed called 'business deals.' I never asked what was going on. I guess you could say I was content to live in ignorant bliss."

"Do you know Millie, the waitress?"

"Oh yes, Millie was promoted recently to food service manager in Covington Commons. Now she oversees all of the restaurants."

I called Michael Ketron after I dropped off Mrs. Weatherly. I disclosed my meetings with Mr. Blessures and Edith Weatherly, and the existence of Milton's letter to his wife written before his death. Michael wanted to see the letter, so I suggested lunching the following day at Antonio's pizzeria in Champaign, an establishment located downtown on Broad Street amidst the slew of shops peddling old junk as antiques.

CHAPTER 30
DISCLOSURE TIME

I arrived thirty minutes early to the pizza parlor and the owner was pleased to see me; James and I were frequent guests of the establishment. The owner was a stocky Italian man named Antonio, who had brought his recipes to America straight from the western coast of Sicily. My favorite was the lasagna with a special spicy red sauce. Antonio showed me to a romantically lit table and asked if I was meeting James. I shook my head no and said I was meeting a business associate named Michael Ketron and that caused Antonio to change course and offer me a brightly lit booth near the cash register. I slid across the plastic-cushioned bench, then I texted James and told him I was meeting Michael at Antonia's Pizzeria. James sent back a smile face, a kiss, and two thumbs up.

When Michael arrived, he immediately asked to see Milton's letter, so I reached into my handbag, retrieved the crumpled copy, and handed it to him after he sat down. His facial muscles strained while he read and his pursed lips tried to hide a smile that began to appear on his face. When he finished reading, his eyes widened, and the smile he attempted to suppress broadened. He asked if I had told anyone about the letter and I said I had showed it to Mr. Blessures. Michael's knee-jerk facial expression to my disclosure conveyed utter satisfaction.

"Why didn't Vicki Milton ever open the letter?"

"I'm not sure," I said, not wanting to discuss Vicki's cockamamie reasons.

"Maybe Milton didn't write it?"

"Vicki said it was genuine. David Clifton gave it to her the day after Milton died. If you think we need to, we could have the letter authenticated by a handwriting expert."

"Sure, we could do that."

I squirmed in my seat, then I divulged, "Mr. Blessures never authorized Andrew Wilson to agree to Cedric's afterhours meeting with Milton at the jail on the eve of Milton's murder."

Michael shrieked, "Blessures is lying! He doesn't want to implicate himself in the death of Theodore Milton, should a further investigation ensue."

"Michael, this is different. I saw Mr. Blessures' reaction to the fact that Andrew Wilson asked the guards on duty to allow Cedric's visit and he was shocked. Mr. Blessures didn't know about the afterhours meeting, and he certainly did not authorize it. Mr. Blessures wants to help us procure a court order to exhume Milton's body for further testing."

"What further testing needs to be done?" Michael asked in a calmer voice.

In response, I explained my oleander poisoning theory.

When I finished, Michael seemed to be restraining himself from a celebratory outburst, then he gritted his teeth and took a breath. "That's nuts. Do you think the authorities will buy your wild theory?"

"I don't know. But I do know things are moving fast and we need more time to gather evidence."

Michael relaxed and cautioned, "I don't want either of us to be in further danger. We're going to have to go to the authorities sooner rather than later."

At some point during our lunch, I began to feel relieved, like a weighty burden had been lifted off my shoulders. Michael was faithfully in my corner; he had no predilections that the Association board members were anything other than base criminals who needed to be prosecuted.

I went directly home after lunch. Star greeted me at the door, so I picked her up and began listening to my messages. Sandy had called. She had obtained the requested contact information. I phoned her back and she gave me a number to call. She said I would be put in contact with FBI agents willing to listen.

I dialed the number and a woman asked for my name. After I gave it to her, I asked with whom I was speaking, and she cryptically replied that she could not give me that information. The woman asked if I could come to the Atlanta offices of the FBI Friday, October 23, 2015, at four o'clock that afternoon. I said, "Sure, but with whom will I be meeting?" She did not answer my question. She just rattled off the address of the FBI offices, which I jotted down on the back of an envelope laying on my desk.

I continued listening to my messages. "This is Roger, Roger Blessures. I'll be out of the office for a few days, but I need you to call me when I get back on Monday, October twenty-sixth—I think that's the date. I'm not looking at my calendar. Thank you, please call me on Monday."

I had another message from Mr. Cobb. "We have not spoken recently, and I was wondering if you had heard anything from the supreme court on the appeal, and I was wondering how the attorney general investigation against the Association is going. Call me next week, if you can. I would love to talk. My schedule is a little busy for the remainder of this week. Bye."

James accompanied me to Atlanta to meet with the FBI agents. He was anxious to bring the matters in which I was involved to a conclusion.

Upon our arrival, a secretary seated us in a conference room with an orangey oak conference table encircled by eight matching chairs. She asked if we wanted anything to drink and I said no, showing her the bottle of water I had smartly brought with me; James likewise declined refreshment. When the woman left and closed the door, James leaned over and gave me a peck on the cheek. His kiss did not quell my anxiety. My eyes darted around the room. It was stifling—there were no windows—and it was confining—the photographs of the FBI director and his subordinates that hung on the walls looked down on us with seeming disapproval.

Finally, after too many minutes of anxious worry, two men entered the room and sat across from us. I gulped and tugged at James' arm when I looked into the eyes of the stoic agents.

I stammered, "I, I, I can't believe it."

James looked at me. "You can't believe what?"

I continued to stutter. "I-it's R-R-Randall Wise and Cl-Claude McCrackin—the investigators I've been working with."

Wise looked at James. "I'm agent Thomas Reed. Your wife knew me as Randall Wise. And this is agent Phillip Goldson, a.k.a Claude McCrackin."

I leaned in, heaved a sigh, and whispered, "I thought you were private investigators. What's going on?"

The investigators had been called in to assist in the investigations of the deaths of the women whose bodies were found washed up on the shores of Carson Lake and Middleton Lake. Wise—no, Reed—revealed he had gone to college with Robert Cobb many years before, so he had contacted him and asked if he had any knowledge about the numbers of young female deaths in Carson County. The deaths were initially thought to be drownings but were later determined to be strangulations. Mr. Cobb did not know much about the deaths of the young women, other than what he had read in the local papers, and he knew nothing about the possibility of a serial murderer in and around Carson County. He did, however, bring up the subject of a rumored prostitution ring, supposedly patronized by wealthy resident men. Mr. Cobb speculated there might be a connection between the prostitution ring and the deaths of the young women, so he came up with a plan by which he could help his dear old college friend and eradicate criminality in Carson County.

Mr. Cobb had told the agents about me and my assiduous attempts to detect the possible financial fraud continuing at the Association. He suggested that the agents act as private investigators and work undercover on my behalf. The men would pose as representatives of a real estate investment firm and pretend the firm was interested in purchasing hundreds of Covington Commons lots. The ultimate goal was for Reed and Goldson to ingratiate themselves into the good graces of the Association board members, discover evidence of financial fraud, and maybe unearth information about the murdered women and the putative prostitution syndicate established to service the well-to-do males in the county.

I gave Mr. Reed and Mr. Goldson a copy of the letter Vicki Milton had given to me, and I discussed my beliefs that Gerald Lavine may have murdered Ed Weatherly and Cedric Holmes may have poisoned Theodore Milton with oleander. I revealed that I had shared my theories with James, Roger Blessures, and most recently, with Michael Ketron. Mr. Reed said he knew all about Mr. Blessures but he was not familiar with Michael Ketron.

I told the men that Michael Ketron had been helping me after I had found his name on a scrap of paper that fell out of one of the public record books I had been searching at the Carson County sheriff's office in Lakewood City. I characterized Michael as an exceptional comrade in discovering information linking Dylan to the prostitution ring.

"Do you have any other evidence that would in fact establish a prostitution organization was operating in Carson County?" Mr. Reed asked.

"Yes, I spoke with a woman named Marjorie Schwartz, Ed Weatherly's former secretary, and she said she knew all about the prostitution—she scheduled the appointments with the prostitutes."

Mr. Reed asked, "Do you have her contact information?"

"Yes. I also recorded the entire phone call. I have an audio copy here on this thumb drive," I replied as I pulled it and a note with Marjorie's contact information out of my purse. I slid the items across the table.

Mr. Goldson left the room momentarily and returned with a laptop computer. He hooked the drive up to his computer and we all listened to the recorded phone call. At the close of the recording, Mr. Reed picked up his cell phone and ordered the listener, "Please prepare a warrant for the arrest of Marjorie Schwartz. She lives in Knoxville, Tennessee, and her address is 34 West Greenbrier Avenue. Goldson will be the affiant on the warrant. He will have his affidavit submitted within the hour. I'm going to need the warrant submitted to the proper authorities in Tennessee for her extradition to Georgia."

I jumped up and exclaimed, "Marjorie will think I double-crossed her! I told her I'd wait until she obtained a lawyer before I told anyone about our conversation. Can't she turn herself in?"

Mr. Reed simply said, "No."

"Please."

Mr. Reed refused. "If she knew the arrest was coming, then she might take off, and if she leaves the country, the FBI may never be able to arrest her."

"Okay."

"You should have told authorities about Marjorie Schwartz way before our discussion here today."

"I'm sorry."

The next call Mr. Reed made was to Virginia Nelson, the Georgia attorney general in Atlanta appointed as liaison on the case because the female bodies had washed up on the shores of two different lakes,

Carson County Lake and Middleton Lake. Since the lakes were each located in two different counties, jurisdiction became a statewide issue and not an issue for the local district attorneys.

"Virginia, do you mind if I put the call on speaker? I have an attorney here who has important information relating to the matters we're investigating in Carson County."

"Yes, put the call on speaker."

Right off the bat, Mr. Reed stated, "I'm going to need a court order to exhume the body of Theodore Milton. He was the man who allegedly killed Ed Weatherly. Theodore Milton was later found dead in his jail cell from a heart attack. I have evidence Gerald Lavine may have been involved in the murder of Ed Weatherly. I want to determine if Theodore Milton was poisoned."

Ms. Nelson laughed sarcastically and said in a raspy smoker's voice, "Are you out of your mind, Reed?"

Unwavering, Mr. Reed confidently itemized the evidence, both direct and circumstantial, that indicated Milton might have been poisoned by oleander, a poison not regularly tested for in toxicology examinations.

Mr. Reed's account of the compiled evidence was received with utter silence for several suspenseful seconds. All we could hear was Ms. Nelson's labored breathing, until the husky-throated woman hawked and demanded, "Text me copies of Vicki Milton's letter and get me an affidavit from Vicki Milton, David Clifton, and the attorney with you, stating they've been the only people in possession of the letter. I'll have to establish a chain of custody."

"Sure," Mr. Reed replied.

"I'll prepare the documents requesting exhumation and I'll present the request to a judge as soon as possible. You people better be right, or I'll look like an ass—and that'll be your fault." Ms. Nelson hung up the phone and a wave of relief swept through the room.

I mentioned to Mr. Reed and Mr. Goldson, "It would probably be a good idea to make sure the exhumation request isn't submitted to Judge McMurray in Lakewood City."

Mr. Reed agreed. "I'll arrange for the hearing to be held before the other Carson County superior court judge, a newly appointed woman by the name of Susan West. She's a former Georgia assistant attorney general who served under Ms. Nelson."

"Is there anything else we can do for you?" Mr. Goldson asked.

"Yes. Why didn't you open an FBI fraud investigation into the Association board and committee members after you obtained evidence of criminal conduct?" I asked.

Mr. Reed said, "Priorities. Our main job is to find out who killed the Jane Does and why. It seemed apparent you were completely capable of connecting the dots and putting together a federal racketeering case against the Association board and committee members and submitting it to the United States attorney general for investigation."

CHAPTER 31
FINAL OPINION

I woke up late the day after James and I met with the FBI. It was five minutes after ten on a windy Saturday when I put my coat on over my pajamas and went outside to get the mail. A thick envelope was tucked between the unsolicited catalogues I annoyingly received on a regular basis, and I knew it was the supreme court's final opinion. I collected the mail and dashed to the front door while brisk gusts tried in vain to lift my coat and expose my slinky gown.

I went inside, tore open the thick letter, and extracted the opinion. I didn't start reading from the beginning; I skipped to the last page and looked for the winning word. There it was: Affirmed! The court-of-appeals decision had been affirmed in its entirety. I won! I won! I started to scream James' name but then I stopped; I had an inexplicable sinking feeling deep in my gut, a feeling that I hadn't won, but that I had lost. I wasn't happy; I wasn't excited.

James peered at me from the kitchen and said, "Did you call me?"

"Uh, no. No, I'm going to take a shower," I replied as I walked upstairs.

In the bathroom, I mindlessly turned on the faucet and stepped into the shower without preheating the water. The ice-cold spray stung my body and revived my memories. I remembered what it was like to lose and the awful feelings that went along with not being victorious. The first federal case I had tried solely by myself occurred four months after James and I married. I represented a woman who worked as a maid for a large company based out of California. The woman was tall, dark-haired, extremely appealing, and buxomly. Her name was Wilma.

Wilma's legal claims arose when she had injured her back while doing some heavy lifting. Another maid had called management and a medical report was drawn up. Wilma visited her chiropractor the same day and he provided her with manipulation relief and a note excusing her from work. Wilma's medical-excuse note, and her request for workers' compensation benefits to pay her doctor bills, was delivered to her manager, a harsh woman who had consistently treated Wilma with inexplicable disdain. Wilma's request for workers' compensation benefits was met with an immediate discharge.

I took the case. The facts seemed self-evident, being discharged after requesting workers' compensation constituted retaliation, an actionable claim in all states. I filed the lawsuit in the state court, but the big-shot defense attorneys removed it to federal court based on diversity of citizenship. I welcomed the removal to federal court; the timeline to conclude a case in federal court was much quicker, so Wilma would get a resolution sooner than she would have in state court.

I fought for months trying to obtain a reasonable settlement, and I even tried to have Wilma reinstated to her prior employment position. However, all my efforts were futile. Lead counsel for the defense thought he had the winning advantage because he had more experience, more money, and more manpower—all inescapably true facts. The case eventually went to trial and James stood in as my assistant; I had no staff.

The trial lasted for three days. The testimony elicited from the witnesses seemed to benefit my client. I was even able to obtain an admission by Wilma's manager, the harsh woman who had fired her, that

Wilma was discharged because she filed a claim for workers' compensation. However, on redirect examination, defense counsel, through savvy manipulation, was able to coax the manager into testifying that Wilma had faked her injuries, rendering Wilma ineligible to receive workers' compensation benefits.

I objected because there had not been any evidence of fraud entered into evidence. The judge agreed and asked the jury to disregard the statement in a flatlining voice—but that did not help. That was the end of our case. The defense attorneys had effectively shot us in the heart with the unsubstantiated claim that Wilma had faked her injuries. The damage was irreparable. Our case died a miserable death. The jury deliberated for less than an hour and came back with a decision in favor of the defense. My client left the courtroom after the final verdict without any compensation for having been wrongfully discharged.

I stood, unmoving, in the shower for more than five minutes, replaying the facts of that trial in my mind. I began to understand why such a devastating trial outcome had consumed my thoughts right after achieving an outstanding win. I needed to remember what it felt like to lose so I could appreciate and savor the win all the more. More importantly, I needed to acknowledge that a loss was not necessarily a loss, and a win was not necessarily a win. From a loss, much could be learned; from a win, much could be forfeited, unless the win was proactively enforced. In other words, I had to make certain that the Association provided the services the court concluded were owed to the community members.

I got out of the shower, dressed, and went downstairs to impart the good news to James. He was thrilled. He had witnessed my hard work for many months, and since he had done so much to help me, he felt the win was his as well.

I called the Wainrights. They were happy and grateful but I still did not let them pay me even though they persisted. Ms. June told me that one day she would return the gift of my service to them. I called Bill after I hung up with the Wainrights. I surmised he would be the best person to get the ball rolling and begin making infrastructure improvement requests so the needed repairs in both Mockingbird Heights and Peacock Plains could commence. I was right. When I phoned him with the news, Bill was ready, willing, and able to start work. Bill was thrilled to have a self-imposed new position. I jokingly told him we should refer to him as the "newly designated infrastructure-improvement czar." I had complete confidence in Bill.

CHAPTER 32
DIG IT UP

The following week, I found myself back in Lakewood City in the Carson County superior court building, sitting in Judge Susan West's chambers with Virginia Nelson. Judge West had decided to convene the exhumation hearing in camera, which meant the hearing was conducted in private precluding public attendance. Virginia Nelson and Susan West were both veteran criminal prosecuting attorneys and it was evident they knew their law. They were neatly dressed, confident women, who exuded an air of professionalism, propriety, and good manners. Ms. West warmly received us when we entered her modest chambers.

At the top of the hearing, Ms. Nelson covered her mouth and expelled a cough that ejected a faint smell of cigarette smoke right before she said, "Marjorie Schwartz has been arrested and is being held in Tennessee awaiting extradition to Georgia." After a brief pause, Ms. Nelson's coughing resumed, then she cleared phlegm from her throat and emitted a hoarse gurgle.

Judge West poured a glass of water, handed it to Ms. Nelson, and asked, "Are you okay? Do you need further assistance or a break?"

"I'm fine, Your Honor. I do apologize," Ms. Nelson said, wiping her nose and mouth with a tissue she had retrieved from her purse.

"Okay, let me know if you need anything," Judge West said.

"Thank you again, Your Honor. Marjorie Schwartz has agreed to testify via closed-circuit TV from her jail cell, but the written immunity agreement is still being reviewed by her attorney. I expect to have a deal on immunity any minute."

"Ms. Schwartz can testify last. That should provide enough time for the immunity agreement to be codified and confirmed by her attorney."

"Vicki Milton, the wife of Theodore Milton, is another witness, she's in the waiting area outside of your chambers should her testimony be needed. And, Your Honor, the lady seated beside me is the attorney who investigated the matter subsequent to the closure of the initial case against Theodore Milton. She is ready to testify as well."

Ms. Nelson looked at her phone and then looked back up at Judge West. "I just received the signed immunity agreement from Marjorie Schwartz's attorney."

Judge West returned, "Okay, let's begin."

Ms. Nelson gave an opening statement outlining the earlier murder trial, then she informally discussed the bizarre circumstances surrounding Theodore Milton's death. Ms. Nelson submitted the requisite chain of custody affidavits, along with the actual letter written by Theodore Milton, into evidence. We all waited while Judge West scrutinized the documents.

Judge West asked, "How will the Theodore Milton letter be authenticated?"

"Vicki Milton will testify the letter was written by her husband since she's personally familiar with her deceased husband's handwriting, and I have a self-proving affidavit signed by a well-respected forensic handwriting expert concluding that the letter was indeed written by Theodore Milton."

Ms. Nelson handed Judge West a pack of documents fastened together with a black clip. "Here's the handwriting expert's affidavit, her curriculum vitae, and a list of the state and federal courts where she has been accepted as an expert witness."

Again, we waited while Judge West perused the paper trail.

When she finished, Judge West turned to me and began asking questions. I told her all I knew. I revealed all the information about David Clifton allowing Cedric Holmes into Theodore Milton's cell afterhours. I divulged how I had come into possession of Milton's last written letter. I explained how Marjorie Schwartz had confessed her involvement in the prostitution ring and how she had heard Mr. Lavine and Mr. Weatherly fighting the day before Mr. Weatherly's death.

At the end of my testimony, Ms. Nelson added in her raspy voice, "It is highly likely Theodore Milton was poisoned in his cell the night before he was scheduled to testify in his own defense. Since Milton wanted to testify that he had witnessed Lavine pull into Weatherly's driveway after Milton left Weatherly's house on the day of the murder, it is a distinct possibility that Milton did not kill Ed Weatherly, and that Milton was poisoned in his jail cell."

"What kind of poison do you expect to find, should the body of Theodore Milton be exhumed?" Judge West asked.

Ms. Nelson responded thoughtfully, "Perhaps a natural or chemically produced substance that can mimic a heart attack." Ms. Nelson did not specifically say oleander, maybe because she thought my theory was somewhat outlandish.

Vicki was called into the room and she testified to the facts of which she had knowledge. She explained how she had come into possession of Theodore's letter, and that she never opened the letter, but instead gave it to me after I contacted her for information. Vicki's testimony was brief and Judge West excused her after asking a negligible amount of questions.

Marjorie's testimony was longer, and formally recorded by video-tape, since it was the first time she was making her claims before authorities. Marjorie testified exactly as she had done when she had earlier spoken with me. Her attorney, who was seated alongside her during the examination, said very little because of the immunity agreement Marjorie had mercifully been granted.

The hearing concluded about an hour later. Judge West ordered the exhumation of Theodore Milton's body. Ms. Nelson told Judge West that the exhumation process would begin the following morning.

I left the Judge's chambers and rejoined Vicki in the waiting room. I told her about the exhumation order and I advised her to be at the cemetery early in the morning. Vicki thanked me as she wiped a tear from her face. She asked if I was going to be at the cemetery, and I affirmed I would be.

The morning was cold and overcast when I drove into the cemetery and parked near Milton's plot. I found Vicki standing alone on the frost-covered ground, looking into a deep hole. Ms. Nelson was there but she did not speak to Vicki or me, she was talking to two men who I assumed were the mortician and the coroner. High-pitched screeching whirrs grew louder and louder as the vault buggy and church truck approached. The gravediggers hoisted the casket from the vault inside the hole and secured it to the vault buggy, then the casket was placed onto the church truck. The coroner and his driver waited while Vicki lightly caressed the casket as she closed her eyes in prayer. Thereafter, the casket was deposited into the coroner's hearse and the driver slammed the rear door. A moment later, the hearse zoomed off with Milton's remains. Ms. Nelson waved to us before she got into her car and left.

Vicki looked at me and said, "I miss him so much. Theo may have done some bad things, but he wasn't a bad person."

CHAPTER 33
BLESSURES' WOUNDS

The phone rang. It was another cold Saturday morning in November. I let the machine answer the call. I had just gotten out of bed and I was still groggy. It was Roger Blessures.

"Sorry we didn't talk last week. I've been doing some digging, and I got in touch with the retired sheriff who was in charge of the Weatherly and Milton investigations. He lives in Florida. His name is Sydney Katz. Sydney retired from the Carson County sheriff's office right after the Weatherly case was closed. He gave me information I think you should hear. Call me as soon as you can."

I rushed to dress, then I ran downstairs and called Mr. Blessures on my office phone. Mr. Blessures was on his way out to take his wife to lunch, and he couldn't talk. He said his wife would be at church the next morning, and he offered to meet with me at his office if I didn't mind meeting him on a Sunday.

It was a far drive to Mr. Blessures office, but I took my time while listening to a local talk radio station. Unfortunately, halfway to my destination, I came upon a traffic jam on the interstate that forced me to re-plot my route and travel the back roads. My GPS indicated I was going to be late—and really late, to boot. My estimated arrival time was half an hour later after the scheduled appointment was set to begin. Since I had adopted a new policy of always being half an hour early, I was embarrassed by my anticipated tardiness, so I phoned Mr. Blessures and explained my dilemma. He was already at his office. He was more than kind. Mr. Blessures said he had a lot of work to catch up on, so he did not mind waiting. He cautioned me to be careful and drive safe.

When I arrived at Mr. Blessures' law office, I walked through the unlocked glass front door into the meagerly furnished waiting area. I called out Mr. Blessures' name, but no one answered so I entered the door that led to the back offices. To my left, I passed a tidy secretary's station, and to my right, I passed a conference room with files strewn all over the tabletop and the floor. The mess in the conference room breached the doorway into the corridor, so I stepped over piles of documents looking for Mr. Blessures. I found him in his private office. His head rested on his desk and his right hand held a gun. There was blood everywhere. Much of it pooled around his head; some of it dripped off the desk onto the floor. Splatter graffitied the walls, curtains, and bookshelves. Lingering gun smoke odorized the air with a burnt acrid aroma. Mr. Blessures' freshly excreted blood humidified the death chamber, leaving it damp and clammy.

I clutched my face with my hands in utter disbelief, then my heart began to pound, and my hands began to shake. I wanted to scream but no one was there to hear me. I turned to run out of the office, but my foot kicked a pile of photographs that had been tossed onto the floor. Instinctively, I bent down and picked up the pictures. The photo on top of the pile showed Roger Blessures walking with Herschel Marks. I gripped the photos tightly to my chest, sprinted to my car, jumped in, tossed the photos onto the back seat, and called 911.

The 911 operator kept me on the line until the police arrived. An officer approached my vehicle and asked if I was the person who had called. I responded in the affirmative, and then he commanded me to wait in my car until further notice. Other police officers began to cordon off the scene. I pulled out my phone and called Mr. Reed. I left a message telling him what had happened. I called James, but he did not answer.

I sat in my car for more than forty minutes, watching police and forensic investigators collect evidence while people gathered in the parking lot and attempted to learn what had happened.

A plainclothes detective knocked on my window after the growing crowd was herded out of the parking lot. "Hello, I'm Detective O'Brien. Do you mind stepping out of the car?"

"Sure, no problem."

"How did you find Mr. Blessures' body?"

"I was here to meet Mr. Blessures. He was waiting for me. I was going to be late, so I called him about an hour before I found him at his desk. He was alive when I called, and I spoke with him, you know, to tell him I was running late. The door was open when I got to his office, so I went in, walked around, and then I found him lying on his desk with blood all around. I ran out right away and called nine-one-one."

"Did you disturb or touch anything in the office while you were in there?"

"No, I didn't touch or move anything at all," I said as I looked directly into the officer's unblinking eyes.

"Why were you here today?"

"I told you, I was scheduled to meet with Mr. Blessures. I was thinking about hiring him to work with me on a case."

"On a Sunday?"

"Yes, it was the only time available for both of us."

"I see."

"Did Mr. Blessures kill himself?"

The detective raised his left brow, tilted his head, and asked, "Do you think Mr. Blessures committed suicide?"

"I don't know anything at all. I've never seen anything like this."

"Okay, let me take down the information from your driver's license and you can leave."

I handed over my license, and when Detective O'Brien finished with it, he handed it back and I said, "Thank you."

"Someone will soon be in touch with you about Mr. Blessures death."

I was stopped by another officer as I tried to exit the parking lot, but Detective O'Brien yelled an order to let me leave.

James called after I had been driving for a while, and rather than answer, I took the nearest exit and pulled into a fast-food restaurant's parking lot. I began to dial James' number but then I remembered the photographs. I started sifting through the pictures. The first eight-by-ten photo pictured Roger Blessures and Herschel Marks walking down what looked to be Main Street in Lakewood City. More photos portrayed them meandering down the same street. Other photos depicted the men amorously embracing and passionately kissing on a side street. Was Roger Blessures being blackmailed? I knew he had a wife and young children. He showed me a photograph of his family perched on his desk when I had met with him and John Simmons.

Mr. Reed returned my call. "My God! What happened?"

"Something terrible. I was scheduled to meet Mr. Roger Blessures at his office this morning, but I found him dead on his desk. I called nine-one-one. The police just let me leave the scene."

"This is unbelievable. Are you okay?"

"Yes, I'm fine. I know he was alive about an hour before I got there because I called to tell him I was going to be late. He was already at his office waiting for me."

"Why were you meeting with him?"

"Mr. Blessures was in touch with Sydney Katz, the retired sheriff who oversaw the Weatherly murder investigation. Mr. Blessures said Sydney Katz had important information and he wanted to convey it to me."

"Let me see what I can find out."

"Maybe someone visited Mr. Blessures between the time I called him and the time I arrived at his office and found him blown away."

"I'll try and obtain any surveillance video at the strip mall where Blessures' office is located."

"Surveillance video?"

"Yes, there's probably videotape," Mr. Reed said.

"Oh sure, yes, I think . . . I think that's a good idea. We should look at the video. I think we should also get in touch with Sydney Katz in Florida."

"Yes, you're right. I'll get on that right away."

I hung up with Mr. Reed and then I called James.

Later, after I returned home, Mr. Reed called to inform me that the gun that had killed Mr. Blessures was Blessures' own gun. He also said there were no videotapes of the strip mall, and no video cameras in Mr. Blessures' office. The owner of the strip mall said the video cameras were broken, and he hadn't had a chance to repair them. I breathed a sigh of relief. If there had been video, the police would have seen me enter the building with only my purse in hand but later leave with a stack of photographs as well. I could have been charged with tampering with a crime scene, or even worse, obstructing justice.

I showed James the photographs. James believed someone had entered Mr. Blessures' office between the time I phoned him and the time I found him dead with a gun in his hand. That same someone had probably shown Mr. Blessures the blackmail pictures of him and Herschel together. Mr. Blessures could have been murdered, and the murderer could have placed the gun in Mr. Blessures' hand. Or, Mr. Blessures could have actually committed suicide at the behest of the murderer in order to protect his family from blackmail and physical threats. Either way, the photographs were left on the floor of Mr. Blessures' office to throw off the investigators, so they would conclude Mr. Blessures had killed himself.

Whoever had killed, or caused Mr. Blessures to be killed, must have known one thing: Mr. Blessures had never authorized Andrew Wilson to permit the afterhours visit of Cedric Holmes to Theodore Milton's jail cell on the night Theodore Milton died. Mr. Blessures was the only person who could have connected those dots. If the visit was unauthorized by Mr. Blessures, then the purpose of the visit was suspect. If Milton was poisoned, the only possible timeframe during which Milton could have been poisoned was during the unauthorized visit. Maybe I had jumped the gun; I didn't know if Milton had actually been murdered. That was yet to be determined.

When we finally went to bed, James spooned me, secured his arm tightly around my body, and said, "It was a good thing you were delayed by traffic today. Had you arrived on time, or even thirty minutes early, you might have been a victim of tragedy as well."

CHAPTER 34
JOURNALISM 101

I woke up late the next morning, Monday, November 16, 2015. James had already left for work, so Star and I tranquilly shared our morning meal. I opened my laptop as I drank my coffee. I wanted to take a look at the Carson County Daily Times news of the day. I had started subscribing to the online version of the newspaper months before in order to keep myself abreast of the local news that might affect my case against the Association. Roger Blessures' suicide was the lead story because he had been Carson County's prosecutor for many years. I slowly scrolled down my laptop screen and was startled by another article.

The author was the editor of the newspaper, Sam Evanson, the chummy buddy of Gerald Lavine, and the killer of truthful stories. The article began by discussing the death of Mr. Cobb's granddaughter, Rebecca Fitzgerald, at the hands of a hit-and-run driver. The story explained that, although Rebecca's death had occurred years before, the Carson County sheriff still had no leads as to who had killed the young girl. Since Susan Fitzgerald had no memory of the tragedy, a plea was put forth to the public to come forward with any information that might be helpful. Evanson concluded the article by reminding the public it was necessary to assist in the investigation for the sake of Robert Cobb Jr., a pillar of the community who often worked pro bono to help the impecunious.

I felt the need to contact the newspaper and confront Evanson. What the hell did he think he was doing, trying to use his newspaper to mislead the public by saying the accident was an anonymous hit and run? Evanson was the one who was holding back the truth that Dylan Matthews was the killer. I tried to call Michael Ketron but my call was weirdly refused. I finished breakfast and speedily dressed while I decided what course of action to take. I resolved not to allow Evanson to get away with covering for Dylan Matthews anymore, so I impulsively set out to rectify the situation and confront the author in person.

I pulled into the parking lot of the Carson County Daily Times building which was unimpressive. The entrance was covered by a rusty metal overhang in need of repair. In the dreary foyer, I approached a graying woman with eyeglasses hanging on a chain around her neck, seated at a desk behind a glass enclosure.

"Hello, I'm an attorney and I've been working on a fascinating case I think is newsworthy. I was wondering if I could run the story by the editor."

"Mr. Evanson should be back from lunch soon. If you want to wait, you can have a seat and I'll let you know when he returns."

"Sure, I'll wait."

I took a seat on a bench at the opposite end of the foyer and I picked up a hard copy of the day's newspaper that rested on a table beside the bench. I re-read the editor's story about the death of Rebecca Fitzgerald, and when I finished, Mr. Cobb entered the lobby with another man. I jumped to my feet, surprised by the encounter, and moved toward the men.

"What are you doing here, young lady?" Mr. Cobb asked as he paternally shook my hand with warm affection.

"I want to speak with Mr. Evanson about publishing a story relating to the Georgia Supreme Court appeal I won against the Association."

"Good idea, here's the man you're looking for," Mr. Cobb declared as he turned to the other man. "This is Mr. Evanson."

Mr. Evanson proffered his outstretched hand, which I shook with no indication I was perturbed by his prior actions. "Hello, Mr. Evanson. I'm happy to meet you."

"I'd love to speak with you about your case. Could you wait a bit so I can finish my business with Mr. Cobb?"

"Sure, that'll be fine," I answered.

Mr. Cobb spoke up. "Sam, I need to be on my way. I am leaving for vacation this afternoon, so we can talk later."

"Where are you going on vacation?" I asked.

"Oh, I have a little place on a small island in the Caribbean. It is lovely this time of year."

"Have a great time," Mr. Evanson said.

"I will. I will be back after Thanksgiving."

Mr. Cobb left in a seemingly cheerful mood. "Have a good day."

I walked with Mr. Evanson to his office, past a massive room that contained the paper's printing presses. There were a number of workers sitting around wooden picnic tables, eating boxed lunches near the presses. Mr. Evanson informed me that the presses were started before dawn and the printing for each day ended before noon. He said several newspaper editions were printed daily because stories were often tweaked throughout the morning as additional information was gathered. The way Mr. Evanson conducted himself made me realize he probably gave numerous tours of the newspaper facility to many of the local school kids and anyone else who wanted to visit. He was clearly proud of his paper and the presses that printed it. I found the presses extraordinary, and I thought how all newspaper presses would be completely obsolete in what was sure to be a short interval of time.

Mr. Evanson's office was boxy and grungy. The honeydew-colored walls were smeared with newspaper-ink fingerprints and his pickle-green metal desk was piled with papers, empty coffee cups, and even dirty eating utensils. Mr. Evanson cleared a pile of papers from a chair in the corner and offered it to me. As I seated myself, I thought my host appeared to be a kind, respectable man, which caused my anger to subside. We briefly discussed my case against the Association. He liked the story, so he picked up his phone and asked a woman named Judy to come to his office. Judy showed up pronto, and Mr. Evanson instructed her to write an article about my case. Judy asked me to accompany her to her writing station, but I deferred, saying I needed to speak to Mr. Evanson about one more thing in private. Judy said she would wait for me at her station, then she left me alone with her boss.

"I read today's article about the death of Mr. Cobb's granddaughter and the search for answers. I'm disturbed by the plea for more information about the hit and run. I know you didn't publish all of the facts at the time of the incident. You intentionally withheld facts from the initial publication."

Mr. Evanson's face contorted. "I don't know what you're talking about."

"That's what was rumored on the internet," I fibbed, not wanting to reveal my connection to Michael Ketron.

Mr. Evanson looked confused. "I'm not following you."

"Some people believe whoever crashed into the Fitzgerald vehicle and killed Mr. Cobb's granddaughter is being protected by the media. You know how conspiracy theories get started."

Mr. Evanson calmed down. "Let me tell you all I know."

He told me a man had come upon the wreck by happenstance late one night just days before Christmas about three years before. The man called 911 and informed the operator he had found a totaled motor vehicle that had been involved in a head-on collision. He said two people were in the vehicle and he did not know if they were alive. He told the operator that the other vehicle must have left the scene because only one car remained on the side of the road. The man waited until the rescue squad came and he later gave a full report at the Carson County sheriff's office.

"Who was the person who came upon the wreck?" I asked.

"I can't say. The authorities have decided not to release the name of the person who made the nine-one-one call to protect his privacy since he was merely a passerby, a Good Samaritan, so to speak."

"Do you have a copy of the nine-one-one tape?"

Mr. Evanson nodded affirmatively. "I have a copy of the audiotape. You can listen to it, if you want. It's now public record because the statement was played on television shortly after the crash."

Mr. Evanson retrieved his copy of the 911 tape and I listened to it intently as I sat in the grimy office. I recognized the shrill male voice on the audio recording. I heard Michael Ketron admit he had found a vehicle with people inside. He specifically reported, "It must have been a hit and run because I only see one car."

When the tape concluded, I asked, "What other evidence was collected at the scene?"

"The sheriff's deputies collected photographs of tire marks from a vehicle indicating it was a late-model dually pickup truck, and they believe that the vehicle was red because red paint was discovered on the Fitzgerald vehicle at the point of impact."

Why had Michael Ketron lied? Why had he made me believe that the editor, Sam Evanson, killed his story about Dylan Matthews killing Rebecca Fitzgerald while drinking and driving? Why did Michael Ketron believe the driver of the vehicle that killed Rebecca Fitzgerald was Dylan Matthews, when Mr. Evanson and the authorities did not know who killed Rebecca Fitzgerald?

I stood up. I felt dizzy. My dizziness caused me to visibly swoon.

Mr. Evanson looked at me with concern. "Is something wrong? Would you like some water?"

"Oh, I'm fine. I have to go right now. I forgot about another appointment I made earlier."

Mr. Evanson led me to the door and gave me his card. "Please contact me soon and I'll have Judy write the story about your case against the Covington Commons Homeowners Association."

"Sure. Thank you."

When I got in my car, my phone rang. It was Mr. Reed. I let the call go to voice mail, then I played back the message.

The autopsy report had come back on Theodore Milton. Milton had been poisoned by oleander. The coroner believed Milton had drunk the poison. Virginia Nelson formally reopened the state's investigation into the Weatherly murder and she opened a new case on the Milton murder. Mr. Reed mentioned that he had informed the US attorney general's office about the matters, should federal jurisdiction become apparent in the future.

My phone rang again. It was Michael Ketron. I let that call go to voice mail as well. Michael did not leave a message. Shortly thereafter, he called again, and again, I did not answer. Michael did not leave a message the second time, either.

I called Bill Collins.

"Hi, haven't heard from you in a while. I'm glad you called, it's always a pleasure to talk to you," Bill said.

"It's always good to speak with you, too," I said, trying to sound upbeat.

Bill guessed something was wrong. "Is everything all right?"

"I'm fine. I can't talk long. I want to ask you a question or two."

"Sure, what do you want to know?"

"What kind of car does Dylan drive?"

"I know exactly what Dylan drives because it became an issue when he was given the job of operations manager for the Association. One week after he was hired, Lavine announced at an open board meeting that Dylan would be provided with a new, fully loaded sports car, bought and paid for by the Association because Dylan needed a vehicle for job-related purposes."

I braced myself for the answer to my next question. "When was Dylan hired by the Association exactly?"

"Dylan was hired right after the new year, January 2013."

"Do you know what Dylan drove before the Association gave him a sports car?"

"Sure, Dylan drove a dually pickup truck his mother gave him."

"Was it red?"

"Yes. How did you know?"

"I'll call you later. I have to go."

I threw my phone onto the passenger seat, then cupped my head in my hands and rested it against the steering wheel.

Dylan had been hired as the Association's operations manager and provided with a fancy automobile just days after he killed Rebecca Fitzgerald. The revelation made me feel as though my brain was being squished between the jaws of a binding clamp.

Three days later, Bill called again. It was one week before Thanksgiving.

"How are you?" he asked.

"I'm fine."

"I called to tell you that Dylan resigned as operations manager on Tuesday. I just found out today."

"Why?!" I cried.

"No one knows why. There was talk he took another job. Haywood Martin is acting as the interim operations manager because Dylan left so suddenly without notice. It'll take time to find a permanent replacement."

CHAPTER 35
WARRANTED ACTIONS

Mr. Reed called before dawn on the Monday before Thanksgiving. He apprised me that the Georgia and Federal Bureaus of Investigation were on the premises of the Association executing a number of warrants issued by Judge Susan West, including one for the arrest of Gerald Lavine for the murder of Ed Weatherly; one for the arrest of Cedric Holmes for the murder of Theodore Milton; and one for the seizure of Association documents, computers, and other items. Further warrants were likely to be executed in the coming days to search the premises of Herschel Marks and the other board and committee members. At the onset, there wasn't enough evidence to issue an arrest warrant for Herschel Marks, but Mr. Reed believed the documents seized at the Association offices might provide needed proof.

Sydney Katz, the former sheriff for Carson County, agreed to sign an affidavit testifying that Cedric Holmes was at Theodore Milton's jail cell afterhours without authorization from Roger Blessures. When Sydney made the discovery, he had confronted Andrew Wilson and David Clifton. Wilson took full responsibility and begged Sydney not to tell Roger Blessures; Wilson wanted to tell Mr. Blessures himself.

Wilson claimed he didn't want to interfere with Milton's constitutional right to counsel, so he independently made the decision to permit the afterhours visit. At the time, Sydney thought Milton's death was unusual, but not particularly suspect, because the autopsy report stated that Milton had died of a heart attack.

"Is there any additional evidence that was uncovered?" I asked.

Mr. Reed sniffed and cleared his throat. "Dylan quietly turned himself into the United States attorney general in Atlanta late last night."

"What?!" I cried.

"Dylan confessed to the hit-and-run murder of Rebecca Fitzgerald, Robert Cobb's granddaughter. Dylan said he'd had too much to drink and he killed the girl who was driving home with her mother right before Christmas on December 22, 2012."

"I can't believe it. Why did he confess, do you think?"

"Well, Dylan realized his arrest for the murder of Rebecca Fitzgerald was imminent. Local authorities recently obtained additional evidence about the girl's death."

"What kind of evidence?"

"A used car dealer came forward after reading a recent article in the Carson County Daily Times and he told investigators that the day after Christmas 2012, Dylan sold him a red dually pickup truck that had been damaged in a wreck. The truck has been recovered and the forensic team is examining it as we speak."

"Did Dylan say anything else about the night Rebecca Fitzgerald died?"

"Yes, he said the road was deserted and no one saw the collision, so he sped off into the dark."

"I still don't understand why he confessed. Why not get a lawyer and fight the charges?"

"Immunity," Mr. Reed replied. "Dylan requested immunity for the hit-and-run murder and the racketeering crimes in exchange for his testimony implicating the Association board and committee members in the fraudulent procurement of Association assets. Dylan also asked for immunity from prosecution in exchange for his testimony implicating Gerald Lavine and Cedric Holmes in the interstate prostitution operation."

"Was Dylan granted immunity?"

"Yes. We had no choice."

"Did you speak with Michael Ketron?"

"No. Why? Should I?" I skirted the question by expressing my gratitude to Mr. Reed. "Thank you for filling me in on the specifics about what's going on in Lakewood City."

"Please don't tell anyone about any of the facts surrounding the cases we're in the midst of investigating."

"I won't say anything to anyone," I solemnly promised.

Bill called about two hours later. I swiped my phone, and I heard him huffing and puffing. It sounded like he was running. Bill said both the Georgia and Federal Bureaus of Investigation were on location at the Association offices carrying out boxes and boxes of evidence.

"Gerald Lavine was arrested but I don't know why. Other Association board members were also taken away in handcuffs."

"Where are you?" I asked.

Bill panted. "I'm with some other residents, huddled together across the street from the yacht club watching everything happen. We've moved several times to different locations because the Association offices being searched are in different places. I saw Millie, the director of the restaurants, handcuffed and placed in a patrol car."

I was sure Bill felt relieved and vindicated for all his hard work. Bill would never be viewed as a troublemaker by anyone at Covington Commons again. In fact, while I was speaking with him, I overheard other community members say, "Bill, you did good!"; "Thanks to you, Bill!"; "Bill, we owe you a lot."

"You should run for president of the Association. You're the man who can clean up the mess and put the Association back on stable financial ground," I said enthusiastically.

He laughed modestly. "We'll see."

Bill gave me a detailed analysis of the events as they occurred. There were at least twenty GBI agents, twenty FBI agents, and many more local sheriff's deputies diverting traffic and holding the public back from the premises being searched. Both local and national news media outlets were at Covington Commons covering the story and interviewing community members. Bill terminated our call because Michael Ketron wanted to interview him for the Carson County Daily Times.

I turned on the television. The local stations had preempted programming with news alerts pertaining to Covington Commons. I flipped through the stations, and there it was—Bill's interview with Michael Ketron. Bill appeared confident and spoke about the widespread fraud and theft perpetrated by the Association board members, committee members, and various other employees. He explained that it had been difficult to expose the fraud because the Association board members would not produce any documents when community members questioned a cost overrun or expense.

"If you can't see the documents, you can't prove your case," Bill acknowledged. "But on the other hand, if you're refused access to the documents, it's likely something is amiss."

"What was the catalyst in finally getting the Association investigated?" Michael asked.

"We were helped by a young attorney who was instrumental in finding the truth."

"Can you tell me the attorney's name?"

"No, she's quite shy and I don't want to put her in the limelight without her consent."

I felt proud I knew Bill Collins, a man of true perseverance and integrity.

I continued watching the non-stop coverage. The local news discussed the arrests of both Cedric Holmes and Gerald Lavine for murder. One news anchor was able to piece together public records with innuendo and speculate that Theodore Milton did not kill Ed Weatherly as originally reported. The reporter opined that Cedric Holmes or Gerald Lavine had killed Theodore Milton. Bits of information trickled out. The reporters were waiting for a press conference scheduled to begin later that evening. When there was a lull in the release of information, the news producers panned over to the empty podium where the press conference was scheduled to occur, ostensibly hoping the empty podium would provide illuminating facts.

News ultimately broke that Herschel Marks was the attorney who represented the Association and that caused numbers of reporters and cameramen to flock to Herschel's home in downtown Lakewood City because he was not in his office at Covington Commons. About an hour after the onslaught began, Herschel appeared on the front steps of his private residence and read a brief, prepared statement to quell the growing mob.

"I am the attorney who represents the Covington Commons Homeowners Association and its board and committee members," Herschel coolly professed. "More specifically, I represent the community interests of the Association and I represent the individual interests of each board and committee member." Herschel continued. "Since I'm the attorney, I cannot make statements about the circumstances presently surrounding the Association or its board and committee members because I am bound by the sacred attorney-client privilege. Thank you."

That was it! Herschel walked back into his house. Reporters looked downcast and began to disperse.

I turned off the television and sank into my sofa. Star jumped up, nuzzled next to me, and began licking my hand. Herschel was absolutely brilliant. He could not be forced to provide any statements to authorities about the Association, the board and committee members, or the business they conducted because all of the testimonial evidence fell within the purview of the attorney-client privilege. Moreover, Herschel could not be forced to disclose any incriminating documentary information because the fabricated documents he produced as the Association attorney to hide the theft of money and assets were likewise protected by the attorney-client privilege. The possibility that the attorney-client privilege could shield Herschel and the guilty Association board and committee members from criminal prosecution for fraud was especially real.

My thoughts turned to Michael Ketron. Michael had lied. He hadn't watched the sheriff's deputies arrest Dylan. Moreover, Sam Evanson had not quashed his story about Dylan killing Rebecca Fitzgerald because of Dylan's affiliation with the Association's powerful elite, who had the ability to protect Dylan and circumvent the law. Why had Michael lied about the events surrounding the hit and run? And how did he know Dylan was the perpetrator well before the local authorities?

I picked up my cell phone and called Michael. He answered despite being busy with the transpiring events. Michael said he would be occupied for the next several days to cover the news at the Association, so we agreed to meet for dinner at the Vidalia Café on Black Friday, the day after Thanksgiving.

James came home early. He said everyone at the hospital had watched the non-stop coverage of the happenings at the Association. He mentioned that the national news outlets had also picked up the story. We ate dinner early and watched the news conference.

During the news conference, Andrew Wilson nervously stood alongside the Carson County sheriff while the sheriff briefed the community about the arrests and the evidence collected to support the allegations of fraud and murder. The sheriff did not say anything about the alleged prostitution ring or the dead females who had washed up on the shores of the local lakes. I presumed the officials didn't have enough facts to substantiate their suppositions regarding those crimes.

CHAPTER 36
THE CABIN

I arrived half an hour early to the Vidalia Café in anticipation of getting the truth from Michael Ketron. It was a shivery Black Friday evening, but notwithstanding the weather, I waited outside the crowded restaurant, slowly oscillating on a white rocking chair, reading the latest news about the Association on my phone. Michael had arrived late, wearing jeans, work boots, and a black T-shirt; he looked as if he was ready to take on landscaping chores in lieu of having dinner at the café. I switched my phone to vibrate and shoved it into my coat pocket just before Michael apologized for his tardiness and sat in the rocker beside me.

"What's wrong?" I asked, sensing his anxiety.

"I'm tired. I've been working relentlessly on the Association case."

I unveiled the specter of incrimination: "I thought you weren't permitted to cover the Association after Gerald Lavine complained about a less-than-flattering article you wrote about Bill Collin's and Alfred Mertz's initial lawsuit."

Michael fumbled the ball but briskly recovered. "Oh, that—what do you mean? Oh, yeah . . . Sam must have forgotten amidst the large-scale investigation occurring right now at the Association."

"Oh, I see." I sighed.

Michael shifted uncomfortably in his seat.

"Can I ask you about the night Rebecca Fitzgerald died?"

"Sure. What do you want to know?"

"Why did you tell me you watched police arrest Dylan at the scene? Then you said Sam Evanson killed your story, and Dylan's crime was covered up and wiped from the record books. Why did you make me believe a story that isn't true?"

"What are you talking about?"

"I met with Sam Evanson and I heard your voice on the nine-one-one tape."

"Are you hungry?" Michael asked.

"No."

"Do you want to take a drive?"

"Where?"

"I have something important to show you. Then you'll understand everything."

"Sure," I said, abandoning my misgivings about my escort because I craved the truth at all costs.

"Why don't you drive with me? I can bring you back to your car later."

"I guess that'll be fine, but where are we going?" I asked as I scooped up my purse and stood, ready to leave.

"I want you to meet a friend of mine who can answer your questions. He's staying at a cabin on Carson Lake."

"Do I know him?"

"Can anyone really *know* anyone else?"

I did not respond to his rhetorically strange question.

Michael drove a back route to the cabin with which I was unfamiliar. He zigzagged through so many winding, circuitous roads, I became a little nauseous during our trek to the mysterious locale.

"I have no idea where we are. Are we still in Carson County?"

"We're almost there. Don't worry, you'll soon have all the answers to your questions."

A short time later, we arrived at a secluded bungalow in a wooded area, which I guessed was positioned somewhere near the most remote location in Carson County—if, in fact, we were still in Carson County. I exited Michael's truck into the bitingly crisp air, stuffed my hands into my coat pockets to warm them, and fiddled with my phone for an instant. We walked toward the cabin and passed the remains of a smoldering campfire that scented the air with a haunting odor of revolting musky meat.

"Where are we?" I asked, moving toward Michael as a chill surged through my body and caused me to shudder with dread. The creepiness of the place shook me with unexpected consternation.

"Don't worry," Michael said when we reached the steps of the front porch.

I looked at a windowless door on which a tarnished brass knocker hung, then I dropped my head and examined my black shoes. They were quite worn, scuffed, and the heels were marked. I needed a new pair. I thought I should have spent the evening buying new shoes instead of traveling to a strange cabin to meet with God knows who; perhaps I could have scored a great Black Friday deal.

I sucked in the stinking air and held it as Michael stepped up to the knocker and pounded it with such force, echoes reverberated in the empty distance.

I waited with nervous expectation, unable to exhale.

The knob jerked with a squeak, a pause ensued, then the door wrenched open.

Mr. Cobb stepped onto the porch with a red glowing cigar in hand. "Hello, young lady. How are you this fine evening?"

The air trapped in my lungs escaped, relieving the built-up pressure that vise-gripped my chest. Seeing the broad, affable face of the attorney I looked up to overwhelmed me with a feeling of welcomed security. "Hi, I'm fine. It's nice to see you. Michael told me you might be able to help answer my questions."

"I will try to help you anyway I can. Please come in," Mr. Cobb said, politely holding the door open.

I passed through the threshold, led by Michael. The cabin was dimly lit and I had to bat my eyelids a number of times to adjust my vision. I found myself in a tiny common area. The room felt dusty. A faded-brown sofa situated between two doors abutted the left wall and a scruffy, reclining lounge chair abutted the right wall. Two broad, uncurtained windows—one over the sofa and one over the recliner— could have been cleaner. The fierce full moon crept into the room through one of the windows and flailed across the rough wooden floor. Opposite the entry was a cast-iron woodstove that emanated a stench similar to yet stronger than the odor discharged from the campfire. The smell was alarmingly comparable to the decaying flesh of the dead opossum James had removed from under our house one summer. Left of the woodstove was a studio kitchenette, and to the woodstove's right was a table with four ladder-back chairs.

Mr. Cobb followed us into the cabin, exhaled a puff of suffocating smoke, and proceeded into the kitchenette.

I made myself at home by resting my purse on the table, then I removed my coat and hung it on the back of a wobbly chair.

"How was your vacation in the Caribbean?"

"It was lovely, my dear. The weather is perfect this time of year. I just got back this morning."

Michael seemed jittery. He dug into his jacket pockets and pulled his hands out, empty, then he said, "I'll be right back. I forgot something in my truck."

"Would you like a drink, young lady?" Mr. Cobb asked after Michael stormed out of the cabin.

"Sure, what do you have?" I asked after sitting down in the chair that served as the hanger for my coat.

"Let me see," he said, rifling through the cabinets.

"I didn't know you and Michael were friends?"

"Oh, yes, we are friends. He told me you needed help, so I obliged."

"Is this your cabin, Mr. Cobb?"

"Oh no, this cabin belongs to a business associate. He lets me use it on occasion when I want to take time off."

"What do you do out here?"

"Carson Lake is a few hundred feet down a wooded path, past three other cabins on the property, so I can go fishing or boating. I also like to hunt."

"What do you hunt for?"

I didn't hear his answer because the dish-clanking sounds had drowned his voice to an inaudible muffle. My phone buzzed, so I pulled it from my pocket and read an email while Mr. Cobb continued to search the cabinets with his back towards me.

It was from Millie, *I got your email address from your website. I wanted to know if you could represent me. I want to confess. Please, I need a lawyer. I found your name on the internet and it said you were the only attorney nearby who knows federal law. I think I'm being charged with federal crimes.*

I sent Millie a return email, *Millie, I cannot represent you. There are too many conflicts. I think you should call Mr. Robert Cobb Jr. in Lakewood City. He is a skilled criminal defense attorney and he is familiar with both state and federal law. I am here with him right now at the cabins on Carson Lake, so I will let him know you will be calling.*

I almost hit send, but Michael returned and distracted my concentration.

"I believe you forgot about her phone, Michael," Mr. Cobb said, still with his back to me, just as if he had eyes in the back of his head.

Michael approached me with an outstretched hand. "Please give me your phone."

"Why?" I asked, pulling back to prevent the confiscation.

Michael pushed me out of the chair, jumped on top of me, and smashed my face onto the floor. He dislodged my phone from my tight grip.

"Please, not so rough, Michael," Mr. Cobb admonished.

"Sorry, sir," Michael said as he pulled me by my hair to a standing position, after which, he forced me back into my seat. Michael swiped through my phone before he smashed it with a hammer he retrieved from a kitchen drawer.

"Michael, forgetting her phone was no good. I hope you did not make a costly error."

"She didn't get any text messages or calls out. I checked her call log, and the last text she sent or call she made was earlier today, hours before we met."

Mr. Cobb calmly procured a pistol from a cabinet and placed it on the counter with the barrel aimed at my face, then he set out a bottle of vodka and three glasses etched with hard-water spots on the table. He filled one and offered it to me. "Would you like some superlative vodka made in the Siberian region of Russia? It is difficult to find here in the United States, but fortunately, I have my contacts. Here, have a drink and we will toast to the future."

"No, I don't want it," I said, then I spat at Michael's face when he moved closer to pick up a drink for himself.

Michael grabbed my hair and pulled my head backward. "I wouldn't disrespect me or Mr. Cobb, if I was you," he said, wiping away my saliva with his shirtsleeve.

"Michael, enough. Leave her alone," Mr. Cobb ordered as he pulled out a chair, set it across from me and seated himself in it.

"What's going on?!" I cried.

"Relax, my dear," Mr. Cobb said soothingly.

I recalled first seeing Perry in Judge McMurray's courtroom on that fateful, windy day in mid-March. Perry was still as animated as ever. His dainty gold chain bracelet glowed in the low light that projected from a rusty metal floor lamp standing in the corner near the dining table.

"Michael, why are you doing this to me?" I asked.

They both looked at me without expression.

"I know what you did, Michael. I know you covered up your involvement with Dylan and I know about the lies you told to cover up Dylan's crimes."

The men continued to look at me without expression.

"Michael, I believe Dylan called you first after he collided with another vehicle on December 22, 2012," I continued. "You arrived at the scene, and you noticed there were no witnesses, so you instructed Dylan to drive away and you assured him that you would call nine-one-one and tell the dispatchers you came upon a hit and run."

Michael smirked an admission without remorse. "That's right."

I looked Mr. Cobb square in the face. "Dylan caused the death of your granddaughter, Rebecca, when he crashed into your daughter's car, while driving intoxicated, on December 22, 2012. I don't understand why Michael covered up the crime for Dylan."

Mr. Cobb responded with a serious expression. I even thought I detected a tear in the corner of his eye after I conjured up the spirit of his dead granddaughter, but he didn't cry. Instead, he began to snicker, and then the snicker turned into a robust laugh. Mr. Cobb laughed and laughed. I was stunned for a moment, until I recollected from my college psychology class that some people responded to emotional pain in different ways; sometimes in reverse of generally expected behaviors.

Feeling sincere empathy for Mr. Cobb, I blurted out, "I'm sorry about the death of your granddaughter. I know you must be hopelessly sad at the thought of her passing. Isn't that why you always wear that gold chain bracelet on your wrist? In tribute to her memory?"

Mr. Cobb stopped laughing. He considered me with a cocked head and a look of disbelief. "I don't wear this bracelet in remembrance of my granddaughter!" he roared, shaking his wrist high in the air.

The man I looked up to paused briefly, then his eyes flamed with malice and he laughed again in a much louder, absurdly sinister voice. His howling resounded throughout the room. My ears absorbed the piercing noise and penetrating fear imprisoned my body. When his laughter had finally ceased, he wiped tears of amusement from his eyes. "My granddaughter died—sure, that was sad, but not for me. The event turned out to be quite fortuitous for me and my side business. Would you like to know about my side business?"

I did not answer. I had lost my voice to feelings of terror, disgust, and sheer sorrow for the pretty little red-haired girl who lost her life three days before the arrival of Santa Claus.

Mr. Cobb sneered, "You see, my dear, years ago I started my side business with the loyal help of Michael Ketron. He regularly hired the girls, brought them here to Carson County, and housed them in one of the comfortable cabins on this property. He even found the men who wanted the services provided by my girls. Ed Weatherly and Gerald Lavine, both louts and thieves in their own right, were merely customers at the onset, but Michael easily lured them into the operational aspect of the scheme.

I found each man's weak nature and greedy temperament distasteful, but I needed employees. Cedric Holmes, another slimy idiot with no chance of legitimate success, also agreed to climb aboard and join the venture. They all wanted a percentage of the action. That was when Michael agreed to sell this lake property to Gerald Lavine so Gerald would have a dog in the race, so to speak. We were also able to lower the percentages paid to those degenerates by allowing them free use of the girls, and I believe they used those girls as frequently as a cook uses a frying pan."

I swallowed hard because vomit began to regurgitate into my throat. Mr. Cobb did not relent; he proudly admitted that all the men worked at his whim. He controlled all of the criminal elements in Lakewood City and Carson County as a silent, omnipresent, unidentified boss. Only Michael Ketron knew of his identity as the proverbial El Patron.

"Early on, before my granddaughter was killed, I thought about hiring Dylan to assist Michael with my expanding enterprise. Everyone knew he was a sniveling Mama's boy who was easily controlled. He was the exact kind of employee I needed. After his DUI arrest, I instructed Michael to go to the Carson County sheriff's office to obtain Dylan's arrest records, under the guise of wanting to report the news. I needed to know every fact that pertained to the case. Since Cindy Matthews couldn't get the sanctimonious Roger Blessures to drop the matter—I offered to represent Dylan free of charge."

"How magnanimous," I scoffed.

Mr. Cobb ignored my comment. "You know the rest. I continued Dylan's case until the malleable Andrew Wilson was sworn in as Blessures' successor. The only reason I did not hire Dylan right after the ink dried on the plea agreement was because I had serious reservations about his ability to keep secrets. After all, it was public knowledge that he had an annoying addiction to drugs and alcohol and addicts are quite often infuriating blabbermouths. Dylan left town for a time, and when he returned, I ordered Michael to cozy up to him and become his friend, in case we needed Dylan in the future."

Soft rumbles of distant thunder prompted me to look out the uncurtained window above the couch into the stark night. Thick, barbed tree limbs oscillated slowly in a fitful breeze while I listened to a supercilious man arrogantly confess his atrocious sins.

"As time went on, it became clear I needed to hire another person. Michael could not continue running the show solely on his own because he had become increasingly occupied by other matters on which

I needed him to focus. I decided the best type of front man for the operation would be someone who had everything to lose, someone I could easily manipulate. The occurrence of my granddaughter's death provided me with such an opportunity. Trusty, loyal Michael called me with the news of the accident right before contacting nine-one-one. That was when I knew Dylan Matthews would be perfect for the job— he could be blackmailed. After the accident, Michael ordered Lavine to give Dylan the job of operations manager of the Association. It was merely a cover for Dylan's real job."

"Why were Ed Weatherly and Theodore Milton killed?"

"I will come to that. All in good time."

"Stop interrupting," Michael commanded.

"It was a shame your inquisitive nature caused you to start digging up records on Ed Weatherly and Theodore Milton. Perhaps if you had kept to yourself, and just represented the Wainrights against the Association for breach of its fiduciary duties, you would be out Christmas shopping with your devoted husband for Black Friday sales."

Mr. Cobb pulled his chair closer and leaned in toward my face. His breath was so offensive, I nearly gagged. It smelled worse than the putrescent stench coming from the woodstove that swirled through the air.

"Michael called one day and advised me there was an attorney from a nearby town who was poking around, looking for information about the deaths of Ed Weatherly and Theodore Milton. Michael said he must have left a note behind, years before when he was asked to obtain Dylan's 2010 DUI arrest records. You know, the note you found in the records room. I was extremely angry with Michael for making such a stupid mistake."

"Sorry about that, sir."

"No need to cry over spilled milk, my boy. Where was I? Oh yes, the blunder. After Michael apprised me of his blunder and disclosed you had contacted him, I immediately recalled seeing you in the courthouse on the day of our first encounter. Do you remember?"

I stayed silent, wishing I had never moved to Georgia.

"I knew about your case," Mr. Cobb snapped. "Everyone in Lakewood City was gossiping about you, an unknown attorney in the community taking on the Association. Everyone agreed you displayed bravery in taking on a case against a mob-like, corrupt organization. Instead of brooding, however, I came up with a delightful idea. I decided to use you and your inquisitive nature to my advantage by feeding you information through Michael Ketron—and lead you down the road to enlightenment."

"You are a loser," I boldly declared.

"That assessment of me is inaccurate, young lady. I am not a loser. To the contrary, I am a winner. I have made millions on my not-so-aboveboard law practice, and I have made even more money off the Association board and committee members because of their love of sleazy prostitutes."

"The women you exploit are not sleazy . . . *you* are sleazy. You took advantage of their misfortune. You are a despicable man."

"Many women make poor choices in life, much to their own disadvantage. I believe I assisted them and provided them with reputable employment. It's a matter of perception, plain and simple."

I began to speak, but Michael yelled, "Shut up, you whore!"

"I can handle this, Michael. Do me a favor, please. Will you go down the road to the gas station and buy some eggs, milk, and coffee for breakfast in the morning?"

"Sure, no problem, sir," Michael replied as he took the money Mr. Cobb offered and left the cabin.

I was petrified to be alone with Mr. Cobb. I began to think about James and how he must have been worried. "What time is it?"

"You shouldn't worry about time, my dear, since you have so little of it left."

"What are you going to do to me?"

"Patience, my dear. I had Michael bring you here this evening because I wanted to let you know that I am giving up my side business and winding down my law practice. I will be moving to my house in the Caribbean very soon. Maybe if you had accepted my amorous advances, you too, could have come with me to live a life of luxury and decadence."

I became sickened at the thought of being with Mr. Cobb.

"I think you asked about the murders of Ed Weatherly and Theodore Milton, correct?"

I did not answer. I again looked out the uncurtained window. The tree limbs had begun to wildly undulate in the turbulent wind that had suddenly picked up speed. I blinked as a jagged bolt of lightning streaked into the room. The blinding flash was followed by a booming thunderclap. Angry rain began to beat on the tin roof while a loathsome fiend continued to recite his demented tale.

"Around 2007, into 2008, Michael began to notice there was a lot of in-fighting between Lavine and Weatherly. It became apparent Weatherly was a loose cannon. He had become an aging man, with a growing conscience, who might confess his sins to attain absolution. Ed needed to go before that happened. Consequently, Michael convinced Lavine to kill Ed because Ed intended on spilling the beans about the fraud committed upon the Association—despite what Ed may have told Lavine. I proposed framing Theodore Milton for the murder because he had motive to kill Ed based on the failed business deal. I knew Lavine was a self-serving weasel, who would lie, steal, and kill to protect himself."

"You are also a hateful weasel—you lie, steal, and kill, or have others kill *for* you to protect yourself," I said with an enraged soul.

"I, my dear, am not a weasel. Identifying someone as a weasel, or any type of animal, is a description that connotes weakness and a lack of intelligence. I am strong and in possession of a genius-level IQ, so your insult is not correct. I will, however, admit that I do not feel empathy or sympathy for people in distress. I only care about myself; that is true. I guess you could say that I am a textbook sociopath or psychopath, depending how one resolves to describe me, but let me be clear, I am proud to be so. It is wonderful to never feel guilt, remorse, or compassion."

The revulsion I felt was inexplicable. I should have guessed that my captor was a deranged maniac when I first saw him in court. It was so obvious. His narcissistic grandstanding coupled with his nauseating egotism should have tipped me off. The psychopathic, larger-than-life Perry resumed bragging about his contemptuous war stories after he slurped his Russian vodka.

"Lavine got a call from Ed on the morning of the murder. Ed said he was expecting a visit from Theodore Milton later that afternoon, so Lavine waited until Milton had left Ed's house, then Lavine executed Ed with Ed's own frying pan. Ed was an easy target; he was a crippled man in a wheelchair. When Milton was charged with first-degree murder, Michael suggested we arrange for Cedric to represent Milton so we could control the influx of evidence and the subsequent trial. Michael's suggestion turned out to be very smart because Cedric learned that Milton saw Lavine enter Ed's house in his rearview mirror just as he was driving away. That information led to the decision to kill Milton. The murder was executed with the help of Andrew Wilson, he arranged for Cedric to meet with Milton afterhours in his cell. Oleander—perhaps the world's best murder weapon. I came up with that idea. Brilliant, right?"

I scowled at my jailor.

"The murders of the two slugs were perfectly covered up. It was all old news until you arrived," Mr. Cobb growled.

Another bolt of lightning lit up the cabin, exposing a layer of dust that begrimed the room. The bright light was followed by another thunder burst as Mr. Cobb loaded more crackling logs into the wood-stove. The rain fell harder and transformed from a shower to a teeming downpour as wrathful wind whizzed around the stink-infested structure. Mr. Cobb paused again to swig his vodka, then he turned to me and flaunted a grotesque smile that exposed his decayed, tar-stained teeth.

"Since you involved yourself in matters pertaining to me, I decided to use you to my advantage. I needed you to discover the truth about Dylan Matthews, Ed Weatherly, Gerald Lavine, Theodore Milton, and Cedric Holmes. I wanted you to determine that Dylan killed my granddaughter and ran the prostitution ring, and that Lavine killed Ed Weatherly and framed Milton for the crime, and that Cedric poisoned Milton with oleander. I wanted all of them convicted so they would cease to be trouble for me or Michael."

I squirmed in my chair; sweat began to dribble down the back of my neck. The temperature in the cabin had risen significantly since more fuel had been added to the fire.

"I sometimes toy with the idea of representing Dylan, Lavine, or Cedric as their criminal defense attorney. Wouldn't that be a fascinating turn of events?"

I refused to answer. I had nothing to say because Mr. Cobb's diabolical thought process was impossible to understand.

"Once Dylan, Lavine, and Cedric are tucked safely away in their jail cells, Michael and I can terminate the syndicate and move on with the rest of our lives. Herschel Marks and the rest of the Association board and committee members will be fighting for their freedom, based on the superb job you did drafting the complaint you submitted to the United States attorney general calling for the investigation into the Association fraud."

"Did you burglarize my home?" I asked as thunder grumbled and churned overhead.

"Yes, Michael and I searched your files to discern whether you had any additional incriminating evidence. It was necessary. I hope we did not leave a big mess; that was not our intent," Mr. Cobb cackled.

"You stole my file with information about Ed Weatherly and Theodore Milton."

"Sorry about that, but I needed to see what you were researching."

Without waiting for a response, Mr. Cobb retrieved my file from a kitchen drawer and threw it on the floor before my feet, causing a haze of dirt to rise and encircle my legs.

"Is there anything else I can do for you, my dear?" Mr. Cobb asked.

"Yes, yes, I want to know if you know anything about the women whose bodies were found washed up on the shores of Carson Lake over the last few years."

"You are forever the investigator, my love," Mr. Cobb stated as he moved toward me and brushed his hand across my face.

I flinched from his disturbing caress.

"Those prostitutes deserved to die," Mr. Cobb snarled.

"Why?"

"It was what needed to happen."

I sat still.

"You know, you are the sole person other than Michael Ketron who can attach me to any of the crimes we discussed tonight."

"How are you going to cover up my murder when you kill me?"

"That is easy. I have laid all the groundwork to frame Dylan for the murders of the prostitutes. I will also leave enough evidence for the authorities to determine that Dylan killed you because you were on his trail. It will not be hard for them to conclude that a serial killer is capable of your murder as well. Very simple, really."

"Dylan turned state's evidence. He was granted full immunity from prosecution while you were on vacation. He's been in police custody for the last couple of days, so you can't frame him for my murder."

Mr. Cobb furrowed his perfectly groomed brow. "You are lying, my pretty."

"No, I'm not. The authorities have kept it under wraps, so no one knows."

Sweat formed on Mr. Cobb's upper lip.

"Do you actually think you can trust Michael to keep your secrets?"

Mr. Cobb's right eyelid twitched. "Michael's loyalty is unwavering."

"Dylan doesn't know about your involvement, but Dylan knows about Michael's involvement, who knows about your involvement. You could be in a heap of trouble. Michael might divulge your participation in the syndicate for a lighter sentence, should the investigation take that course."

Still standing near my chair, imprisoning me with his towering physique, Mr. Cobb leaned down and slapped my face. The smack stung long after the blow. "Shut up!" decried Mr. Cobb. "I will rape, torture, and kill you the same way I raped, tortured, and killed those deplorable prostitutes."

Michael returned from the store, soaked by the rain, holding a bag of groceries. He had begun putting the groceries away, when Mr. Cobb seized the pistol that rested on the counter and aimed it at the back of the young man's head. Mr. Cobb pulled the trigger, detonating an explosive blast. That was it. Michael fell dead to the ground, not knowing what had hit him. He died instantly. The high-velocity back splatter from the inflicted wound sprayed onto my hair and shirt, and stained Mr. Cobb's face like nightmarish warpaint. I quaked with uncontrollable fear. I knew Mr. Cobb would kill me next.

"Well now, Michael will not be a problem for me anymore," Mr. Cobb triumphantly said as he wiped away blood that dribbled from his bulbous nose with his immense hand. He grabbed a kitchen towel and reseated himself opposite me, then he wiped blood from the barrel of his pistol.

I looked away from the animalistic psychopath and fixed my eyes on the uncurtained window. The rain had subsided to a light drizzle and the wind ceased to blow. The tree limbs were still and dripping. The cabin in the woods was noiseless—the eerie calm before the cryptic end had begun.

"You were right. Michael needed to go. He made a mess of the entire Blessures episode. I asked him to kill Blessures, but rather than doing what I told him to do, Michael blackmailed Blessures into killing himself by threatening to expose those photos of his affair with Herschel Marks. I had a photographer take those photographs years ago because I was going to blackmail Blessures myself and force him to drop the original DUI charges against Dylan. However, when the Association backed Andrew Wilson in the succeeding election, the blackmail became unnecessary."

Mr. Cobb guzzled more vodka. I looked down and stared at my bloodstained file that had been thrown at my feet. I struggled with my thoughts, hoping I lived a life spreading happiness and kindness to all of the people with whom I had come in contact. I tried to think only of the good in the people I knew. I did not want to die with thoughts of negativity passing through my brain and emotions of discontent passing through my heart. I thought of forgiveness and those who I wished would forgive me. I thought of James and second chances.

"Are you listening, my dear? You seem to be disoriented."

I lifted my head upwards and looked into the eyes of a man who had caused so much pain. "I'm here."

"Michael did not handle the Blessures matter well. He did not do what he was told to do. He stupidly dropped the photographs in the hallway on his way out so the police would believe Blessures committed suicide in response to blackmail. That was an idiotic decision that will no doubt put the authorities on the trail of a blackmailer. Michael thought no one could be charged with murder if the police determined Blessures killed himself. Michael should never have left the photographs. So I am glad you told me about Michael's possible disloyalty. Michael can thank you for his early demise."

Mr. Cobb's dainty gold chain bracelet shimmered in the low light as he emptied the remaining contents of the vodka bottle into his glass and swilled the last of the liquor.

"As soon as the rain stops, I will restart the campfire. The weather forecasters reported earlier today that the storms this fine Black Friday evening would merely be fleeting. You know, I used to have the prostitutes' bodies dumped in Carson Lake and other nearby lakes, but they kept washing ashore. So I started to incinerate them on the campfire and in the woodstove."

"Can I ask you a question?" I whispered. Fatigue had set in; I barely had the strength to speak.

"Why of course, my dear. You know you can ask me anything, young lady. I am at your service."

"You said earlier that you don't wear the gold chain bracelet on your wrist in remembrance of your granddaughter."

"Yes, that is right."

"Then why do you wear it all the time? It seems too small for you."

Perry smiled sweetly, flashed his decayed, tar-stained teeth, and revealed, "It belonged to my first victim. I killed her many years ago. I wear it as a reminder of the power I wield in this world."

CHAPTER 37
JAMES' WORRY

I was fully ready to meet my maker. I tried not to feel scared. I pitied Mr. Cobb.

After he had revealed the meaning of the dainty gold chain bracelet, he picked up his pistol and pointed it at me. "Where would you like to be shot?" he asked matter-of-factly.

I was not going to answer. I decided to leave the planet without making that decision—but then there was no need to answer. Chief Sullivan busted past the front door, gun in hand, and aimed at Mr. Cobb.

"I wouldn't do that if I were you, officer, or you will be liable for this young lady's death. Please put your weapon down on the floor in front of you," Mr. Cobb said as he held his pistol fixed on my face.

Chief Sullivan did as instructed.

"Thank you, Chief—Sullivan, is it? I remember meeting you in the past. You do a fine job in Champaign. But why are you working a shift in Carson County?"

Chief Sullivan did not answer.

"My, my, so quiet, Chief. Did you call for backup?"

Again, Chief Sullivan did not respond.

"Of course, you did! You know your job well. And I am sure you know you have no jurisdiction in this county. You cannot arrest me or you will be guilty of abuse of power."

Chief Sullivan remained silent.

"What time do you think the Carson County sheriffs will be here?"

Chief Sullivan did not move or speak.

"I assume I have minutes at most. Or, perhaps you didn't call the sheriffs. Maybe you stupidly came here without calling for backup. Is her husband with you, waiting outside, perhaps?" Mr. Cobb said, steadfastly pointing his pistol at my face.

Chief Sullivan said nothing, but he was discernably vexed, given his inability to act. He stared down Mr. Cobb and did not look at me. A chill wafted through the air and zipped up my spine. Mr. Cobb racked the slide of his pistol and it produced an unmerciful clicking sound that amplified like a cursed alarm, notifying all present that the time had come.

I looked out the same window I had been looking out all evening, and I thought I saw James' reflection, but the lights inside the cabin had flickered to a dull glow, which made it difficult to see anything clearly. When the lights brightened, no one was looking in; my mind had seen a hallucination of the man I loved.

"Would you like to say anything, young lady? Your last words?" Mr. Cobb chuckled with despicable depravity.

I glanced at Chief Sullivan.

He looked at me with pitiful fear.

"You will be next Chief Sullivan. Of that, I am sure you are aware," Mr. Cobb jeered.

Neither I, nor Chief Sullivan responded to Mr. Cobb's certain threats.

Doom filled the cabin. The lights flickered once again. I squeezed my eyes shut to keep out the evil, then—all at once—a monstrously loud blast, intermixed with the sound of shattering glass crashing to the floor, quaked the cabin and produced a life-ending explosion.

I fell deaf. I could not see. Blackness had shrouded the cabin.

The lights flashed back on.

My eardrums beat with rhythmic aches and agonizing ringing.

Mr. Cobb writhed on the floor, grasping his blood-spurting upper-right thigh with his right hand. His pistol laid out of reach.

I looked out the window; the pane was smashed out.

Chief Sullivan raced to my side.

James entered the cabin, holding a shotgun.

Clenching his decayed, tar-stained teeth in visible pain, Mr. Cobb seethed. "You bested me at my own game, young lady. Congratulations. To the victor, go the spoils."

James removed his jacket and ripped it into strips, then he made a tourniquet and fastened it to Mr. Cobb's gaping thigh to stop the profuse bleeding.

Backup officers from the Carson County sheriff's office stormed the cabin.

James pulled me aside, and the officers surrounded Mr. Cobb's debilitated, shaking body.

I told the officers what had happened to Michael Ketron, and one of them called the coroner.

An ambulance arrived, and Mr. Cobb was transported to a future without freedom.

The dreadful night was unending. I refused to go to the hospital; I hated hospitals. James and I were taken to the sheriff's office to meet with officials from the Georgia Bureau of Investigation and the Federal Bureau of Investigation.

James held my hand and listened intently while I told my story. Afterward, I held his hand and listened intently while he told his story.

James recounted that it was about midnight on the evening of my captivity when he had driven to the Champaign police department and asked to speak with Chief Sullivan. The officer on duty said Chief

Sullivan was not available, but James persisted and explained that an emergency had arisen. Chief Sullivan met James at the station and as a result of James' dogged conviction, a missing person's case related to my disappearance was formally opened, even though I had only been off the radar for a short time.

James revealed that when he had failed to reach me by phone earlier that evening, after repeated attempts, he checked my email on our home computer and discovered the message Millie had sent. My response was recorded as a draft. James showed the email and drafted response to Chief Sullivan. Chief Sullivan knew of a former fishing village on the north shore of Carson Lake that consisted of several rural cabins. He told James the cabins were under investigation as dwellings used for prostitution. Since Chief Sullivan knew of no other cabins on Carson Lake, the men took a chance and headed there.

The night was frigid. Murky fog had set in. Visibility was low, less than ten percent.

James goaded Chief Sullivan to hurry, but the weather conditions rendered his request impossible.

When Chief Sullivan and James arrived, they parked several hundred yards away from their destination because a sudden jolt of police presence announced by a car's roaring engine might stun somebody inside and precipitate a catastrophic occurrence. Hence, subsequent to parking, the men walked quietly toward their target until they happened upon a cabin illuminated by an ominous interior light. Smoke billowed from the glowing fire near the entrance; they smelled the same stench I had been exposed to for an inordinate amount of time. James suspected the smell was burning animal or human remains, so Chief Sullivan decided to penetrate the cabin, even though backup had not arrived. Chief Sullivan gave James the keys to the patrol car, instructed him to wait outside for ten minutes, and told him to call for help on the radio scanner if he did not emerge within the time allotted.

The minutes slugged by at an intolerable pace. James heard nothing but crackling embers fighting extinguishment from the moisture that filled the dark woods. Fearing the worst, James could not wait for any more time to pass, so he returned to the patrol car and used the keys to unlock the shotgun from the vertical front-seat mount, then he racked the slide and released the intimidating noise before he came within earshot of anyone inside the menacing cabin. He snuck past the front door, moved around the left side of the building, and looked into the smeared window. The lights flickered to a faint dimness and illuminated a dreadful scene. The lights brightened, and James ducked out of sight. The lights flickered again, and James took aim at his deservingly wretched target. He pulled the trigger at the exact instant the lights went out. He didn't know if he had hit his mark. He circled around the cabin, entered through the front door, and discovered he had shot Mr. Cobb, disabling him with precision as intended.

At the close of James' statement, I remarked, "You really were telling the truth at JollyWorld when you said you were a great shot. I thought you just got lucky that day."

James smiled and replied, "I think I got lucky this day."

The ordeal was over. The corruption at the Association was uncovered and would be prosecuted, the cases involving the deaths of Ed Weatherly and Theodore Milton were solved, and a serial murderer was captured. My ascent from within the stifling rabbit hole that had ensnared me for too long had materialized.

CHAPTER 38
THE RECKONING

I watched replays of the news footage wherein officials forced Robert Cobb Jr., Herschel Marks, Gerald Lavine, Cedric Holmes, Cindy Matthews, and the other board and committee members to make their perp walks. Each abhorrent criminal looked scared and tearful—all except Mr. Cobb. He made his perp walk with pride and grandeur, pushed in a wheelchair by an attractive young nurse. He laughed and broadly smiled to the cameras when they came in for a closeup. His decayed, tar-stained teeth exemplified his decayed, tar-stained soul. David Clifton was the guard on duty when the perpetrators were escorted into the jailhouse to be booked for the crimes they had allegedly committed. He held the jail door open for each criminal as they crossed over the threshold from freedom to incarceration. David Clifton did not look at his former lover when Herschel paraded past with his head hung in shame.

The wrongdoers were arraigned two weeks after James and Chief Sullivan had saved me from the clutches of Mr. Cobb. The arraignments were held in the Carson County superior courthouse in Room 113, the exact room where my case against the Association had been dismissed on a windy, cool day in mid-March. James and I entered room 113 half an hour before the commencement of the proceedings. The room smelled sweet, like lemon-scented furniture polish. I sat down on the same smooth bench that I had sat upon before. I gazed at the painting of the Carson County superior courthouse that hung above the judicial bench. It was not crooked. It hung properly positioned, straight on the wall. It was no longer dirty; the painting seemed bright and clean. The entire room was immaculate. A janitor emptied the trashcans before court convened.

Bill Collins entered the courtroom, accompanied by Alfred and a tall woman about forty years old, with graying auburn hair. The mysterious woman had a pale complexion and woeful brown eyes. She walked with her shoulders hunched forward and she seemed irreversibly crestfallen. The defendants' attorneys arrived and seated themselves inside the bar to wait for their clients. Numerous members of the press began filing in and taking seats alongside the family members of those accused. The bailiffs ushered the defendants into the courtroom. Each defendant was clad in an orange jumpsuit, accessorized with a heavy set of silver handcuffs. Mr. Cobb was wheeled in last. In addition to the orange jumpsuit and silver handcuffs, he wore complementing leg irons. I winced when he turned and gave me a sinister smile and a thumbs-up as he passed by.

I recalled that I had met all of the evildoers on three prior occasions in three separate courtrooms—when Judge McMurray had dismissed my case; when I'd delivered the first oral argument to the court of appeals; and when I'd defended that decision in the Georgia Supreme Court. Sometimes evil congregates in places that should be reserved for truth and divine justice. That day, however, in a criminal context, I was grateful to see them all there.

The bailiff called the room to order and the spectators rose.

Judge Doyle McMurray, already wearing his robe, entered the courtroom through a side door behind the judicial bench and seated himself underneath the aligned, bright painting of the courthouse. His mane was gone. Judge McMurray's locks were neatly trimmed into a version of a pompadour that exposed his receding hairline. His oversized sideburns had been shaved off. It was difficult to recognize Judge McMurray. He looked starkly different. Respectable, but weaker and more feeble. He no longer appeared to be tyrannically in control of his surroundings.

After the arraignments concluded, Bill and the mystery woman approached James and me in the lobby of the courthouse. Bill introduced the woman and I shook her cold, limp hand. The woman was Susan Fitzgerald, Mr. Cobb's daughter.

"I'm in town winding up my father's affairs, and I wanted to thank you for what you've done."

I felt complete sympathy for the woman and I wanted to erase her pain.

"I left town after Rebecca's death and relocated to California. I stopped practicing law. I only got a law degree because it was my father's dream, not my own. I'm sorry that my father hurt so many people."

I put my arm around her and gave her a squeeze. I wanted to tell her not to blame herself, but I realized that was her lot in life—she would probably always blame herself, and no one could do a damn thing about that.

Bill escorted Susan to her car and James and I followed behind. Susan's horrific misfortunes caused me to resolve—right then and there—to always make an effort to be happy.

James and I were about to drive away from the courthouse parking lot when an exotically bewitching brunette knocked on James' car window. James put the car in park and opened the window.

"I'm Jan Blessures, the wife of Roger Blessures. Can I speak with you both? Just for a minute, if you don't mind."

I opened the door, jumped out of my seat, and walked around the car to meet Jan Blessures. She began to cry. James tried comforting her by putting his arm around her shoulders.

"I'm sorry for the loss of your husband," I said.

Jan Blessures grabbed my hand. "I appreciate all you two have done to bring wicked people to justice."

"We're happy to help any way we can," James said.

Jan Blessures handed me her card. "I'll always be indebted to you. If you ever need anything, call me."

When I got back into James' car, I looked at Jan Blessures' card. She was a psychologist. Her card read, *Jan Blessures Counseling Services, There is life after adultery. Marriages can heal.*

Later that night, James lit a fire in the fireplace in our den. I retrieved the photographs of Roger Blessures and Herschel Marks in their compromising positions and I tossed them into the fire one by one as James watched in silence. The fire quickly consumed all the evidence of the illicit affair between the two men. Jan Blessures and her family had been through enough; sometimes people do not need to know every single thing about their beloved partner.

An independent federal prosecutor was assigned to prosecute what became collectively termed the "Association cases" because the crimes implicated the defendants under the Racketeer Influenced and Corrupt Organizations Act. Dylan was riding high; he was the only person who would not be prosecuted. He was, however, required to testify at the trials of Gerald Lavine, Cedric Holmes, his mother, and many of the other Association board and committee members.

I filed an affidavit with the prosecutor testifying how Millie was a victim herself and that resulted in a sentence of probation. Marjorie Schwartz received a three-year reduced sentence, despite cooperating with authorities because her criminality was uncontroverted.

Haywood Martin and Cindy Matthews accepted plea agreements and testified against numbers of the board and committee members. Haywood Martin received a seven-year prison sentence and Cindy Matthews received a ten-year prison sentence. Gerald Lavine and

Cedric Holmes both pled guilty to malice murder and both received life sentences without the possibility of parole. Andrew Wilson resigned as prosecutor and relinquished his license to practice law. Judge McMurray retired from the bench after conducting the arraignments and moved to a Florida golf community. It was much better for him. Judge McMurray didn't want to work anymore; he just wanted to play golf.

Herschel was not able to hide behind the attorney-client privilege and escape prosecution because many of the board and committee members waived their rights to the privilege, hoping to secure leniency from the court in exchange for testifying against him. Herschel was the quintessential enabler. He enabled the corrupt board and committee members to steal, cheat, and lie to the community members. Herschel Marks pled guilty to a number of lesser-included fraud counts in exchange for probation, and he permanently lost his license to practice law.

Mr. Cobb received the death penalty, but when the sentence was handed down, I predicted he would never be executed. I believed that he would die before his appeal rights were exhausted—and that was exactly what occurred. Mr. Cobb only served two years and eight months in prison when he was stricken with an incurable and unusually aggressive form of lung cancer; he died four weeks after his diagnosis.

After the dust settled, Bill Collins, Alfred Mertz, and the other honest community residents were assigned positions as interim board and committee members of the Association. Bill asked me if I wanted to assume the role of attorney for the Association, but I respectfully declined. I felt that I had done my part. The Association needed to regroup and rebuild with individuals who had the time and desire to make it a great organization again.

Also, once the plea deals were inked and the trials concluded, Bill invited James and me to a dinner party at the Covington Commons yacht club. The Association had held a recent election and they were going to announce the results at the soiree. The dinner was a fun and fabulous potluck. All of the invitees brought delicious dishes to share. We ate off paper plates, drank out of plastic cups, and used disposable utensils. It was the most refined dinner party I had ever attended.

The Wainrights sat at our table. Mrs. Wainright handed me two packages wrapped in white shiny paper, each tied with a pink bow. I opened the first package like a child on Christmas morning. It was a tiny sweater. I must have looked confused when I examined it because Ms. June explained, "It's for Star."

I looked at it more closely. "It's so pretty."

Ms. June said, "Star can wear it when she goes outside on chilly nights and mornings. Star is the reason why the cases were solved. Remember, the oleander? Bill told us the story at a community meeting a few weeks ago."

I smiled and slowly closed my eyes to thank God for Star. "This sweater is lovely. I remember. I told Bill the whole story. Thank you."

"Please open this one too," Ms. June said as she handed me the second gift.

It was an artfully embroidered white linen tablecloth with matching napkins she had meticulously needle-crafted with her own hands. Emblazoned on the linens were pineapples—the southern symbol for home, hospitality, and friendship.

Sensations of joy and gratitude spread through my body when I said, "They're just like the beautiful linens that were on your table! Thank you, again."

John Simmons approached me with an outstretched hand and I stood to clasp it.

"I appreciate your help," I stated.

"I want to thank you. The Association recently hired me as the new maintenance director."

"Congratulations! The Association hired a trustworthy man."

"Yes, congratulations!" James agreed.

A young, attractive woman walked over to our table and stood alongside John. "This is my wife," he said. "We got married last month."

Everyone at our table chimed, "Congratulations!"

I shook the young woman's hand, and then I shook John's hand again. "Good luck to both of you."

At the end of the dinner, Bill rose and named the newly elected board members. I was disappointed that Bill's name was not mentioned. I guessed he had lost his bid for election. Bill turned to me and loudly exclaimed, "I want to recognize our friend, the attorney who helped save our community! If it wasn't for her tireless devotion to our cause, we might not be where we are today. So thank you so much."

I blushed as all the members clapped. In response, I whispered, "Thank you all."

Bill left the podium and walked toward me. I asked him, "Why weren't you elected as a board member?"

"I'll be actively volunteering my time in any capacity needed, but I didn't think it would be appropriate to put my name on the ballot in this election, since I've been serving as interim president."

"You are a really good man," I said.

Alfred walked towards us, and he and Bill thanked us once more.

"Where do we go from here?" James asked as we left the party.

"First, we're headed home," I said with a giggle. "I'll give you heads up on my next project as soon as one comes across my desk."

As I fell asleep that night in my warm, safe bed, I thought, *Thank you means so much, it acknowledges your passion, validates your hard work, and counsels you to close the book on a job well done.*

EPILOGUE

The better part of being a hero is when no one knows your name.